BLOOD ON THE MONEY

J-Blunt

Lock Down Publications and
Ca$h Presents

Blood on the Money

A Novel by **J-Blunt**

J-Blunt

Lock Down Publications
P.O. Box 944
Stockbridge, Ga 30281

Visit our website
www.lockdownpublications.com

First Edition September 2020
Printed in the United States of America

This is a work of fiction. Names, characters, places, and incidents either are products of the author's imagination or are used fictitiously. Any similarity to actual events or locales or persons, living or dead, is entirely coincidental.

Lock Down Publications
Like our page on Facebook: Lock Down Publications @
www.facebook.com/lockdownpublications.ldp
Cover design and layout by: **Dynasty Cover Me**
Book interior design by: **Shawn Walker**
Edited by: **Jill Alicea**

Stay Connected with Us!

Text **LOCKDOWN** to 22828 to stay up-to-date with new releases, sneak peeks, contests and more…

Submission Guideline.

Submit the first three chapters of your completed manuscript to ldpsubmissions@gmail.com, subject line: Your book's title. The manuscript must be in a .doc file and sent as an attachment. The document should be in Times New Roman, double-spaced and in size 12 font. Also, provide your synopsis and full contact information. If sending multiple submissions, they must each be in a separate email.

Have a story but no way to send it electronically? You can still submit to LDP/Ca$h Presents. Send in the first three chapters, written or typed, of your completed manuscript to:

LDP: Submissions Dept
P.O. Box 944
Stockbridge, Ga 30281

DO NOT send original manuscript. Must be a duplicate.

Provide your synopsis and a cover letter containing your full contact information.

Thanks for considering LDP and Ca$h Presents.

Acknowledgements:

For me, acknowledgments are the most difficult part of this book to write. That's why I've never done it in my previous 12 books. There have been so many people that played a big part in my life and I didn't want to forget nobody. But I decided to write one this time because there are some special people that need to know how much I appreciate them. Like everybody that was raised to believe in something higher than themselves, I gotta thank God for blessing me with the talent to write and for keeping me alive long enough to reach my potential. Shot out to Ca$h, CEO of Lockdown Publications, for having the vision and creating a platform for the voiceless to be heard.

To my beautiful mother, Marcella Williams, thank you for the unconditional love and support. I don't know what I would've done without you. Pops, you my dude and I appreciate everything that you are. To my son, Mooka, you are loved and you have the potential to be great. I'ma always be there for you. To my baby girl, Pria, you stole my heart the first time I seen you and I love you. Keda, thank you for our two blessings. You a Queen and I wish you enough.

To my sisters, Shawntale and Kim, thank y'all for accepting my phone calls, working my social media, and putting up with me even when I was irritating the hell out of y'all. We gon' do it big when I touch down! C-Lo, you know you my dude. Thank you for being my champion and holding the fam down. I know the world gets heavy sometimes, but you got big enough shoulders to carry it. To my li'l brother Johnnie "Big Jay" Jones, I know you in a better place. One day we gon' see each other again in Thugz Mansion.

To my niggas Mike Flowers, Sam, 3rd, T-Murda, Whiskey, Dank, Black Rob, Lo-Dog, and C-Roc, thank y'all for the real love and support. Antonio & Binky, words can't express how much I appreciate y'all showing me love from around the world. Sand, you are an angel. Big shot out to my boy Keith Bump at Hawkstar tattoo shop for the art work and K-Dog for answering my millions of questions about Chi Town. And last but certainly not least, to Christina, thank you for showing up on time and restoring my faith in good and strong women. You are amazing. Let's be great!

A special thank you to the fans and supporters of J-Blunt. None of this would be possible if y'all didn't go out and buy and read my books. The reviews you leave on Amazon are golden. Thank you.

Connect with me online at:

Facebook: Author J-Blunt

BOOK I: BURNING DESIRE

TO LONG FOR, CRAVE, OR COVET. TO WISH FOR.

WHEN A MAN REALLY WANTS SOMETHING, HE WILL STAKE HIS LIFE TO OBTAIN IT. THE KNIGHT WILL RISK HIS LIFE TO SLAY THE FIRE-BREATHING DRAGON AND WIN THE HEART OF THE PRINCESS.

THE HUSTLER WILL RISK FREEDOM TO SECURE THE BAG.

THE QUEST FOR RICHES BEGINS WITH A STATE OF MIND. IT IS THE BURNING DESIRE FOR MONEY THAT DRIVES US TO CREATE PLANS FOR GETTING IT.

BE WARNED THAT BEFORE SUCCESS COMES IN ANY MAN'S LIFE, HE IS SURE TO BE MET WITH TEMPORARY FAILURE OR DEFEAT. BUT BURNING DESIRE GIVES YOU PIT BULL DETERMINATION AND PERSISTENCE THAT WILL KEEP YOU GOING WHEN YOU MEET THESE OBSTACLES.

AND ALWAYS REMEMBER, EVERYTHING HAPPENS FOR A REASON.

J-Blunt

Prologue

The ten-year-old is stirred awake by his bladder demanding to be emptied and the cries of his baby brother. After sitting up in bed, Carl wipes the sleep from his eyes, gathering his bearings. He is in the bedroom he shares with his twin brothers, Chris and Charles. Through the moonlight creeping through the window, he can see the twins aren't in their cribs. He steps into the hallway and notices the bathroom light is on. That's where the cries are coming from. The crying gets louder as he walks to the door. What he sees scares the piss out of him - literally.

The urine drips down Carl's legs when he sees his mother covered in blood. She is holding a knife while kneeling in front of the tub. His little brother Chris is naked, lying on the floor and crying his eyes out. The other twin is floating in the tub half-filled with bloody water. His throat is slit.

Carla doesn't notice Carl behind her as she lifts the other twin up from the floor. She looks at him lovingly, tears streaming down her face. Then, in an instant, her look changes from love to hate. And then fear.

"You are the devil's baby. They told me this is the only way to save you," she mumbles, bringing the blade to the child's throat.

For most of her life, Carla knew she was different. She grew up having what her mother and father called "episodes", hearing voices and seeing things that weren't actually there. But her case went unreported for most of her life. In her family, metal health was misunderstood and not considered a priority. She didn't get diagnosed as a paranoid schizophrenic until she was twenty-four years old. She was prescribed medication and mostly functioned as a normal person. But emotional reactions could trigger psychotic reactions so severe that the medication didn't work. Tonight, the medication would not save the children.

"Mama!" Carl shrieked.

Carla spun to face her oldest son, a deranged look in her eyes as she continued to hold the knife to the crying baby's throat.

"C'mere, baby. They want us to come home. He gon' save all of us and reunite us in heaven."

Carl is frozen with fear. "No, Mama. You gotta take yo' medicine. What did you do to Charles?"

Carla looks to the dead child floating in the tub. "Jesus got him. And now Jesus wants you."

Carl begins backing away from the door, flight mode kicking in.

"Come here right now, Carl!" Carla demands, pointing the bloody knife at the boy.

The sight reminds Carl of a scary movie and he takes off running.

"Carl? Carl!" Carla calls angrily.

When the boy doesn't respond, she gets angrier. The child in her arm continues screaming. The voices are telling her that she must send him to God, so she plunges the knife into his chest before tossing him in the bloody water.

"Carl! Where you at, baby? Mama needs her li'l man right now," Carla calls as she searches the house for him. When she sees the front door open, she panics and runs into the hallway. Carl is banging on the neighbor's door. He is going to ruin their plans.

"Gwen, help! Gwen, is my daddy in there?"

Hearing the name of the woman in the apartment next door makes Carla angrier. Gwen is the cause of her psychotic outbreak. Gwen is fucking Carla's boyfriend! The voices tell her to kill.

"Get over here, boy!" Carla calls as she approaches.

Carl stares at his mother with wide eyes as he continues beating on the door. "Gwen! Daddy! Somebody open the door! Help!"

When Carla is a few feet from the boy, she lifts the knife over her head and swings. Carl lifts an arm to block the knife and the blade cuts his arm before plunging into the boy's chest.

"Ahh!" Carl screams.

Carla yanks the knife from the wound, about to stab him again, when the door swings open. Jason, Carla's boyfriend, appears, wearing only a pair of boxer briefs. He is so horrified by what he sees that he gets stuck. He can't believe that he just saw Carla stab their son. And before he can react, Carla turns the knife on her man.

"You did this to us!" Carla screams.

Jason can't move away from the knife swinging at his chest. He lifts a hand to block, but is too slow. The blade dives into the left side of his chest, piercing his heart. Jason stumbles backward, falling into the apartment. Carla leaps on top of him and begins stabbing him in the chest repeatedly.

"Ahhh! Carla, stop!" Gwen screams.

When the murderess looks up and sees the pretty light-skinned woman only wearing a bra and panties, her anger is kindled times ten. Carla leaps up from Jason's dead body as the voices scream louder inside her head.

Gwen tries to run, but doesn't get far. The knife plunging into her back sends the mistress crashing into the wall. Carla continues driving the knife into the woman's back over and over until she falls on the ground. In a rage, she stabs Gwen over a hundred times, until her arm gets tired.

Out of breath, Carla looks around at the gory scene. She is kneeling on top of Gwen's bloodied corpse, Jason is stretched out in a bloody mess a few feet away in the living room, and Carl is laid out by the front door. She has done what the voices have told her. Now she has one last task to complete. She lifts the knife to her own throat and makes a deep slice from the left side all the way to the right, creating a bloody smile. Blood pours from her neck as her strength and conscious fade.

In her dying moments, she watches as Carl rises from the hallway floor.

Oh no! She failed.

J-Blunt

Chapter 1

November 7th, 1994

I was awakened by a burning in my chest.

Every time I had the dream, my scar itched and burned like I had been stabbed again. I opened my eyes and looked down at the three-inch scar on the right side of my chest. It was dark brown and fully healed. Nine years ago I thought it would kill me as I lay on the hallway floor bleeding and barely able to breathe from a punctured lung. I had another longer scar on my forearm from trying to block the knife. I still couldn't understand how my mother could bring so much evil upon her children. Her creations. Her blessings. Not wanting to start my day off in a bad mood, I pushed thoughts of my family's darkest moment from my head and sat up in bed.

Home for me was my Nana's house, my father's mother. My room was in the basement. It wasn't exactly a bedroom. Nana knew I was getting older and would need my own space, so she gave me the entire basement. I threw some couches, a TV, and a bed in it and turned it into something like an efficiency apartment, minus the plumbing. Had to go upstairs to use the bathroom and shower. I threw on a pair of cotton shorts and slipped into my house shoes before climbing the stairs. I could smell the breakfast food as I neared the door. When I opened it, my little brother Chris was walking by.

"Happy birthday, Carl!"

"Thanks, li'l punk," I nodded.

Chris survived my mother's psychotic episode, ending up with a scar on his chest similar to mine and missing one lung. Even with one lung, he was a healthy ten-year-old boy and I loved my li'l nigga. Even when I didn't act like it.

"I ain't no punk, pussy-ass nigga."

The curse words stopped me in my tracks and I spun to face him. "Fuck you just say to me, li'l nigga!?" I mugged, ready to beat his li'l ass.

He smiled like it was a game. "You heard me, punk-ass nigga."

I lunged at him.

"Nana!" he screamed and he took off running towards the kitchen.

I chased him, but couldn't catch him. He ran into the kitchen and right into my grandmother's hedge of protection.

"Why are you two screaming and runnin' in my house?" she scolded.

"Carl tryna hit me," Chris told her.

"Li'l snitch!" I mugged.

"Hey, don't call your little brother names!" she scolded again. "We don't play that in this house. Y'all is all each other got. Family is the most important thing in this world. When I'm gone, it's just gon' be y'all two and y'all can't be tryna beat each other up all the time. Now stop."

"Yes, Nana," I mumbled.

"Now come gimme a hug, baby. Happy birthday!" She smiled, opening her arms.

I walked over and allowed my grandma to wrap me in a warm hug and kiss my cheek. My Nana was a short, big-boned woman who was originally from Little Rock, Arkansas. The family migrated north when she was still a kid and landed in Chicago, Illinois. She had light skin, big brown eyes, and short graying hair that she normally covered with a wig. The fifty-three-year-old queen was the best thing that ever happened in my life and I loved her like she had birthed me. She nurtured me and Chris, giving us the maternal love that we never got from Carla. When I was in school, she sat down and did homework with me. She taught me to pray and how to understand the Bible. When puberty hit, she told me about girls and how to protect myself from STDs. The only thing she couldn't do was teach me how to be a man. And since I didn't have a father or worthy father figure to look up to, I would have to learn this on my own.

"Thank you, Nana."

"Sit down and let me make you some breakfast. So, now that you are nineteen, what are you going to do with yourself? You are not a little boy no more and you have to figure out what you want to do. If you don't come up with a plan, you've already planned to fail."

"I don't know, Nana. I'm still figuring that out."

"You said the same thing when you turned eighteen. Why don't you get a job and enroll in college? You're obviously smart. You graduated high school with a 2.9 GPA," she said while preparing a plate overflowing with eggs, pancakes, and bacon.

"I don't know what I want to do. I'm just playin' it by ear, I guess."

She tugged on my ear lobe as she sat the plate in front of me. "Well you need to stop playing it by ear and play it smart. Chicago is a dangerous city for a young black man with no direction. I don't want you to get caught up out there with those gangs and end up in jail or dead. I know it seems like I'm harassing you, but I'm not. I don't want you to end up like your uncle Harold. He was smart and good at football. But this city didn't give him a chance. Learn from your uncle."

The tears in her eyes made me want to change the direction of my life and straighten up. "I'ma figure something out, Nana. I'ma be somebody one day. Somebody you can be proud of."

She stared at me lovingly for a few moments. "I know you will. I just need you to hurry up and figure it out. You are smart and very talented. You can do anything you want if you put your mind to it. The life God put in you is bigger than the life you're living," she said before kissing me a top the head. "I'm taking your little brother to the doctor with me for our appointments at 10:00. Don't have your friends in my house while I'm gone."

"I won't," I mumbled between bites of food.

"And here's fifty dollars. Happy birthday."

After eating the big breakfast, I went to shower and get dressed in the birthday gear I got a few days earlier. Carolina blue Jordan's, Blue Jean Guess pants, Michael Jordan's North Carolina college jersey over a white T-shirt, and a white and blue North Carolina brim. When I stepped outside, I knew I was the freshest nigga in the hood. My hood was on Chicago's South Side. Rag Town. 119th and

Hausted, one of the city's most violent neighborhoods. I walked two blocks over to my nigga Rideout's crib and banged on the door.

"Who dat?" Rideout called.

"Carl."

The locks clicked and the door opened a few moments later.

"What's hannin', li'l folks? Happy birthday, nigga!" He smiled, showing off the single gold front tooth before embracing me.

Rideout was what we called blue-black, skin so dark that he looked blue. He stood a little over 6 feet tall with a nice cut from the workouts he did while in Cook County Jail. He was four years older than me so as far as the streets went, he was my big homie and I did as he did.

"What's good, fam-a-lam?" I said coolly.

"See you got geared up, boy. I wanna sport that J-Bone jersey too, nigga. That mug cold. C'mon in."

I stepped past him and into the house he shared with his girl-friend, Sherry. She was sitting on the couch braiding a dark-skinned female's hair. There was another brown-skinned female on the couch across from them. And my nigga, Crash, was sitting on crates near the corner smoking a Newport.

"What's hannin', nigga! Happy birthday, boy!" Crash said, standing up and giving me an aggressive hug.

Crash was brown-skinned, about my height with my same slim build. He had been my nigga since we was wearin' Ninja Turtle draws. We was the same age and clicked instantly when I moved to my Nana's house. We went from flipping on pissy mattresses in back alleys to getting our grind on by any means necessary.

"Good lookin'. Good lookin', fam."

"What's up, Carl? I didn't know today was yo' birthday, nigga. Happy birthday," Sherry said.

"Thanks," I nodded, playing it cool in front of the females that was checking out my fresh Jordan 'fit.

"I like yo' shoes. Happy birthday," the brown-skinned female said.

I nodded. "Thanks."

"You nineteen, right?" Rideout asked, looking me up and down.

"Yeah, nigga. You know that. What you looking at me like that for?"

"'Cause I wanna make sure I hit you the right amount of times. Whoop that nigga!" he yelled before punching me in the chest.

I wasn't ready for the blow and all I could do was flinch and cover up. Rideout gave me rapid hard body blows. A few seconds later Crash, Sherry, and the two females I didn't know jumped in. I tried to keep my balance, but there were too many fists. I fell onto the couch as they beat my ass. But I didn't stay there. I kicked Rideout off of me along with the brown-skinned female. Then I started swinging wildly, not caring who I hit or where I hit them. Caught the dark-skinned female in the mouth and she backed up. I continued kicking and swinging as I thrashed around on the couch, eventually making enough room to get to my feet. Everyone was hesitant to rush me when they seen I was trained to go. Everybody except Rideout. He rushed me, throwing body blows. I threw them back and for a moment, we stood toe to toe exchanging punches. When the rest of the people seen I was distracted, they jumped back in. They beat me back onto the couch and made me fold.

"A'ight! A'ight!" I yelled when I had enough.

"Damn, nigga. Yo' light-skinned ass got hands," Rideout said, huffing and puffing as he fell on the couch across from me.

"Nigga, you kicked my homegirl in the face," Sherry said.

I looked to Sherry's friend. She was sitting on the couch across from me holding the side of her face, looking pissed off. "She shouldn't have been hittin' me," I defended myself. "When it's one of y'all birthday, I'm stomping y'all ass out."

"We don't put our feet on the folks," Crash said as he settled back onto his crate.

"Fuck that. I'm puttin' feet, hands, sticks, and bats on anybody that act like they want it. I ain't goin'," I said.

"I ain't mad at em," Rideout said. "Ay, y'all come in the other room and lemme put ch'all up on some game."

Me and Crash walked into the bedroom and took seats on the bed.

Rideout sat on the dresser and started talking. "Check the steelo. I got a nice li'l move that's gon' set us straight for a few. Mawg over in Harvey gettin' to it. He an op, so it don't matter what we do to 'em. I heard the nigga got a nice li'l chunk of change in there. Four or five thou."

Hearing the amount made my eyes light up. "On what?"

"On er'thang I love," Rideout confirmed.

"Let's get that bitch, then," Crash said, ready to move.

"Y'all know we in there tonight. We gon' lamp around here until later. I got the Mossberg and the Nina. Y'all know how we do."

After leaving the room, I hit the bathroom to check myself over and make sure my clothes was still fresh. I was only in there a couple seconds when there was a knock on the door.

"Yeah," I called.

"I gotta use the bathroom," one of Sherry's friends called from the hall.

"A'ight. Here I come."

When I was satisfied that my shit was still tight, I opened the door. I locked eyes with the brown-skinned female. She was pretty. She had plump cheeks, brown eyes, and juicy lips. She was tall and wore a pair of tight jeans that showed off her curvy body.

"Hey, birthday boy." She smiled.

"What's hannin'?" I asked, biting my bottom lip while looking her up and down lustfully.

"I gotta pee. Move," she said, pushing past me.

"Want me to help you get them pants down?"

She smirked. "You can't handle what's inside my pants and I just don't give my stuff away."

"I ain't too proud to beg," I said, hitting her with the TLC song title.

She laughed. "That was good. Talk to me when I get out. I gotta pee," she said before closing the door.

I walked back into the living room and joined the party, waiting for her to come back out. A few seconds, later she joined me on the couch.

"What you know about TLC, birthday boy?"

"Stop playin'. Creep off with me and I'll show you that Red Light Special," I said, continuing to hit her with TLC titles.

She laughed again. "I like the way you did that. You good, Carl. Where yo' girlfriend at?"

"Prolly with yo' man. What's yo' name?"

"I'm Marie and I don't got a man."

"And I don't got a girl. You wanna be my girl?"

"Yeah right, Carl. You got too much game, nigga. You probably got too many girls."

I gave her a serious look. "Do I look like a liar?"

She stared into my eyes for a moment. "Hell yeah!" She laughed.

"Look at dis nigga thinkin' he a mack!" Rideout laughed.

"Damn, nigga. Why you blowin' up my spot?" I mugged.

"'Cause a real mack don't worry 'bout they spot gettin' blew up, li'l nigga. I'm a real gangsta mack. Can't no bitch tell me shit," Rideout bragged.

"A'ight, gangsta mack," Sherry spoke up. "Don't get fucked up," she warned.

Rideout blew her off with a wave of the hand. "You know what it is. Act like you crazy in front of yo' friends, but you know," he laughed. "I got some gin and juice in the kitchen. Y'all ready to get fucked up?"

I kicked it at Rideout's house for the rest of the day, smoking weed, drinking, and kicking it with the females. By the evening, we was all faded and horny. Crash was on the couch with the dark-skinned chick, Tasha. Sherry and Rideout was damn near fucking on the recliner. And I was all over Marie, trying to get some birthday pussy. I was whispering all kind of nasty shit in her ear and she was almost ready to go.

"I never got no pussy on my birthday. And you so fuckin' sexy and fine. I know you got some good pussy. My dick hard as a muthafucka right now. Feel it," I said, grabbing her hand and setting it on my lap.

"No, Carl." She pulled away. "Everybody can see us."

"You see everybody doin' they own thing. They ain't thinking about us. Come to the bathroom with me."

"Why don't we leave? Do you got somewhere we can go?"

I thought about my room in the basement, but it was too early. Sometimes Nana tripped when I brought females home and I wanted to wait for her to fall asleep. "Yeah, but we can't go there right now. I gotta make a move with my niggas in a li'l while."

"Okay. I'll be here when you get back. Then we can leave."

That wasn't good enough for me. "But I need some right now. What we doing tonight is dangerous and it ain't no guarantee I'ma come back. Let me see what it's like just in case."

She stared at me through intoxicated and lust-glazed eyes. She wanted it just as bad as I did, but she needed some coaching.

"Okay. Let me go first. You come in a few minutes."

I watched her phatty until she disappeared down the hall. When I looked around the living room, it looked like both of my niggas was trying to get some pussy and not paying me no attention. After counting to sixty in my head, I went to the bathroom. As soon as I stepped in, me and Marie started kissing and feeling each other's bodies. I reached under her shirt and started squeezing her titties while she reached in my pants and stroked my dick.

"Let me see it," she said, breaking the kiss.

I stepped back and pulled off my T-shirt and jersey before pulling down my pants and boxers. My dick stood out like a light-skinned flag pole.

"Let me see yours."

She unbuttoned her pants and started doing a little shimmy as she slid the pants down to her ankles. Then she sat on the sink and opened her legs. Her pussy was hairy and fat. I was thirsty to get in and rushed between her legs. Because she didn't take her pants all the way off and couldn't open her legs all the way, I was only able to get a little bit in. But she had some bomb-ass pussy.

"Ssss!" She moaned, grabbing my back.

I started humping like a mutherfucker, trying my hardest to get deeper in that pussy. But I couldn't because her legs wouldn't open.

"Turn around," I told her.

She hopped off the sink and bent over.

I took a moment to look at her pretty brown round. Her ass was nice, plump, and phat. I moved behind her and spread those cheeks apart, exposing that hairy pussy and diving in.

"Mmmhhh!" she moaned

"Damn!" I breathed, shoving my dick all the way in. Her pussy was so wet and tight. Shit felt like a waterfall. I wanted to control myself, but couldn't. I started tearing that shit up.

"Wait, Carl! Slow down. Oh, shit," she moaned.

I couldn't slow down. Her pussy was too good. And when my nut started building, I didn't even try to prolong it. I kept hitting it and snatched out right before I busted.

"Aw shit!" I moaned, unloading my seed into the toilet.

Marie watched me. "That was fast," she smirked.

"You got some bomb," I said while stroking the rest of the sperm out.

She pulled up her clothes and started talking shit. "You talked a lot of shit about fucking me and then you turn out to be a two minute brotha."

I laughed. "That was just a quickie. I just wanted to see what you was working with. When we go to my house later on, I'ma show you how I put it down."

She rolled her eyes. "I told you that you can't hang with what's in my pants, Carl."

I gave her a serious look. "After I take care of my business, I'ma take you to my crib and make you tap out."

J-Blunt

Chapter 2

We left Rideout's house at around 9:00 and hopped in his hoopty, a maroon 1984 Pontiac 6000. We rode to Harvey, Illinois, a suburb on the outskirts of Chicago. We parked a couple houses down from the spot we were running in, checking the block for potential hostiles or witnesses. Since it was November and winter was getting close, the cold air kept most people in the house.

"Y'all know how we doin'. We going in buckin'. Carl, you got the gator. Be ready to let it go if shit don't look right. You hear me?"

I grabbed the Mossberg pump and made sure there was a slug in the chamber. "I know how it go, nigga. I'm ready to get this chicken. Let's go."

We pulled ski masks over our faces as we hopped out the hoopty and speed walked to the house. I hid on one side of the door and Rideout was on the other. Crash rang the doorbell.

"Who dat?"

"This Murda, Joe. Y'all straight up in there?"

There was a pause. "I don't know no Murda. Ain't nothing hannin'."

"Aw, c'mon, Joe. I ain't on no bullshit. I'm out here by myself. Look out the peephole. Lord n'em on Lamera said y'all was gon' serve me."

There was another pause. Then the locks on the door clicked and the door opened a crack. A dark-skinned nigga with French braids stuck his head out. "Who you say sent you?"

"Big Lord over on——"

Crash didn't even get the chance to finish the lie before Rideout made his move. He jumped from the hiding spot and started sparking. He shot the nigga that answered the door in the chest before running into the house. I followed behind him, ready to let the gauge buss. There were three niggas sitting around the living room. One of them tried to run and I let the gauge go.

Kaboom!

The slug hit him in the back, sending him face planting to the floor.

"Put ch'all fuckin' hands up! Where that shit at, nigga?" Rideout screamed at the niggas sitting on the couch.

"In the kitchen!" one of them told.

Rideout snatched him up by the collar. "Take me to it. Bet' not try no bullshit or I'ma buck yo' bitch ass!"

I kept the gauge on the nigga that was sitting on the couch and snuck a few peeks at the nigga I shot in the back. He was groaning in pain, his body starting to shake. I never killed nobody before. I had shot a few niggas, but it wasn't no doubt in my mind that it would change tonight. I didn't have time to dwell on my first body because Rideout came running from the kitchen holding a box of cereal.

"I got it, nigga! Let's go!"

I backed out of the house, keeping the gauge pointed at the nigga on the couch. As soon as I stepped onto the front porch, I booked it! Crash was already in the car with it running. As soon as we were in, Crash peeled out.

"That's what I'm talkin' 'bout, Carl! You fucked that nigga up. Put a big-ass hole in that boy's back!" Rideout yelled, geeked up from the robbery and shooting.

"He shouldn't have moved. Stupid-ass nigga," I said, not showing the remorse that was starting to creep up inside of me.

"Fuck them hook-ass niggas. What you got in that box?" Crash asked.

"We hit a lick, folks!" Rideout yelled as he poured the contents of the box onto his lap.

It was money, all kinds of bills from ones to hundreds.

"How much is it?" I asked, eager to know.

"Hold on, nigga. Let me count it," Rideout said.

I watched from the backseat as he counted out seven thousand dollars. We had been doing robberies for about a year and this is the most money we'd ever hit for. Me and Rideout got 2,500 apiece since we did the dirty work. Crash was cool getting two thousand. We drove back to Rideout's house, still geeked up from shooting them niggas and the amount of money we took. When we walked in the house, the females was all over us.

"I see you made it back." Marie smiled.

"I was thinking about that rematch. I'm ready for round two," I cracked.

"I hope it was better than the first because I don't like no minute man."

After kicking it with my niggas for a li'l while longer and smoking another blunt, I showed them some love and took Marie to the crib. It was past eleven o'clock when I unlocked the back door, so I knew Nana was sleep. I took her to my room in the basement and broke out a bottle Seagram's Gin and played TLC's *Crazysexycool* tape.

"This is my shit, boy!" Marie started snapping when "Red Light Special" came on.

"You don't know nothing 'bout that," I teased.

"Whatever." She rolled her eyes. "What y'all do that was so dangerous that you didn't think you was gon' come back from?"

I thought about the nigga I shot in the back. "I get it how I live, baby," I said before taking a swig from the gin bottle and passing it to her.

"Sherry said y'all be robbing niggas."

"Sherry don't know what she talking about. Don't believe everything you hear."

She took a sip from the bottle, staring into my eyes like she was trying to read me. "You look different from earlier. What happened?"

I laughed. "What is you talking about?"

"Yo' eyes look different."

I stood up and took off my jersey. "Don't worry about my eyes."

She looked over my body, stopping at the scars on my chest and forearm. "How you get them scars? What happened?"

"Don't worry about my scars. You need to be worried about my dick."

"Why? You can't hang with me." She giggled.

I pulled off my pants. "I'ma fuck the shit out of you. Get naked."

She handed me the bottle of gin and pulled off her shirt. Her titties were big, perky, and firm. Nipples hard. When she shimmied out of her pants, her titties bounced and jiggled like crazy. After she was naked, I looked her over. Marie's body looked flawless. Flat stomach. Small waist. Thick thighs. Hairy pussy.

"Why you lookin' at me like that?" she asked.

"Because I'm finna fuck the shit outta you!" I said, grabbing a jimmy hat from the drawer and putting it on. Then I grabbed her around the waist aggressively and threw her on the bed.

"Damn, nigga!" she grumbled.

I acted like I didn't hear her as I got on top and wrapped a hand around her throat and tongue kissed her aggressively. She purred like a kitten and let me have my way. Next I started kissing my way down her neck to her titties. I went back and forth, sucking and licking both nipples.

"Mmmhhh!" she moaned.

While I was sucking her titties, I slipped a finger inside her good-ass pussy. It was hot and wet.

"Mmmm, Carl. Yeah!"

I got her open with the foreplay, fingering her while I sucked her nipples.

"Oh, yeah! Oh, yeah!" she moaned.

Even though I was young, I knew how to fuck. I had a good teacher that taught me how to make a female cum. I paid attention to Marie's moans and the way she was wiggling beneath me. She wanted more, so I slipped a second finger inside.

"Ssss! Oh, Carl! Oh, damn! I ain't never felt this before."

When she started lifting her ass off the bed to get more of my fingers, I knew she was close. I pressed my thumb against her clit and she went crazy.

"Oh, God! Oh God!" she screamed.

Shit was so loud that I had to reach a hand up to cover her mouth. But I didn't stop giving her pleasure. I shoved two fingers in and out of her roughly while wiggling my thumb across her clit and sucking her nipples. Her body went stiff as her pussy clenched and got super wet.

"OH GOD! OOOOHHH!" she screamed.

Even though I had my hand over her mouth, that shit was still too loud and I hoped she didn't wake up my Nana.

"Shhh!" I said, trying to get her to calm down.

She kept on screaming until the orgasm passed her body.

"Damn, girl. You tryna get me in trouble!"

Her chest heaved and she was out of breath like she just ran from the police. "Oh my God, Carl," she panted. "I'm sorry, but I couldn't help it. I didn't know you knew how to do that."

I smiled. "I told you I'ma fuck the shit outta you. Can you handle it, or you want me to stop?" I teased.

Defiance shone in her eyes. "Fuck you, nigga."

"I'ma show you what this gin finna make me do to you," I said, grabbing the bottle and taking a big sip. Shit burned on the way down my throat.

After wiping the dribble from my lips with the back of my hand, I got between her legs and dove in. The liquor and the rubber took away just enough feeling from her good-ass pussy so that I could last longer.

"Oh, yeah!" Marie moaned.

I started off with slow strokes, going halfway in.

"C'mon, Carl. Gimme some more," she begged.

I gave her what she wanted and started drilling that pussy with long strokes. A few minutes later I put her legs on my shoulders and went deeper.

"Oh, God! Oh, God!" Marie screamed.

I put both of my hands over her mouth and got down on her pussy like I hated her. When I felt my nut rising, I flipped her into her stomach and put a pillow under her hips, tooting that ass up just right. Then I slipped in that pussy and drilled her from the back. She put her face in another pillow and screamed. That gin kept me going like the Energizer Bunny. She busted one more time before I finally busted my nut.

***

I woke up at around 11 o'clock the next morning and sat up in bed. When I seen the empty gin bottle sitting on the table, a flashback of last night popped into my head. I fucked the shit out of Marie most of the night. Made her cum four or five times and had her whipped on my shit. She wanted to spend the night, but I didn't wanna have to explain why a female was in my room to my granny. So I sent her home in a cab at around 4 o'clock in the morning.

After stretching, I got dressed and went upstairs to freshen up. I took a shower and went to the kitchen to make a bowl of cereal. I was sitting at the table eating Honey Smacks when I heard footsteps coming towards the kitchen. It was Nana.

"Good morning, sleepy head. Had a long night, huh?" She smiled.

"Something like that," I answered.

She sat down at the table. "You only turn nineteen once. Gotta enjoy them younger years while you got 'em," she said, staring at me like she wanted to say more.

I waited. She didn't say nothing. Just kept staring.

"You didn't have to go to work today?"

She continued staring at me like she didn't hear what I said. Then she snapped back. "I'm sorry, baby, what did you say? I had a senior moment."

"You didn't go to work today?"

"No. I took the day off. I gotta take care of some things and clear my head. I didn't wanna be stuck in no office building today."

"What's going on? Why do you need to clear yo' head?"

She gave me the stare again. I could see that she wanted to tell me something.

"I just have some things on my mind. I'm okay."

I didn't think she was okay but since she didn't want to talk about it, I left it alone. "How was the doctor's appointment?"

"Your brother needed a booster shot. He's fine."

"What about you?"

She paused slightly before answering. "I'm fine. I need you to come with me to church this Sunday."

"C'mon, Nana," I whined. I loved and believed in God, but I hated going to church.

"Oh, stop whining, Carl. You haven't been to church in a while. You need to come so you can repent and ask God to forgive your sins."

I thought about the nigga I killed last night. Did she know? How? "I still know how to pray. I ask God for forgiveness all the time."

"But it's not the same as when you in the house of God worshipping with the saints. I want you to come so I can pray for you."

"C'mon, Nana. I really ain't tryna go. Church is long. I'ma be falling asleep."

She gave me a serious look. "I need you to do this for me one last time. I want you to be there with me this Sunday. I won't ask you no more after today. I promise."

The look in her eyes told me something serious was going on and she wasn't taking no for an answer.

"Okay."

She smiled and patted me on the arm. "Thank you, baby. I have to make a run and meet with a lawyer. Don't have no more girls in my house," she said knowingly before getting up and walking away.

***

When Sunday came, Nana woke me up at 7:30 in the morning. I took a shower, ate breakfast, and got dressed. We hopped in the car and I was forced to listen to Nana and Chris sing along to gospel songs by the Mississippi Mass Choir. We pulled up to the church at 8:30. My grandmother didn't believe in being late for nothing especially church. Nana had been going to Saint Ebenezer Baptist Church for over twenty years. Everyone in the church knew and respected Sister Elenore White. She walked through the aisles hugging, kissing, and God blessing everybody. Since the service didn't start for another thirty minutes, I found a seat in the corner and closed my eyes. Wasn't long before I felt a presence hovering over me. I opened my eyes and seen Deacon Jones's wife. Sister Jackie was a beautiful and stacked forty-year-old woman that drew attention from every man in the church when she walked by. She always wore tight clothes that showed off her Coke bottle figure and big-ass titties.

"Hey, Carl. Long time no see."

"Hey, Jackie," I mumbled.

"Nuh-uh, baby. Sister Jackie. We in church," she corrected.

"My bad," I apologized.

"I need you to help me move these boxes. Come to the basement with me real quick."

I got up and tried not to look at her big bouncing booty as I followed Sister Jackie to the back of the church and down the stairs. The basement was filled with churchy stuff. She led me towards the back and into an office. I didn't see no boxes.

"Why haven't you called me?" she demanded, walking in my face.

I backed up until I ran into the wall. "I been busy."

She closed the distance between us, pressing her big ass titties into my chest, our lips close enough to kiss. "Oh, so you too busy to call me? You got one of them little trifling heifers getting my time?"

"C'mon, Jackie. It ain't like that. And you married."

"Don't you worry about my marriage. You still belong to me. I told you that when I took your virginity. You is mines and this is my dick," she said, gripping my crotch.

I moved her hand and grabbed her by the throat, forcing her against the wall. "You betta calm yo' ass down, Jackie. You tripping. We in church. My Granny upstairs and so is yo husband."

The gravity of our situation shone in her eyes and she lost some of her edge. "Okay. I'm sorry. You know how I get when I don't see my man."

I let her go and backed up.

"I found a way for me to keep in touch with you," she said, going into her purse and pulling out a beeper. "I bought this for you. My code is 69."

I took the pager and slid it in my pocket. "A'ight. I got you."

She stared at me like she was trying to intimidate me. "Don't play with me, Carl," she warned.

"I ain't. I'ma hit you back."

She stared at me a little longer. When she was satisfied that she had me under control, she smiled. "Okay. Now gimme a kiss."

I tried to peck her on the lips, but she grabbed me by the jaws and stuck her tongue down my throat. After a long tongue kiss, she backed away.

"Grab that box of Bibles from behind the table and come back up."

When I got back upstairs, the choir was starting to line up and the music began. A few minutes later, the service was in full swing and people were dancing in the aisles catching the Holy Ghost. After a few songs, Mother Robinson got up to read a scripture and say a prayer. When she was done, Pastor Robinson took the podium.

"Good mornin', church family!" he yelled.

The congregation shouted back good mornings.

"We are gathered here today to give thanks to the Lord for allowing us to wake up with breath in our lungs and in a right state of mind. Amen."

The church gave him his amen back.

"Before I begin today's message, I wanna invite our dear Sister White up to the altar. Sister White, please come up here."

I looked at my Nana as she scooted past. She caressed my face and smiled before making her way to the altar.

"Church family, I want us all to come together to say a special prayer for Sister White. She has been a faithful servant of the Lord and a dedicated member of this church for over twenty years and unfortunately she got news from the doctor that she has been diagnosed with cancer in her pancreas. The doctors say..."

I didn't hear any more words spoken by Pastor Robinson after he said that my Granny had cancer. It felt like I got punched in the chest by God. Everything inside hurt and it felt like I was going to faint. All I could do was stare at the woman that saved my life and cry.

J-Blunt

Chapter 3

I couldn't process the thought of losing my grandmother.

She had been the only stable thing in my life since Carla tried to kill me. She saved me and Chris from the Chicago Child Protective Services and gave us a home. And now she was dying. We were back at home, sitting at the kitchen table talking about her final plans.

"I don't know what to do without you, Nana," I cried.

"That's why I always told you to make plans, Carl. I knew I wasn't going to be around forever but I never imagined it would happen this fast," she said, wiping tears from her eyes. "Now it's time for you to grow up. Chris needs you now more than ever."

"You sure it ain't nothing they can do about it?" I asked, not wanting to accept that it was the end for her. "Can't you get some medicine? Or go to another doctor and see what they say? You don't even look sick. You sure they didn't make a mistake?"

She put her head down for a moment, gathering strength. When she looked up, I could see that she had accepted her fate. "I got a second and third opinion. I can't get another pancreas. Ain't nothing nobody can do. I had a hard time accepting it, too. But you are stronger than you know, baby. I know it all seems hard right now but you will get through this. Now listen because I need to show you some things."

She pulled a set of papers from her purse.

"This is the deed to the house. I seen a lawyer and I'm giving it to you and your brother. I'm behind on the mortgage and I also had to take some loans out on it. There's a lien against it for almost twenty thousand dollars. I need you to keep up the payments so the bank can't take it from the family. I have a life insurance policy and you and Trisha are the beneficiaries. The policy is for fifty thousand dollars. You take twenty to pay off the house then split the last thirty between you, your brother, and Trisha. I tried to get more, but they wouldn't let me because I was already sick. When you get the money, make sure you are responsible with it and don't go buying nothing stupid."

"I won't."

"I'm going to switch all the bills over to your name. You are going to have a lot on your plate, but I know you can handle it. You have to do this for your brother. He needs you to be an example. Show him how to be a good man. Promise me that you will raise him right?"

"I promise I'ma raise him right, Nana."

She smiled at me proudly. "You're going to be okay, baby. And so am I. To be absent from the body is to be present with the Lord."

I didn't want her to be with the Lord.

"I'm leaving you the car, too. I still owe about twenty five hundred dollars so you will still have to make the payments if you want to keep it. Otherwise the repo man will come and take it. I'll keep paying it until I can't pay anymore."

"I can pay off the car," I mumbled.

She laughed. "You got twenty-five hundred dollars?"

"Nah. I spent some of the money but I got two thousand."

She looked surprised. "How did you get two thousand dollars, Carl?"

"I been saving up?"

She stared at me like she was trying to see through me. "If you got that money doing something illegal, I don't want it."

"It didn't come from nothing illegal," I lied. I felt bad about lying to her, but I knew she wouldn't take it if I told her the truth. "I just been hustling over at Jew Town and on the L. Doing what I can when I can."

She stared at me again before reaching out and grabbing my hand. "Okay. I'll put it towards the car. You'll be okay, baby. God doesn't put more on us than we can bear."

I wanted to believe her but accepting her leaving seemed too heavy of a burden for me to carry.

***

The next couple of days went by in a cloudy haze. Knowing that I was losing my grandmother put me in a funk. All I wanted to do was mope around and get drunk and high. I think I was depressed, but niggas in the hood didn't acknowledge that kind of shit so I stayed fucked up.

"What's good, my G?" Rideout greeted as we shook hands.

"You know you got it."

"Come in and lock the door behind you," he said, letting me in the house. "Crash told me about yo o'girl gettin that monster. That's fucked up, fam."

"Yeah. They only gave her like six months and ain't nothing they can do about it. That shit got me fucked up," I mumbled before flopping down on the couch.

"You know they say God don't put more on a nigga than a nigga can handle. You got it, li'l folks. Yo' li'l brotha need you."

"She told me all the same shit. But fuck that. I ain't tryna be all fucked up and cryin' and shit. What's goin' on?"

"Shit. Lamping around the spot. Marie been sweating Sherry 'bout you. You ate that booty, didn't you, nigga?" He grinned.

I looked at him like he was crazy. "Fuck kinda nasty ass shit you on, fam? Hell nah, I ain't eat no booty."

He busted out laughing. "Only way bitches sweat niggas like that is if you lick the pussy or eat the booty. You did one of 'em, nigga. I ain't tryna hear that shit."

I waved him off. "Stop playing, nigga. You talk that gangsta mack shit, but I do it. I get that bumpy face in my system and blow a bitch back out. I ain't eating nothing that bleeds or sticking my tongue where shit come out of. That shit nasty."

Rideout busted out laughing. "Yeah, that shit sound slick to a fat bitch."

"You ate Sherry's booty before, didn't you?"

His voice got high-pitched. "Hell nah, nigga! I'm a gangsta."

I stared at him for a few moments. His serious face began to break and he looked away.

"You nasty as fuck, G!" I yelled.

A knock on the door made Rideout get up. "Ay, get off that bullshit," he grinned.

I couldn't let it go. "My nigga, you be eating Sherry's ass?"

"Hold that shit down, nigga," he said before answering the door. "Who dat?"

"Crash."

Rideout's eyes got big. "Don't say nothing, Carl. On the G, my nigga."

"Fuck that shit. Open the door. Let him in," I laughed.

He got serious. "Carl, don't say shit."

I wasn't going to keep it to myself. "Open the door, my nigga. Let Crash in."

"Open the door, nigga! Fuck you doing?" Crash called from outside.

"On everythang I love, that nigga lyin'!" Rideout said as soon as he opened the door.

"Fuck you talkin' 'bout?" Crash asked as he walked in the house.

"That nigga eat ass!" I blurted.

Crash looked Rideout from head to toe. "On what?"

"On everythang I love, he be eating Sherry's ass!" I laughed.

"Ole nasty booty mouf-ass nigga!" Crash teased.

Rideout mugged us. "A'ight. Laugh niggas. Yeah, get y'all laugh on 'cause y'all ate ass too smoking and drankin' with me."

Our faces grew sour.

"That shit ain't funny now, is it?" Rideout laughed.

"You nasty as fuck, G. You can't never hittin' my blunt or my bottle again," Crash sulked.

"Ole shitty mouf-ass boy!" I ribbed as my pager started beeping.

"When you get a beeper, nigga?" Crash asked.

"Couple days ago," I said, checking the number. It was 69.

"Oh, you a baller now?" Rideout asked, quoting the movie *Menace II Society*.

"Nah. Lemme see yo' phone."

I grabbed the cordless phone and called Jackie. "What's up?"

"Hey, boyfriend. I need to see you. Where you at?"

"I'm with my niggas right now."

"Well, you can hang out with them later. The deacon is working late and I'm coming to pick you up. You at the boy Rideout's house?"

"Yeah."

"I'ma be there in about an hour."

"A'ight."

When I got off the phone, Crash and Rideout was all in my smitty.

"Damn. Fuck you niggas on?"

"That was that fine-ass yellow church bitch, wasn't it?" Crash asked.

"Yeah. She finna come swoop me."

"You definitely be eating her ass or pussy, li'l folks. Ain't no way you hittin' that without lickin' that," Rideout said.

"I told you I'm a real mack, booty eatin'-ass nigga. Ladies love cool Carl," I joked before turning to Crash. "Hit the liquor store with me, fam. I would ask Rideout, but ain't no way I'm drankin' nothing after that nigga no more."

"On everythang!" Crash laughed, following me to the door.

"Fuck both of you li'l niggas," Rideout called behind us. "Grab me a 40!"

We walked a block over to the liquor store and grabbed three forty ounces of Old English 800. We had just stepped out of the store when a white 1977 Cadillac Eldorado came to a skidding stop a few houses from the liquor store. The pearl white L-Dog got everybody's attention. The gold grill, gold side mirrors, and gold trim around the Caddy made it stand out. The clean whip was also sitting on thirty's with True and Vogue tires. Tupac's "Me Against the World" was bumping from the sound system.

Jewels hopped out of the car looking like the definition of a successful street nigga. His permed hair was freshly done up in finger waves with gold glitter making it shine like real gold. He wore a thick herringbone chain with a medallion made up in the head of an Egyptian woman. On one wrist was a gold watch, on the other, a gold bracelet. And he had iced-out pinkie rings on both fingers. He wore a Gucci shirt, slacks, and snakeskin shoes.

"No, Jewels! Get back in the car!" a fine-ass woman that looked like she could be in movies called as she got out of the car to chase her man.

"Get back in the car, Glenda! I gotta take care of some business!" Jewels yelled.

Glenda stood near the Caddy and watched as Jewels stormed up the stairs of a white house and banged on the door like he was the police. Someone inside must've asked who was outside, because he started screaming.

"It's Jewels, muthafucka! Tommy Guns, get yo' muthafuckin' ass out here right now, nigga. I got some holla for yo' ass!"

The door opened a moment later and Jewels grabbed a tall, skinny nigga by the neck and snatched him outside.

"No, Jewels! Get in the car!" Glenda called.

Jewels ignored her and pulled a big-ass revolver from his pants and put it in the nigga's mouth. "You tryna play me out my shit, nigga?"

Tommy guns mumbled something that I couldn't hear.

"Let me find out you tryna play me, Tommy, and I'ma come back over here and knock yo' muthafuckin' noodles out!"

Tommy guns did some more mumbling before Jewels threw him down on the porch and pointed the gun in his face.

"If I don't get my shit by 9:59 tonight, I'm coming back and lighting this bitch up like it's the 4th of July!" he threatened before kicking Tommy in the face.

I stood in awe watching Jewels get down. That shit looked like something out of a movie and I loved it. Jewels was known all over Chicago as somebody you didn't fuck with. He was also known for getting money and keeping some of the finest females in Chicago in the passenger side of his cars. We made eye contact as he walked around to get in the L-Dog. Then he acknowledged my presence with a wink and a smile. And just like that, he was gone.

"You know Jewels?" Crash asked.

"Nah. But real macks know another mack when they see one," I jacked.

Blood on the Money

We went back to Rideout's spot and sat around drinking 40s until I heard Jackie's horn. After showing my niggas some love, I stepped outside and seen the pink Benz coupe parked at the curb. I strolled coolly towards the car as Jackie got out looking like a black queen. She wore high heels and a tight gold dress that showed all of her body parts.

"Hey, boyfriend." She smiled walking up to kiss me. "Ugh! You been drinking beer?" she asked, making a sour face.

"Yeah. My bad."

"Next time chew some gum or eat a peppermint. You know I don't like beer," she fussed.

"A'ight. Where we going?" I asked.

"Wherever you drive to," she said before getting in the passenger seat.

I hopped in the driver's seat and pulled away from the curb.

"Where are the Jordan's I bought for your birthday?" she asked, undoing my pants.

"I wore 'em on my birthday. I can't wear 'em every day."

She pulled out my dick and began stroking it. "Tell me how bad you want to fuck me, Carl."

This is why Jackie cheated on her husband. She could act out her wildest fantasies with me and be who she really is: a straight-up freak!

"Every time I see you, I wanna stick my dick in you and fuck you til you cum. You got the best pussy I ever fucked and I wish I could fuck you all the time."

A shiver ran through Jackie's body like she was having an orgasm as she hiked her dress up to her waist. "Yes, Carl! I love when you talk nasty to me. Tell me some more."

"I want you to play with that pussy while you suck my dick. And I want you to gag. Do it now."

Jackie leaned over and started sucking the shit out of my dick while fingering herself roughly. She started gagging and choking like I told her, using so much slob that I could feel my dick hairs getting wet. I grabbed her head and pushed it down some more. She gagged like she was about to throw up, but I know she loved it.

"Keep suckin', and I want you to swallow my nut. Swallow all of it. Bet' not waste a drop."

Jackie sucked my dick harder and faster, continuing to gag and slob all over me. Shit felt so good that I was having a hard time concentrating on driving. When she came, she started moaning on my dick, sending vibrations through my shit. Felt too damn good and I skeeted.

"Aw shit!" I groaned, gripping the steering wheel.

Jackie kept on sucking until I was drained. When she lifted her head, there was slob all over her face.

"Take me somewhere right now and fuck the shit out of me," she demanded.

We ended up at a cheap motel on 79th and Stony Island. I parked at the back so I could hide her car, ready to get out and grab a room.

"Where you going?" Jackie asked, a crazed look in her eyes.

"We gotta get a room."

She started yanking at my pants. "Pull them all the way off. I need some dick right now."

I took a look around. It was almost six o'clock and just starting to get dark. "You sure?"

She leaned over and started trying to recline my seat. "Push the seat all the way back and recline it."

I did what she said and she climbed on top of me reverse cowgirl. She held the steering wheel and lowered herself onto my dick.

"Oh shit, Carl! I missed you so much, baby," she moaned as she rode me.

"I missed you too, Jackie," I talked back, noticing the small string hanging out of her ass. She wanted the lawnmower.

"Do you like the way my pussy feel, Carl? Is it good?"

"You got that bomb, baby. You know I love yo' pussy. Yo pussy is my pussy, ain't it?"

"Yes, Carl. It's yo' pussy, baby. Yeah. It's yours," she moaned, riding me faster. She was going so hard that the shocks began squeaking as the car bounced. A few minutes later, she was at her peak.

"Gimme the lawnmower, baby! Pull 'em out!"

I grabbed the string that was hanging out of her ass and pulled like I was starting a lawnmower. When the string of medium-sized anal beads slipped from her ass, Jackie started screaming at the top of her lungs.

"Oh God! Oh my God! Oh my God!"

She sat down hard on my lap as the orgasm gripped her body. It took almost a minute for it to pass.

"Damn, Carl," she breathed. "I love your little young ass."

"I know. Do you still want me to get the room?"

She climbed off me and into the passenger seat. "I ain't through with you yet, li'l nigga. I gotta suitcase in the trunk. Grab it for me and go pay for the room."

J-Blunt

Chapter 4

Nana's health was fading fast.

Two weeks ago she was on her feet and looked healthy. Now she barely got out of bed and complained of pain most of the day. My aunty Trisha came over almost every day to check on her and talk to the home nurse that was given by the healthcare company.

"What's gon' happen to us when Nana dies?" my little brother asked.

I looked up from my pager and seen tears in Chris's eyes. "Nothing. We gon' keep doing what we been doing. We still gon' live here and you still going to school."

"Who gon' pay the bills and cook the food? Who gon' help me with my homework?"

"I'ma do all that?"

"How? You don't even got a job."

"I don't know. I gotta figure it out."

We looked towards the hallway as Trisha walked in the living room. "I'm tired of this shit," she complained, throwing some papers on the floor and wiping tears from her eyes.

"What up, Aunty?" I asked, picking up the paper.

"These muthafuckas tryna stop the in-home nursing assistant from coming over if we don't pay them eight hundred dollars. My mama about to die and they don't even care. All they thinking about is they money."

I read the letter from the insurance company. Nana's insurance wouldn't cover the nurse visits. It would have to come out of pocket.

"This don't make no sense," I mumbled, reading the letter again. "Why won't the insurance pay for it? I thought that's what having insurance was about."

"Not when you about to die and costing them money. They don't wanna spend they money on somebody that can't pay the premiums."

Seeing the helplessness on my aunt's face and the tears in her eyes made me want to do something about it.

"How long we got to give 'em the money?"

"The letter say by the first of December. It's the holidays. How they expect us to get the money that fast?"

I grabbed my Chicago Bears Starter pullover coat. "I'ma get the money," I said before walking out the door.

The cold Chicago hawk slapped me in the face when I stepped onto the front porch. Winter was here and a fresh layer of snow covered the ground, crunching under my Nike boots as I mobbed over to Rideout's house.

"What's hannin', family?" he answered the door.

"I need eight hunnit dollars," I said, kicking the snow from my boots before walking in the house.

"You spent that shit we took from them ops in Harvey?"

"Shit been gone. I had to pay off the car for Granny. Now they tryna take her nurse unless we pay them the eight hunnit."

Rideout shook his head. "That's some fag-ass shit."

"Hey, Carl," Sherry greeted, walking out of the bedroom.

"'Sup, shorty." I nodded before turning back to Rideout. "Who can we jack real quick? I need that shit right now."

He thought for a moment. "I don't know. Shit, maybe one of these liquor stores or somethin'."

I liked the idea. "I never liked them Arabs on Stony Island. Let's get they ass."

Rideout nodded. "You know I'm G. I'm always down to take somebody shit. Let me get the Mossberg."

I fingered the shotgun as we crept through the wintry Chicago night in the Pontiac. My thoughts were mostly on Nana. She needed somebody to take care of her while she was on her way out and I was going to do whatever was necessary to pay for that nurse.

When we got to the liquor store, Rideout drove past the front so we could take a look. We didn't see nothing crazy, plus the snow and cold cut down the traffic in and out of the store. After parking around the corner, we put on ski masks and I tucked the Mossberg in my pants leg. Rideout led the way as we jogged to the liquor store. When we got to the door, he was the first one in.

"Everybody get the fuck down!" Rideout screamed, shooting in the air.

There were a few people in the store and they hit the floor as soon as the shooting started. I pulled the shotgun from my pants and watched over the customers while Rideout went to the counter.

"Gimme the money out that drawer, you Arab muthafucka!" he demanded.

The little brown-skinned man behind the counter looked terrified. "Okay! Okay! Don't shoot!"

"Shut the fuck up, bitch, and gimme the money!" Rideout screamed.

I continued watching the people on the floor.

"Put it in a bag, bitch! Put it in a bag!"

The clerk fumbled putting the money in the bag.

"Gimme this shit, stupid muthafucka! Here, folks," he called, tossing me the bag. "Gimme some of that top shelf, bitch!"

I didn't catch the bag cleanly and some of the money spilled onto the floor. I bent down to pick it up while Rideout had the clerk putting the expensive liquor in a bag. Movement near the back of the store caught my eye. I looked up as another Arab came from the back holding an M-16. He didn't see me because I was bending down. But he seen Rideout.

"Rideout, wa——"

Tat-tat-tat-tat-tat-tat!

Rideout fell into the counter and dropped his gun as the assault rifle bullets tore him up. I stood up, lifted the gauge, and let it ride.

Kaboom!

The 12 gauge slug tore into the Arab's stomach, lifting him off his feet and knocking him on his ass. In all the commotion, I didn't notice the Arab behind the counter pick up Rideout's gun until he pointed it at me and started shooting.

Pop, pop, pop, pop!

I dropped to the floor, hiding behind a rack of potato chips and crawling to the door.

The clerk kept shooting, sending potato chips raining down all over me.

When I got to the door, I stayed low, keeping cover behind the rack. I couldn't see the clerk, but I figured he was still at the counter. I cocked the gauge before lifting it over my head and letting it blow.

Kaboom! Sh-sh. Kaboom! Sh-sh. Kaboom!

I took off from the store, the gauge in one hand and bag of money in the other. I slipped and slid in the snow as I made my get away. I had just got to the corner when the shooting started again.

Pop, pop, pop, pop!

I dipped behind a car and peeked my head up. The clerk was walking towards me holding the gun out. I cocked the gauge again and got on his ass.

Kaboom! Sh-sh. Click. The shotgun was out of bullets, but that was okay because the clerk was lying on the ground with a slug to the chest. I took off running, disappearing down a side street. I tucked the gauge in my pants and half walked/half ran while watching my ass. I was so busy looking behind me while crossing the street that I didn't notice the car coming towards me. I looked up too late and all I seen was headlights. Next thing I knew, I was flying. I hit the cold hard ground and rolled a little bit, but my adrenaline had me back on my feet with the quickness.

"Nigga, what the fuck wrong with you?" a man yelled, jumping from the driver's seat.

I recognized him immediately. It was Jewels.

"My bad," I said, trying to walk away. That's when I felt the pain in my leg and buckled over. "Ahh shit!"

"You a'ight, young blood?" he asked.

I reached down my pants and tried to pull out the bent up shotgun that was stabbing my leg.

"Hold on, li'l nigga!" Jewels yelled, pulling out a big-ass revolver.

"I'm not on that!" I screamed, lifting my hands. I had a broken gun and no bullets. I wasn't trying to go out like Willie Lump Lump.

"Fuck wrong wit'chu, boy!? You tryna pull a gun on me?" He yelled.

"Nah. It's stabbing my leg. I gotta take it out."

He looked me over suspiciously. "Let me see yo' face, boy. Take that mask off."

I took the mask off. Recognition flashed in his eyes.

"You look familiar. Where I know you from?"

"I was walking past when you fucked up Tommy Guns. Listen, Jewels. I gotta get the fuck outta here. I'm hot. And this gun is stabbing me."

He lowered his gun. "A'ight. Gimme that gun and get the fuck outta here," he said, nodding towards the sidewalk.

I wasn't about to give him the gun that I just put some bodies on and had my fingerprints on. "I can't give it to you."

Sirens in the distance got both of our attention. Then it all dawned on him.

"Oh shit. You just put in work?"

"Yeah. Can I get a ride?"

He looked like he was about to say no.

"Hurry up and get in. And you bet' not bleed on my peanut butter interior."

I pulled the mangled shotgun from my pants as Jewels drove away. Police cars sped towards the liquor store from all directions.

"What you do?" Jewels asked.

I didn't want to say. "I hit a lick."

He glanced over at me. "So you ain't no dummy, huh? Know not to talk how you walk."

I nodded.

"I respect that. I like when niggas keep it gangsta. You know my name. What's yours?"

"Carl."

"You from the South Side, right?"

I nodded. "Yeah. 119th and Hausted."

He chuckled. "You one of Larry's boys, huh?"

"Yeah."

"What's yo' hustle?"

"I get it how I live."

"Did you leave any witnesses?"

"Yeah. But I wore a mask."

"Robbery, huh? Hittin licks?"

I shrugged. "I get it how I live."

He glanced at me again. "How much you get?"

I wasn't sure if I should tell him.

He seen my hesitation.

"I don't want yo' money, young blood," he said, pulling a knot from his pocket and setting it in the ashtray. "My last lick got me fifty thousand. That's five of it right there. How much you get?"

I reached in my underwear and pulled out the brown paper bag. After dumping the money on my lap, I counted it. I had 437 dollars.

"Look like chump change. How much is it?" Jewels asked.

"Four hunnit."

He looked disappointed. "Think about everything that you just went through to get that money and then tell me if you think it was worth it."

Visions of Rideout getting shot flashed in my head. I wasn't a hundred percent sure, but I knew he was dead. And so were the Arabs.

"Nah."

"You know how much time you would be facing if you got caught?"

I wasn't sure how much time I would be facing for two bodies and a robbery.

"I don't know."

"That's yo' first mistake, Carl. You don't know what the fuck you doing. You know how to recite lit and fall in line, but you don't know shit about gettin money. And that's sad. You ready to give up yo' freedom for four hunnit dollars. And just so you know, for that robbery, you would be facing fifteen years. But based on the way all those police cars was flying by, somebody died. For a body and a robbery, that's an extra twenty five to thirty years."

We rode in silence for a while and I thought about everything Jewels said. I never thought about how much time I would be facing if I ever got locked up for a robbery. And I never considered if what I was robbing niggas for was worth my freedom. I was just trying to get a li'l money to meet a few needs.

"What you want, Carl?" he asked, breaking the silence.

I wasn't sure how to answer. "What kinda question is that?"

"That's the question you need to ask yo'self before you run around out here robbing and shooting people with shotguns for a few hundred dollars. What do you want? What are the desires of yo' heart? You don't gotta answer that right now. That's not a question you should take lightly. I'm just giving you something to think about."

We got quiet again. I was thinking about what I wanted. I never been asked the question and I was stumped.

"Okay, Carl. This yo' stop. Where you want me to drop you off at?" Jewels asked.

I didn't want him to know where I lived, so I stopped him at the corner. "You can let me out right here."

He pulled to the curb. "I wanna give you my pager number. When you figure out the answer to my question, gimme a call. Make yo' code 119 so I know it's you. Here go some advice. Get rid of that gun. Break it in pieces and throw it in different sewers or parts of the lake. Also, get you an alibi. Take yo' girlfriend out in public so you can have people back y'all up. The way those police was moving tells me they finna be looking hard for the shooter. Peace, young brotha."

I got out of the Cadillac with a bunch of mixed feelings. I was happy that I met Jewels and got some game from him, but fucked up about losing my nigga, Rideout. And it was really fucked up that he died over four hundred punk-ass dollars. I had to tell Sherry the news, and that was a conversation I wasn't looking forward to having. And I still needed four hundred more dollars to keep Nana's nurse.

After stashing the shotgun in the bushes behind Nana's house, I limped over to Rideout's house. I gathered my strength before knocking on the door.

"Who is it?" Sherry called.

"Carl."

She opened the door with a puzzled look on her face. "Where Rideout?"

Even though I practiced what I would say on my way over, I couldn't get the words out.

"He got caught?" she asked, her body language deflating.

I shook my head. "Nah. He... He got shot. I don't think he made it."

It looked like she didn't hear what I said. Her eyes grew wide and then squinted really small. Then she looked confused. "He didn't make it?"

"The Arabs killed him," I mumbled.

I seen her worst nightmare come to life in her eyes before she collapsed to the floor. "Nooooo!"

I walked in the house and wrapped her in a hug.

"No, Carl! No! He not dead, Carl. He not dead!" she cried.

**

As soon as my eyes opened, I thought about Rideout. My nigga was gone. Ever since Jewels pointed out how petty the lick was, I kept comparing a money amount to the value of life. I wasn't sure how much I was worth. Made me think about what I learned about slavery in school. During those times, black life wasn't worth shit. And as I thought about all the niggas that got locked up and killed in Chicago every year, I realized that not much changed since the 1800s. My nigga died over four hundred dollars. That shit was fucked up.

Movement from Marie got my attention. She stretched and yawned before looking to me.

"G'morning," she mumbled.

"'Sup, shorty?"

"What time is it?"

I looked to the clock on my dresser. "8:56."

She stretched again. "Damn, I'm still tired. Why you woke so early?"

"I was thinking. I got a question for you. How much is yo life worth?"

She thought for a moment. "I don't think you can put a value on life. You only live once, so it's precious."

I had to think about what she said. That shit was deep.

"You thinking about that because of what happened to Rideout last night?" she asked, turning to look at me.

"Yeah. I never really thought about life being precious. Niggas get killed every day, but I never stopped to think about it until last night. My nigga died over a couple of hunnit. That shit just feel fucked up."

"When you think about it like that, it is. But y'all been doing that for a while so he knew what he was doing."

"I know. I just wish I coulda seen that muthafucka. I was supposed to watch his back but I got distracted picking up the money. We was supposed to get the money so I could pay for my Nana's nurse, but he wanted to get some liquor. That shit threw everything off."

We grew silent for a few moments.

"You ever thought about leaving Chicago?"

I looked at her like she was crazy. "And go where? The city is all I know."

"I'm getting ready to move to Wisconsin with my sister. She said it's better than here. You can come with us."

I shook my head. "I gotta be here for my Nana. Plus, I don't know nobody in Wisconsin. I ain't going nowhere that I don't know nobody."

"Well, whatever you decide to do, I hope you stay safe. Don't let this city take you under. You a good nigga, Carl, and your life is worth more than you think. You are precious."

"I appreciate that. So, you really leaving Chicago?"

"Yeah. My sister found a good job and I live with her, so I gotta go."

"Damn. So this probably gonna be the last time I get some of this good-ass pussy, huh?"

A lustful fire lit in her eyes. "Yep. So what you gon' do about it?"

Damn. I didn't have no more rubbers, but I wanted to fuck. I decided to roll the dice and climbed on top of her. "I'ma fuck you like it's the last time."

Chapter 5

I stood at the door of Nana's room and watched her for a moment. She lay in bed covered by several blankets. She looked fragile and weak, like death was knocking on her door. The dresser had been converted into a pharmacy, all kinds of pill bottles lining the oak surface. The scene was heartbreaking and it took all of my strength not to cry as I went to her bedside. Her eyes were closed.

"You asleep, Nana?" I whispered.

Her eyes opened slowly. She looked weary. "Hey, Carl," she whispered.

"Hey. How you doing? You need anything?"

She offered a weak smile. "I need you-" her words were cut short by a bout of harsh coughs.

I grabbed the glass of water from the bedside table and held it to her lips. "Here, Nana. Take a drink."

She lifted her head and took a small sip. "Thank you, baby." She grimaced. After taking a moment to gather her strength, she tried to speak again. "I need you to be strong for your brother. He don't understand everything that's going on right now and it's making him angry. I need you to help him deal with the anger so he won't take it out on the wrong people."

"I got him, Nana. I'ma talk to him about it when he come back home."

Nana let out heavy breath. "I'm getting so tired, baby."

I didn't want to cry, but the tears came on they own. I grabbed her hand and held on tight. "Just stay with us as long as you can, Nana. I love you so much."

She reached a hand up and wiped my tears. "It's okay, baby. To be absent from the body is to be present with the Lord."

***

The police was looking for me. Two Arabs died along with Rideout and they were showing video from the robbery on all the news channels. They showed close-ups of me and my clothes. Luckily I wore the ski mask so they didn't have my identity. But they were asking all around the city about the robbery and offered a reward for any information leading to my arrest. The only people that knew about the move was Sherry, Marie, and Crash. I knew they wouldn't tell, but I was hot as fuck and had to lay low.

"I'm done with this petty robbing shit."

Crash looked up from the TV. We was in his room playing Killer Instinct on Nintendo 64. "How you gon' get money? You gon' pick up that nation sack?"

"Nah. I ain't finna be hustling for no other niggas."

"So, what you gon' do then?"

I set the joystick down. "When I was running from the liquor store, I ran into Jewels. He gave me a ride to the crib and asked me a question that got me thinking."

"On what, you was with Jewels? What he say?"

"He asked me what I wanted. Why I was jackin'."

"You told him for the money, right? That's why we do it, nigga. For the bread."

"That wasn't what he was talking about. He asked me what I wanted out of life. Is we supposed to spend the rest of our life jackin' and killin' niggas for a few G's, or do we want more? Rideout died over four hunnit dollars and some Hennessey. That shit just don't seem right."

"I think you looking at it the wrong way. He didn't die over four hunnit dollars and some liquor. He died hustling how he got it. That's what we do. We take niggas' shit. He died like a gangsta."

I shook my head. "Life supposed to be precious. We only live once, my G. Think about it like this. If you had the last diamond in the world, wouldn't you protect that shit? You wouldn't just give it away. We more valuable than diamonds, my nigga. It's only one me and it's only one you. We irreplaceable. We ain't gon' find another Rideout. He gone, G."

Crash was quiet for a moment. "Damn. I never thought about it like that."

"Me either. Not until I rode with Jewels. Everything he said was on point and I been thinking about that shit ever since. We can't be trading our lives and freedom for chump change."

"So, how we gon' get paid? What we gon' do, rob a bank or somethin'?"

I shrugged. "I don't know. Jewels told me to page him when I found out what I wanted."

"Do you know what you want?"

I nodded. "Yeah. I wanna make a lot of money, but do it a smarter way. He told me his last move paid fifty G's. I want in on that."

"So what you waiting for, nigga? Page him."

***

I paged Jewels and left my code, 119. He called back about fifteen minutes later and told me to meet him at the pool hall on 87th and Ashland. Me and Crash hopped in my Nana's black 1987 Oldsmobile Park Avenue and drove over.

The pool hall was filled with older people who gave us the eye when we entered. I ignored them and looked around for Jewels. I spotted him at a table near the back shooting pool with two fine-ass females. One of them I'd seen with him before, when he pulled the gun on Tommy Guns.

"Young Carl!" Jewels called when he seen me walking over.

"'Sup, Jewels?" I nodded, loving the stares I was getting from his female company.

"What's going on, young blood? I'm glad to see you no longer limping," he said before turning to Crash. "What's up with you, young blood?"

"I'm good. What's poppin'?" Crash nodded.

Jewels gave him a long look before turning back to me. "Do you know about billiards?"

"I know a li'l something about it."

He looked surprised. "Do you now? Give him yo' stick, Valerie. Let's see what the kid knows. Let me rack 'em."

After racking the balls in the triangle, he pulled a quarter from his pocket. "I'ma flip a coin to see who break. Call it in the air."

"Heads," I called, grabbing the pool stick from the woman.

Jewels caught the coin out of the air and flipped it onto the back of his hand.

"Heads it is. Break 'em."

I set the cue ball on the white dot and leaned over the table, taking aim with my stick. When I was satisfied, I hit the cue. The white ball smacked into the other balls, scattering them around the table. Two striped balls went into the holes.

"Good break, young blood. You got stripes," he said before turning to the women. "Y'all get us some drinks. Matter fact, tell Steve to give me a bottle of King Louis and a couple glasses."

Me and Crash watched the women's phatties. I loved watching them walk away.

"Valerie and Glenda are sisters," Jewels said. "And I'm fuckin' both of 'em and they know it."

I was surprised. "For real?"

"Damn, you a real mack," Crash nodded.

"Do y'all know what a mack is?"

I answered that. "A nigga with flavor."

"Almost." Jewels smiled. "Macking is the art of persuasion. The flavor that you talking about is confidence and charisma. If you know what to do with those two qualities, you can have anything you want. Even sisters. Your shot."

I took a moment to chew on his words while lining up my shot.

"Did you think about the question I asked you?" Jewels interrupted.

I cracked a ball into the corner pocket before answering. "Yeah. I want to get money, but also be around to spend it."

He nodded before turning to Crash. "And what do you want?"

"Same thing as Carl. We wanna make some money."

I lined up another shot, but missed.

The women came back with the liquor and poured us drinks.

"Why do you want the money? You answer first, Crash."

Blood on the Money

"'Cause I'm tired of asking for a ride. I need my own Cadillac. I want some jewelry too. Like a Rolex and a herring bone."

Jewels dismissed him and turned to me. "What about you, Carl?"

"I got responsibilities. My Nana dying from cancer and we gotta pay her doctor bills. I gotta take care of my li'l brother, too."

Jewels nodded before bending over the table and sinking a shot. I took a sip from my drink, watching and waiting for him to continue speaking.

"I was like you, Crash, when I first started hustling. I wanted the finer things and I spent most of the money I made. The problem with that is I didn't have any money left after I bought all the cars and jewelry. So what did I do? I had to hustle it all over again. It was a never-ending cycle. It took me a while to learn this principle: there are few things in life worse than a fool with money."

After saying the line, he sank three straight balls.

"The hustle is not meant to be forever. You get what you need and get out so you can live to enjoy the fruits of your labor. This is the first lesson. Come up with a plan."

While giving us the lessons, he continued to sink shot after shot until there was only the eight ball left. Instead of winning the game, he stood to talk some more.

"I'm going to put y'all on a move. Should put a nice piece of change in ya pockets. This ain't no liquor store robbery, bloods. I'ma show y'all what real money looks like. Depending on how good y'all do is gon' help me decide if I want to take y'all on my last move that I'ma ever need."

After pausing to stare at us, he turned back to the game. "Eight ball, corner pocket."

***

I'm not gon' lie. I was scared as hell.

It was 4:40 in the evening and the sun was just starting to go down. I was in Calumet City, a suburb outside of Chicago filled with white people. The one thing most niggas didn't do was commit crimes in white neighborhoods or against white people. History taught us that was a no-no. Emmit Till got killed for whistling at a white woman. And niggas that got caught or framed for committing crimes against white people were thrown in prison with sentences as long as phone numbers. Yet here we were, me, Crash, and Jewels, sitting in a stolen Pest Control truck outside a white family's house playing Russian roulette with our freedom.

"You with me, Carl," Jewels directed, slipping on a pair of black leather gloves. "Crash, wait until we get inside and then you park this van around the corner and walk back."

"I got it," Crash said.

We got out of the van dressed in tan jumpsuits. I was hoping I didn't piss or shit myself because my stomach was doing summersaults from the fear.

"You okay?" Jewels asked as we walked up the walkway.

"I'm good," I lied.

He saw through me. "Fear is good. It keeps you sharp and aware. What you can't do is let it paralyze you. I'm scared every time I make a move. But it's okay. Fear and do it anyway," he said before ringing the doorbell.

"Who is it?" a white lady asked from inside.

"Quality Pest Control. We're here about your pest problem," Jewels called.

The door opened and a blonde-haired white woman appeared behind the screen. "I didn't call a bug company. Are you sure you have the right house?"

Jewels checked the clipboard. "Looks like the call was made by Christopher Maddow."

"That's my husband, but we don't have a pest problem."

Jewels looked confused. "Okay. Well, we came out. If you don't need our help, I need you to sign this and we'll get out of here. It's a form saying you don't need our services."

The woman opened the door and took the clipboard. "Where do I sign?"

Jewels pulled the gun. "Get back, lady!" he said, forcing his way in the house.

"No! Stop! Somebody help!" the lady screamed.

"Shut up, bitch!" Jewels yelled slapping her to the floor. Then he turned to me. "Go get the kid!"

I ran through the house, checking all the rooms, and found a seven-year-old boy in the back playing a video game.

"Who are you?" he asked.

"I'm a friend of yo' daddy. Come with me."

He didn't move fast enough, so I grabbed him by the arm and led him to the living room. Jewels had the woman sitting on the couch at gun point. I sat the boy next to her.

"What do you want?" she asked, holding the boy in her arms.

"We are not going to hurt your family as long as you cooperate," Jewels spoke up. "As soon as your husband gets home, I'll explain everything. For now, sit tight. What time does he get home?"

"He should be here soon. What do you want?"

The doorbell rang. Jewels gave me a nod and I went to check the peephole. Crash was on the porch.

"How did it go?" Jewels asked.

"We good."

"Okay. Everybody relax and let's wait for Mr. Maddow," Jewels said before sitting down on the couch across from the mother and son.

I couldn't relax, so I paced and checked the windows to watch for the husband. At 5:36, a gray Grand Prix pulled into the driveway.

"Here we go," I said, pulling my gun and standing behind the door.

Crash hid in the hall while Jewels remained sitting on the couch looking calm. I heard a key being inserted into the lock on the door before it opened.

"Honey, I'm home!" the man called as he stepped into the house. When he saw his family sitting on the couch looking scared and Jewels sitting across from them, he got angry. "Who the fuck are you?"

Crash appeared from the hallway holding a gun while I closed the door and put the gun to his head. "Chill, man."

"Mr. Maddow, come have a seat next to yo family," Jewels gestured.

"Did they hurt you?" he asked his wife as he sat next to his family.

"They fine. All we ask is that you cooperate and nobody will be hurt," Jewels explained

"What the hell do you want?" the man asked angrily.

"We don't want nothing from your house, Mr. Maddow. We came for the money in the safe at your job. Me and my boys are going to stay the night with you and your family. As long as you cooperate and nobody tries to play hero, we'll be gone in the morning. Don't risk the life of your family for something that doesn't belong to you."

We stayed in the living room with the family all night. They eventually fell asleep, but we didn't. When the morning came, Jewels woke the husband.

"Let's go, Chris. Me, you, and my partner are going to get the money. I'm going to leave one of my boys with your family and as long as you don't do nothing stupid, everythang will be fine."

After assuring his wife and son that everything would be fine, we went to the car. I laid down in the backseat while Jewels rode up front. When we got to the check cashing place, me and Jewels put on masks and went inside with the manager. He led us to the back and cracked open the safe. Inside was fifty-six thousand dollars. My eyes got so big that it felt like they was about to pop out of my head. I had never seen so much money in my life. After putting the money in a bag, Jewels used the phone to call the Maddow's house to tell Crash to get the fuck out of there. After tying up the manager, we made our way to the getaway car parked on the next block.

"That's how you get money without risking your life." Jewels nodded as we got in the car.

Chapter 6

I walked away with ten thousand dollars cash money!

When I got home, I spread the one hundred 100 dollar bills out on my bed and just stared at it. All the bills were crispy like they just came from the bank. And nobody got shot or killed for it. It was so easy that I couldn't believe we hadn't thought about it before. The entire lick felt too good to be true. But I knew it was true because I had the proof laying on my bed. I didn't know what I was going to do with the money. I didn't even want to spend it. If I could, I would've looked at it every day all day. But I had responsibilities and shit to do.

After a night of the best sleep I had in a long time, the first thing I did the next morning was pay for my Nana's home nurse. I also hit the bank and opened a checking and savings account, dropping a thousand dollars in each one. For the first time, I felt like a grown man. I had a car that was paid off, money in the bank, and a house in my name. I was growing up fast as hell. Shit didn't seem real, but it was.

I was heading back home when my pager started beeping. I checked the number and seen the code 69. It was Jackie. I stopped at a payphone to hit her back.

"What up, baby?"

"Hey, boyfriend. What are you doing?"

"I'm about to be doing you if you say the right words."

"Mmmhhh," she moaned. "You know how to read my mind, don't you?"

"I can do more than read yo' mind, baby. I know how to talk to yo' body. I'm finna get the same room we had last time. What time you getting off?"

"Right now. The building is being fumigated and I have the rest of the day off. I want you to fuck me until I can't walk. You think you can do that?"

"You ain't said shit, baby. You know what they say. Once you go black, you gon' need a wheelchair."

After ending the call, I hopped in the Park Avenue and went to the liquor store to grab a pint of Seagram's gin before getting the room. I smoked a blunt and drank half the pint before there was a knock on the door. I went to answer dressed only in my boxers.

"Hey, boyfriend!" Jackie smiled devilishly as she stepped into the room. She was wearing a pink pants suit with her hair flowing past her shoulders.

Damn she was fine!

"That ain't how you greet yo' man, baby. Do it right."

She dropped her purse on the floor then went to lock the door. I stood where I was as she dropped to her knees and pulled out my dick. She kissed the head then looked up at me. "Hey, boyfriend. Can I get undressed, or do you want me to suck it?"

Damn, she looked so fuckin' good on her knees with my dick in her hand. "Get up and take them clothes off."

She looked disappointed, like she wanted to stay on her knees. "Look in my purse. Do you know what to do with those?"

While she undressed, I grabbed her purse from the floor and poured out the contents on the bed. There were four sets of handcuffs and a vibrating dildo. When I looked at her, there was a fire in her eyes.

"Cuff me to the bed and do whatever you want."

After she was naked, I made her lay on her back with her head hanging off the foot of the bed, then I cuffed her wrists and ankles to the bed post. After taking off my underwear, I stood before her, checking out her body. She was stretched wide, her big-ass titties spread out, nipples hard. Her pussy was shaved and thick thighs wide open.

"What are you waiting for?" she asked, staring at me upside down.

I walked up to her about to crawl on top and 69 but when she reached her head up and sucked my sick in her mouth, I stopped and let her do her thang. She was upside down so she couldn't polish my knob like she normally did. But that was okay. I took over and started shoving my dick deep down her throat, my balls slappin her nose every time I thrust forward. I grabbed her nipples between my thumb and finger and began pinching them and she started moaning. And that's when my pager started beeping. I ignored it, but it went off again. And then again.

"Wait, baby. Let me look at it."

"No, Carl. Bring that dick back over here!" Jackie demanded.

"Here I come," I said, grabbing the pager from my pocket and checking the number. It was my aunty Trisha's work number with the code 911. Images of my Granny flashed in my head.

"No, no, no!" I panicked as I grabbed the phone.

"What are you doing, Carl? Get your ass over here right now," Jackie said, getting mad. "Who are you calling?"

"It's my aunty Trisha. I think something might've happened to my Nana," I explained while dialing the number.

"Hello?"

"Aunty Trisha, this Carl. What's going on? Is Nana okay?"

"Yeah, my mama is fine. It's Chris. I just got a call from his school. He had a fight and got suspended. I need you to pick him up for me." The emergency page no longer seemed like an emergency.

"You need me to go get him right now?"

"Yeah. He suspended and I'm in the middle of something. I need you to take him home."

I looked at Jackie. She was eyeing me like a hungry cat watching a mouse.

"Okay. I got it." After hanging up the phone, I turned to Jackie. "I gotta go, baby. I gotta pick my li'l brother up from school."

She looked pissed. "No, Carl! Hell nah! You better not leave."

I grabbed my underwear. "This my little brother. I can't leave him. He had a fight and got suspended. I gotta go."

"You little mutherfucker! Uncuff me right now," she yelled, struggling to get free.

When I took one of the cuffs from her wrist, she grabbed my underwear in her fist. "You not going nowhere until you fuck me, mutherfucker!"

"Let me go, girl! You tripping," I said, trying to snatch away from her.

She ripped off my underwear. "Get your ass back over here, Carl!"

I grabbed my pants and started putting them on. "I just told you I gotta go get my brother. I'ma come back after I drop him off at home."

"No, Carl! I want to get fucked right now, dammit!"

I blew her off and continued putting on my clothes.

She grabbed the key and started unlocking the cuffs. "Oh, you think I'm playing with your light-skinned ass!"

I got dressed before she could get the cuffs off and hit the door.

"Carl! Carl, wait!" she called after me.

I was almost to the car when she came to the door naked. "Carl, wait. I'm sorry. Come back, baby, please!" she begged.

"I gotta grab Chris. I'ma come back after I drop him off at home."

I drove to my little brother's school a little pissed off that he fucked up my time with Jackie. When I went inside, I made my way to the principal's office and found my brother sitting in a chair outside the door. From what I could tell, all he had was a busted lip.

"What happened?" I asked, looking him over as my beeper started beeping.

"Greg was talking junk about Nana and I beat his ass," he explained.

I pulled out my beeper and seen it was Jackie. I was about to speak when an older black man with a gray afro walked over.

"Are you Chris's brother?" he asked.

My pager went off again.

"Yeah. What happened?"

"I'm Principal Meadows. Chris beat up another boy for talking about his grandmother. I understand that your family is going through a hard time, but Chris cannot beat up other kids. I'm suspending him for a couple of days so he can think about what he did. I won't tolerate violence in my school."

My pager went off again.

"I understand, Mr. Meadows. I'ma talk to him. Like you said, we going through a lot and he don't know how to handle it."

The principal looked understanding. "The school has counseling. If you want, we could give him a grief counselor to talk to. That can help."

My pager went off again.

"Do you need to get that?" The principal asked.

I turned it off. "I'm good," I said before looking to Chris. I didn't know shit about counseling, but if it could help him stay out of trouble, I had to give it a shot. "Yeah. That's cool. He needs all the help he can get."

"Okay. I'll arrange that to begin when the suspension is over. I have to get to another class. Excuse me."

"Let's go," I told Chris, leading the way to the door.

"Man, why you tell him to gimme a counselor?" he whined.

"Because it might keep you out of trouble. You can't keep getting suspended."

"Then they bet' not say nothing else about Nana. I don't wanna talk to no counselor. The other kids gon' talk about me."

"You can't be worried about what they say, man. And you can't keep on getting suspended. Nana gon' be mad when she find out and she don't need to be worried about this. She got enough problems."

We walked to the car in silence.

"Nana said you angry. Why?"

He stayed quiet but the tears that rolled down his face told it all.

"I know it's hard losing her, man, but it ain't nothing we can do. And fighting and being mad won't help. That's only gon hurt you. You know she don't want you fighting and getting suspended. Right now, you gotta do what's best for her and forget how you feel."

"But it ain't fair, Carl. Why she gotta die? She all we got," he sobbed.

"I hear you, man. And I feel like you. I don't want her to go either. But I'ma be here with you, man. I got you. She did her part, and now God want her to come home."

"Fuck God," he cursed

"Ay, don't say that shit no more, boy!" I snapped. "God is the reason we still alive when Mama tried to kill us. He brought us to Nana. Don't say no shit like that again or I'ma beat yo' ass."

He smacked his lips but didn't say anything else. The rest of the ride home was quiet. When I pulled up in front of the house, I turned to him.

"Listen, man. I'ma take care of you, li'l brah. I promise, I got you, my nigga. But you can't be fighting and shit. Trisha gon' holla at you when she get off work. And you wasn't wrong for kickin' that li'l nigga's ass for talking about Nana. I woulda did the same thing. But no more fighting. If you go two weeks without getting in trouble, I'ma buy you some Jordan's. Bet?"

He smiled for the first time since I picked him up. "Bet."

After my little brother went in the house, I checked my pager. There were a million pages from Jackie and one from Jewels. I drove to a pay phone and called him back.

"What's up, Jewels?"

"Hey, young blood. What you up to?"

"I just dropped my li'l brother off at home. He got suspended for fighting. Li'l kid was talking shit about our granny and he whooped that ass."

Jewels laughed. "Sounds like the young nigga was in the right to me. Niggas talk shit, they get dealt with."

"Yeah. I hear you."

"Yeah, listen I need you to come by my house. I got a few things I wanna run by you. This is my address."

Jewels lived in a nice-ass condominium on 12th and State. Big-ass floor to ceiling windows allowed me to see the entire Chicago skyline.

"Hey, Carl." Valerie smiled as she let me into the plush apartment.

As far as looks go, she was super fine. Light brown complexion, wide brown eyes, high cheekbones, and juicy lips. Her hair was long, thick, and curly, and her body was banging. She was wearing a little white silk nightgown with a lace bra and pantie set. The robe was opened and when I looked hard enough, I could see her areolas through the sheer fabric.

"'Sup, Val." I nodded.

"Jewels is in the shower. Come sit down. You want something to drink?"

"I'm good on the drink," I said, copping a squat on the white leather couch. The TV was on and music videos were playing.

"Well, I'm having a drink," she said before switching away.

I looked away from the TV to watch her ass bounce in the damn near see-through panties.

"Hey, Carl!"

I looked to my right and seen Glenda walking from the bedroom wearing only panties and a bra. I couldn't decide which sister was finer. Glenda's skin tone was the same as Valerie's. She also had long curly hair and a pretty face. They looked similar, except Glenda had a beauty mark on her chin.

"What's up, Glenda?" I nodded, trying not to stare at her jiggling body parts as she walked towards me.

"You are what's up, Carl. It's all about you, baby boy," she said, sitting down next to me and staring at me like I was Michael Jordan.

I didn't know how to react to my nigga's girl being so close to me half-naked and looking at me like she wanted to fuck.

"Why am I what's up?" I asked.

She twirled a finger through her hair, continuing to look in my eyes. "Because you are playing in the big leagues now. No more little games with little boys and little girls," she said before leaning close. "Now you need grown women," she whispered, sucking my earlobe into her mouth.

I moved my head. "What you doing, shorty?" I mugged. I couldn't believe she was all over me with Jewels in the bathroom. No way was I about to fuck his girl after everything I was learning from him.

"What's wrong? You don't like me?" she asked, rubbing my thigh.

I got up. "You trippin', Glenda. Jewels my nigga and I don't get down like that."

She looked sad. "That's too bad."

"What about me?" Valerie asked, taking off her robe and throwing it at me.

I threw the robe on the couch. "Man, y'all on some bullshit."

The women busted out laughing.

"What's funny?" I asked, looking to both women.

"You passed," Jewels said as he walked into the living room.

I looked at the women and then back to Jewels. He was fully dressed and didn't look wet.

"What's up with the test? You don't trust me?"

Jewels stared at me as he sat on the couch between the half-naked women. "Do you trust me, Carl?"

"Yeah."

"Why?"

"Because you giving me game. You just put ten thou in my pocket."

He nodded. "I did that, but that doesn't mean you should trust me. If someone telling you a few truths and using you to make their pockets fatter makes you trust them, then you will be easily manipulated. You trust too easy, Carl. And that could be your downfall one day. The early bird gets the first worm, but the second mice gets the cheese."

I didn't get it. "What?"

"Don't worry. It will all make sense in due time. For now, you're good. Have a seat. I want to talk to you. Valerie, get him a drink."

"I offered him one. He said he didn't want it."

"Well, go get him one anyway," he said before turning to me. "Do you toot?"

"Nah. I'm good."

Jewels reached under the couch and pulled out a mirror. On it was about a quarter ounce of cocaine, a rolled up 100 dollar bill, and an Ace of Spade. "This is a rich nigga's high. Shit will have you thinking you can touch the sky," he said, using the Ace of Spade to make a line. Then he picked up the bill and snorted the dope before passing the plate to Glenda.

"Whoo!" he yelled, sniffing repeatedly. "That's flake."

I remained quiet.

"Where is Crash?"

"I don't know. I ain't talked to him today."

"Do you know what he did with his cut?"

I laughed. "Bought a car and some jewelry."

He nodded knowingly. "What about you? What did you do with your cut?"

Glenda sniffing a line of coke interrupted us.

"Opened a couple bank accounts and paid off some of my Nana's medical bills."

He smiled proudly. "You are a sharp young nigga, Carl. With the right guidance, you will be great. The reason I called you over is because I'm planning a big move and I'm recruiting you. Your boy, Crash, didn't make the cut. Don't tell him nothing that we talk about. Don't even tell him about our next move. You hear me?"

I nodded. "I got you."

"Good. My next move will make the one we did the other day look like peanuts. You have the opportunity to become a very wealthy young nigga."

I didn't know what to say. All I could do was smile. "What are we doing? When?"

"You don't need to know that right now. Just know that it's happening soon."

"Here's your drink," Valerie said, giving me a glass half filled with cognac.

"Now, to celebrate this partnership, I want you to get your nose dirty with me," Jewels said, taking the plate from Glenda and offering it to me.

"I'm good, man," I declined.

Jewel's eye contact became serious. "I wasn't asking you, Carl."

I didn't want to snort that shit, but I also didn't want to offend or piss off the nigga that was about to take me to the next level.

He seen my hesitation. "It's okay, young blood. Trust me."

The way he said trust him unnerved me. There was also a gleam in his eyes. It was the look of a smarter or more powerful person manipulating someone inferior. But I pushed it to the back of my head and grabbed the plate. I used the card to make a line then picked up the dollar bill. When I looked up, Jewels and the women were watching me eagerly.

"Go ahead," Jewels nodded.

I stuck the bill up my nose and sniffed. The line of white powder went into my nose and my eyes began watering.

"There you go, young blood," I heard Jewels say.

I continued sniffing as the cocaine had an instant effect. My throat began to numb and a euphoric feeling came over me. My body started to vibrate and tingle.

"How do you feel?" Jewels asked.

I tried to wrap my mind around the feeling but struggled. "I don't know."

Jewels laughed. "That means you're high. I have to make a run, but I want you to say here until I get back. Valerie and Glenda will keep you company," he said before turning to the women. "Ladies. Entertain my guest."

The women walked over and sat next to me. Glenda grabbed my face and started kissing me while Valerie went for my zipper.

"Hold on!" I stopped them.

"Relax, Carl," Jewels said. "Have a good time. And get used to this. This is how a real boss kicks it."

The women picked up where they left off at when Jewels walked out of the condo. As soon as my dick was free, Valerie started sucking it. I was high as fuck and her mouth felt too good. Glenda continued kissing me, grabbing my hand and moving it to her pussy. I slipped two fingers into her wetness and she began moaning while sucking on my tongue. This was my first threesome and it was kicking off with a bang.

"Stand up and take your clothes off," Valerie said.

I stood and got undressed.

"Stay right there," she said, grabbing the mirror and putting a line of coke on my dick. Then she grabbed the bill and sniffed my shit clean.

"It's my turn," Glenda said, putting more snow on my dick and snorting it off.

Then she started giving me head. My dick started tingling and went numb.

Valerie grabbed the Ace of Spades and put some more girl on the corner and brought it to my nose. "Here. Take some more."

I took a big-ass sniff and it felt like that shit tickled my brain. Next thing I know, I was lying on the couch with Glenda sucking my dick while Valerie rode my face. About ten minutes later, we stopped to do more coke and change positions. Glenda rode me while Valerie sat her pussy on my face. Another pause came a few minutes later and we sniffed more dope. When we started back fucking, Valerie lay on her back with her legs spread and Glenda started sucking her pussy. That shit got me geeked and I got behind Glenda and started tearing that pussy up. When I busted my first nut, I knew that this experience would be the first of many.

J-Blunt

Chapter 7

A week later, I was back in the company of Jewels, riding in the passenger seat of the Cadillac, headed to Foster Park. There were some people there that he wanted me to meet. It was the team that he put together to pull off the next move. Even though I didn't know the niggas, I still wanted in on the move. Jewels convinced me that this would be the last robbery I ever needed and I wasn't going to pass up this opportunity, no matter who the niggas was.

"Do you remember what I said about the early bird and the worm?" Jewels asked as he pulled into the park.

"Yeah. The early bird gets the first worm and the second mouse gets the cheese."

"Did you figure out what it means?"

"I haven't really thought about it."

He parked the car. "Tell me what you think it means."

I thought for a moment. "If you want something, you gotta out-work or outsmart the competition."

Jewels nodded. "That's good, but it's more to it than that. Some-times you gotta let somebody else get there early and sacrifice them-selves so you can walk away with the prize. The first mouse that gets to the mouse trap will die. But the second one will get the cheese."

"I get it." I nodded.

"Good. The meeting we're going to will introduce you to your teammates. It's three of them. None of you know each other and I did this on purpose so nobody would fuck up the plans. I seen some-thing in all of you, but you have way more potential than the other three. And because of that, I'm going to give you an advantage. This move is going to make us rich. Probably a quarter of a million dol-lars. Do you know how much money that is?"

My mind was blown away by the amount. "Yeah. Two hundred fifty thousand."

"That's right. As it stands, you four will split one hundred thou-sand. That's twenty five thousand apiece. The other one fifty is mine. Now if you want, you can make them all the first mouse and pick them off after they do their job. If you kill them all, you can have the entire one hundred thousand. It's up to you. If you want, you can be the second mouse."

I turned to look at Jewels to see how serious he was. He stared back at me with that gleam in his eyes. I remembered what he said about not trusting niggas. All three of my teammates probably trusted him, and he was putting their lives in my hand. And I was tempted to kill them all.

"How can I get away with it?"

"I'm going to give y'all silenced pistols. Do to them as you see fit."

I took another moment to think. "I want to meet 'em first."

"Their names are Tech, Fresh, and Smoke. All of them are your oppositions and none of them know what you are. That could be an advantage." He smiled.

After getting out of the L-Dog, we strolled through the park. My teammates were already waiting in the bleachers near the basketball court.

"Gather round, young bloods," Jewels said, waving them over. "I told y'all I had something to say and now is the time. The move is going down tomorrow night. You four are the team. Introduce y'all selves."

After we all said our names, Jewels started talking again.

"I have a man inside and he will get y'all the straps. The money is upstairs in the back. Y'all gon' have to pop a cap in a couple fools to get to it. All y'all guns will have silencers so they won't hear y'all coming until it's too late. I done been in the club a hundred times and the money will be in that back room. They gon' have security at the front and back doors. Two of y'all kill the ones at the back door to clear the way for the niggas that's gon' run in the room. The niggas at the front door won't even know what going on until it's too late. It's a simple plan, my niggas. Get in and out, and y'all gon' have twenty five G's apiece."

***

Later that night, I got up with my nigga Crash. He wanted to go to The Rink and skate.

"What Jewels say about another move? I need some more money," Crash said, whipping the Cutlass through traffic.

"He didn't say. Slow down, nigga, before you crash."

"Yo' scary ass." He laughed. "The Cutti don't go slow, nigga. Fuck a speed limit. I go as fast as I wanna go."

"You gon' get us sweated by the dicks and I got weed on me," I said, looking around for the police.

"Fuck the dicks, the Jakes, the fags, the po-po, and er'body else. Muthafuckas can't fuck wit' a real gangsta. Just focus on that fake-ass mack shit you be talking 'bout and let me drive."

Twenty minutes later, we pulled into the parking lot of The Rink. The outside was packed, niggas and females all over the parking lot. We climbed from the Cutlass and walked to the door. Crash wore a gold herring bone with a big-ass six point star on it so we got a lot of looks. I paid for us to get in and we went to the counter to rent skates. After putting on the rollers, we went to find some of the guys from the 90s and seen the OGs, TJ and Lex.

"What's up, li'l folks?" TJ said, showing us love. "Ooh! Let me sport that bone, li'l nigga!"

We spent three hours at The Rink, drinking and kicking it. Everything was going good until some niggas from the 80s started tripping when Lex started macking on his girl. About twenty niggas from both sides of The Rink started piling out onto the floor. It was about to go up.

"You see that?" Crash pointed as niggas started gathering on the wood.

"Yeah," I mumbled, not wanting to get caught up in the bullshit. I had a lick to hit tomorrow and I wasn't trying to end up in jail or shot. "Let's get the fuck outta here."

Crash looked at me like I lost my mind. "Yeah, right. We gotta put in work. Let's go."

When Crash skated towards the action, I followed, wishing I wouldn't have come to The Rink. Before we could get out onto the floor, shit hit the fan. Niggas started throwing punches and a brawl kicked off. I thought about leaving, but seen a nigga rushing towards me out the corner of my eye. He was coming at me fast with a skate in his hand. I ducked out of the way as he swung. He missed, tripping and falling on the floor. I didn't have my skates on tight for this very reason and I kicked them off with the quickness. Before he could get up and swing the skate again, I was on his ass, throwing lefts and rights. He did the only thing he could do and ran. I looked around for Crash and seen him throwing blows with a nigga a few feet away. I ran over to help and we partied that nigga.

"Break it up! Break this shit up!" Security yelled, jumping in the mix.

The security guards at the rink were beasts, big swole-ass niggas that looked like they spent all their off time in the gym. There were eight of them and they jumped in the middle of the fight and started beating niggas' asses. That was my cue.

"Let's get the fuck outta here," I told Crash.

When he seen how security was handling niggas, he followed me to the counter. We changed our skates for shoes and got the fuck outta there. We made it to the Cutlass, about to get in, when some of the niggas from the 80s ran up.

"There them niggas go!" one of them yelled.

I looked over and seen a fat dark-skinned nigga pointing a revolver.

"He got a blower!" I warned Crash before ducking.

Pop, pop, pop, pop, pop, pop!

I stayed low until I heard footsteps running away. I got up slowly and seen them niggas booking it. "Bitch-ass niggas," I cursed, looking around for Crash. "Crash, you good? They gone. Where you at?"

When he didn't answer, I looked around and spotted a body lying on the ground by the driver's door. Crash was bleeding from a hole in his neck.

"Crash! Hold on, family! Hold on!" I yelled, kneeling beside him and putting pressure on the hole in his neck. "Where the keys? Where the keys?"

He couldn't answer me. His eyes were wide with shock and his body was starting to shake.

"Hold on, nigga!" I said, pulling him into the car and searching his pockets for the keys. I sat him in the passenger seat, holding my hand against his neck as I sped out of the parking lot. I got about a block from the scene when Crash's body went limp.

"Crash? Crash?" I called, slapping him in the face. "Wake up, my nigga. Crash!"

He didn't answer me back.

***

I didn't get home until almost three o'clock in the morning. I was so physically and emotionally exhausted that I fell asleep in bloodstained clothes. When I awoke later that day, a vision of Crash's body slumped in the passenger seat of his Cutlass popped in my head. I couldn't believe that I lost my two closest niggas in a matter of two months. And my Granny was upstairs in her room waiting to die next. Everywhere I looked, death was there. It seemed like it was chasing me and gaining on my ass. I didn't know who would be next. Me?

I forced myself out of bed and took off the bloody clothes before hitting the shower. After getting dressed, I fired up a blunt and hit the liquor store for a pint of gin to escape the pain. Before I knew it, I was at Jewels's condo, lying on the couch with my eyes closed. I spent the rest of the day in that spot, only getting up to use the bathroom.

"How you feeling, young blood?"

I opened my eyes and seen Jewels standing over me, a concerned look on his face.

"I don't know," I mumbled. "All this shit getting heavy. I don't know how much more I can take."

He let out a breath and sat next to me. "I'm not gon' lie, Carl. You gotta raw deal, li'l brotha. Both yo' niggas dead and yo' ole girl on her way out. I wish it was something I could say to make it better, but I can't think of nothing. There are some fires that you can't put out. Sometimes you gotta let it burn."

I didn't have a response.

"It's about that time, and I need to know if you can get yo' head in the game. This is enough money to change your life. Give you a new start. You can move to a place where nobody knows you and start over. What you wanna do?"

I didn't feel like doing shit but laying my ass on the couch. But I had the potential to make a hundred thousand dollars. It didn't matter who died last night. I would be stupid to turn down that much money.

"I'm in."

"My nigga!" He smiled. "Listen, there are more plans that I haven't told you about. The office with the money will be locked and you won't be able to get in from the outside. But I have people inside. They will let you in and get you the money and security tapes. I need you to make sure that nobody walks out that room but you."

The club was called Slick Rick's. It was one of the hottest spots in Chicago and it was no secret that the niggas who ran it moved plenty of product out of that spot. Nobody ever tried to rob it because it was suicide. And that was exactly why we were hitting it. Nobody would expect the attempt.

Jewels dropped me off in front and I found my team standing in line waiting to be let in.

"Y'all ready to get this money, self?" Fresh asked.

"Let's eat, lord." Smoke grinned.

I remembered that they were all brothers and they didn't know what I was. Some of their kind killed Crash last night. Wasn't a doubt in my mind that I was walking away with all the money.

After paying a cover fee, we were pat searched and wanded with a metal detector before being let in the club. We went directly to the bathroom and found four pistols with silencers on them in Ziploc bags under the garbage can. After tucking our heat, we split up and watched the scene. All kinds of drugs were being moved by two niggas. They constantly went up and down the back stairs. There were two security guards at the front door on the inside of the club and two outside. There was also two more guarding the back door. Jewels had people in the room with the money and drugs that would assist me. After I got the shit, I was going to kill everybody.

At 12:30, my pager started vibrating. That was my cue. I looked around for my team. Fresh stood near the front door, Tech was by the back door, and Smoke was near the stairs. I gave Smoke a nod as I walked by him and up the stairs. It was his job to kill the hustlers and guard the stairs. When I was halfway up the stairs, I seen one of the bodyguards by the back door look at me. Tech pulled out his silenced pistol and started clapping. The music was loud so nobody heard the shooting and only the people nearby seen what was happening. I ran to the door, pulling my pistol. As I knocked, Valerie opened the door. I was thrown off for a moment, but got my shit together. I ran in the room and seen a nigga sitting behind a desk. Glenda sat next to him. Without hesitating, I shot him in the face.

"I'ma get the tapes," Valerie said and started fucking with the monitors.

"The money is in the drawer," Glenda said, opening a big bottom drawer and handing me a duffle bag filled with money.

I felt bad for what I was about to do, especially since they gave me my first threesome.

"Here go the tapes," Valerie said, handing me a small bag.

I took everything and headed for the door. Right before I stepped into the hall, I turned around and lifted the gun. I seen surprise light the sisters' eyes when I started sparking. They screamed as the silenced pistol clapped. I shot them each twice in the head before running from the room. I ran down the stairs and seen the clubgoers scattering. A flood of people were running out the front and back doors.

A couple bodies lay on the floor by the back door: two security guards and Tech. I turned to look for Smoke and Fresh. They were headed towards me, looking over their shoulders towards the front door. I went for the back door, mixing in with the people trying to get out. Fresh and Smoke followed behind me. Jewels was waiting for me in the getaway car two blocks away. I needed to make sure I showed up by myself.

"Y'all niggas good?" I asked as we jogged down the alley.

"Yeah, lord. Tech ain't make it," Smoke said.

"I seen him," I said, trying to think of a way to kill these niggas. It was so many people running with us that I didn't know what to do. So I slowed down a little bit. Smoke and Fresh ran a couple steps ahead of me.

"You good?" Fresh asked, looking back to check on me.

I lifted my pistol and shot him in the face. Fresh collapsed. Smoke tried to lift his blower, but it was too late. I hit him up and left him a few feet from his brother. When I got to the getaway car, I was by myself.

"You good?" Jewels asked, looking around as I climbed in the passenger seat.

"Yeah," I breathed, slightly out of breath. "I'm by myself. Go."

"You did good, young blood. Did you get everybody?" He asked, pulling away.

I thought about the looks on Valerie and Glenda's faces. "Yeah. Tech got hit by the security. I got Fresh and Smoke. Why Valerie and Glenda? I thought they was yo' girls? You didn't trust them?"

Jewels showed that devilish look. "I told you not to trust nobody. This was too much money and too much blood got spilled. The less people that walked away, the better chance I have of getting away. Remember what I said. The early bird gets the worm but the second mice gets the cheese."

When I noticed the pistol in his hand, it was already too late. I grabbed for the door handle as he lifted the pistol to my head. I heard the gunshot and felt the fire burn the back of my head. The last thing I remembered was falling out of the car and my face hitting street.

Chapter 8

I thought I was dead.

I opened my eyes to blinding white light. Shit made my head hurt so I closed them again. And that's how I knew I wasn't dead. You didn't get headaches in hell. I think.

I opened my eyes again, more slowly this time, and took in my surroundings. I was in the hospital, hooked up to all kinds of machines. My head felt swollen and heavy. How the fuck did I get in the hospital? Then it all came back to me in a whoosh.

Jewels tried to kill me. He had been playing me all along, grooming me to do his dirty work. I trusted a snake and it bit me. When I found that nigga, I was going to kill him slowly. I tried to sit up in bed only to discover that my arms were cuffed to the bed.

"What the fuck?"

There was a nurse call button laying next to me. I pressed the button repeatedly. A few moments later a nurse walked in the room followed by a police officer.

"Mr. White! You're awake," the nurse said

"Yeah," I groaned. "What up with the handcuffs?"

The po-po answered. "The detectives want to talk to you. I'm going to call them right now."

"The detectives?" I asked.

"Don't got nothing to do with me, man. I was just told to call them when you woke up," he said, going to the phone beside my bed and making a call.

"How do you feel?" the nurse asked, pulling out a flashlight and looking into my eyes.

"My head hurts," I said, focusing most of my attention on listening to the phone call.

The fag told a detective I was woke and then hung up. "Detectives are on the way," he told me before turning to the nurse. "You need me for anything?"

"No, I got it. I'm checking him over before the doctor comes," she told him before turning back to me. "Where does your head hurt?"

"All over. Can you gimme something for the pain?"

"You've been sedated since you came in. We weren't sure if you were going to survive. You have a very serious head injury, Carl. You were grazed by a bullet in the head and something gave you a concussion. Do you remember what happened?"

I remembered, but I didn't want to tell her. "Nah, I don't remember."

"It is a miracle that you are still alive. You must have angels watching over you."

"So, what's gon happen? Am I good?"

"You will probably get a lot of headaches and temporary memory problems. Other than that, you're fine."

When the nurse left the room, I stared up at the ceiling and thought about everything she just told me. I couldn't believe I was still alive. Jewels had me. When my head started itching, I tried to lift a hand to scratch, but the cuffs didn't let me. What the fuck did the police want? Did they know about the club robbery? Was I about to get charged with all those bodies? I didn't have to wait long to get my answers. The door opened about twenty minutes later and two white men walked in wearing suits.

"It's a fuckin' miracle," one of them said, stopping to look at me like I was baby Jesus in the manger. He was tall with a slim build and dark hair graying around the edges.

"How do you feel?" the short pudgy one asked.

"Why am I sporting these cuffs?" I asked, ignoring their question about my health.

"So you won't get away," the pudgy one laughed as the men approached my bedside. "I'm Detective Ashcroft and this is my partner, Detective Rivera."

"Who shot you?" Detective Rivera asked.

"I don't know. Am I getting arrested?"

"Most likely," Ashcroft answered nonchalantly. "Maybe one of your accomplices shot you for that prize money."

Shit! They knew I was a part of the club robbery. I was cooked. But I played my role. "I don't know what you talking about. I don't remember what happened."

"Right, right," Rivera nodded. "The husband and wife already identified you. That scar on your wrist is almost as good as a fingerprint. And we already got those, too."

I looked down at the scar on my forearm and then back up at the police. "What the fuck is you talkin' about?"

The cops stared at me for a moment.

"Either that bullet really fucked up your head or you are involved in so much shit that you don't know what we're talking about," Rivera said.

"I think it's the latter. That would explain the bullet to your noggin," Ashcroft said. "Where were you on the night of November twenty-ninth?"

A sinking feeling entered my gut. That was the night we held the manager and his family hostage. "I was at home with my family. Why?"

"Oh, we playing this game?" Rivera asked.

"What game? I was at home," I said, sticking to my guns.

He nodded. "Listen, Carl. I'm going to be honest with you. This case is basically a slam dunk. Let me explain to you what good detective work is. That husband and wife that you and your boys kidnapped remembered that scar on your arm. Light-skinned black male, average height, between the age of 17-24, can be anybody in the city. But that scar on your arm drops the number down significantly. And we took your prints while you were asleep. They came back a match to the ones found in the backseat of the husband's car."

He paused to let the words sink in. I was fucked in the game. They was about to fry my ass.

"We have your balls in a vice and I'm about to make it tighter." Ashcroft smiled. "The only reason we're having this conversation is because we want the other two that were with you. Give up your accomplices, and we'll cut you a deal. This is a one-time offer."

"I told y'all I was at home with my family," I repeated. Even though Jewels just tried to kill me, I wasn't about to become a bitch-ass snitch. I would do life before I told on anybody.

"So, you wanna spend the next twenty years in Pontiac for your gangbanger friends, huh?" Rivera asked. "You know they won't write or send money. This is going to be on you and your family. If you have any family. Give up your guys and you could be out in five. This is the best deal you're going to get."

I didn't have nothing else. "I wanna talk to my lawyer."

***

I stayed in the hospital for another day. They were calling my condition a traumatic brain injury and the doctors wanted to keep an eye on me. When they felt I was stable, I was taken to Cook County Jail and put in the infirmary. My injury was still serious and they didn't want me in general population yet. I was being charged with armed robbery and kidnapping and faced sixty years in the pen. I called my aunt Trisha and told her about the five thousand stashed in the basement so she could get me a lawyer. That was the only call I made for the first couple of days. When I could no longer take missing my Nana, I called home. Chris answered.

"What's goin' on, li'l brah?"

"Why you in jail? Aunty Trisha said you robbed somebody."

"That's what they say I did. But I'm fighting it."

"Did you do it?"

The phone calls were recorded. "Nah, I didn't do it."

"So when they gon' let you out?"

"I don't know. I gotta go through the process."

"How long that's gon' take?"

"I don't know. But I don't wanna talk about that right now. How is Nana?"

"She in her room asleep."

"Do she know I'm in jail?"

"Yeah. She didn't say nothing to me about it though."

"Take her the phone so I can talk to her. I only got a couple minutes."

"A'ight. But I need you to come home, Carl. When Granny leaves, all I'ma have is you. You said you was gon' take care of me. Please come home."

Hearing the need for me in my little brother's voice almost made me cry. I had to find a way to get out of here. "I'ma be home, man. For real. I got you."

"Okay. Here go Nana."

It took a few moments for him to get her the phone. When she spoke, her voice sounded raspy and tired.

"Carl, is this you?"

"Yeah, Nana. It's me. How you doing?"

"I'm trying to hold on. But forget about me. Why are you in jail? Trisha said they charged you with robbery."

It broke my heart to tell my ole girl the truth. "Yeah."

"Why, Carl? Why would you put yourself in that situation with everything that's happening to me? Chris needs you. Why would you do this to him?"

Hearing the pain and disappointment in her voice was killing me. "I can't say too much on the phone, Nana, because these calls is being recorded. But I'm working on trying to get out. I might need to put the house up for my bail."

"No, Carl. I am not putting my house up to bail you out. I will not get my stuff involved with you doing crime. I love you, baby, but I am not going to risk losing this house because of you."

"But Nana, you not gonna lose the house. I'ma go to court. I just need collateral to help me get out."

"I know I won't lose it. Because I won't be putting it up to help you out," she said before sniffing.

Damn. I had made my Granny cry.

"I am so disappointed in you, Carl. You have so much potential. You are so smart. But what you did was stupid. You let Chris down and broke my heart."

When I got off the phone, I felt like shit. I had let down the two most important people in my life. I had to figure out a way to fix this shit. I needed to find a way to get out of Cook County Jail.

I went to a bail and arraignment hearing the next day. I was officially and legally charged with robbery and kidnapping, and my bail was set at one million dollars. The DA and judge agreed that the crime was too serious, I was too dangerous, and potentially a flight risk. That's when I realized I probably wasn't going home anytime soon.

***

I was in the infirmary for thirty days before they released me to general population. I had a serious felony charge so I was sent to unit 1, a max unit where they housed Chicago's most violent criminals to await their day in court. I was escorted from the medical unit by a guard, all of my belongings wrapped in my linens. We stopped outside of a big metal and Plexiglas door. The lock clanged open and I stepped inside. There was another door ten feet ahead. Another lock clanged and I stepped onto the pod. There were about fifty niggas scattered around the pod, some playing dominoes, some in the TV area, some on the phones. But as soon as I stepped through that door, all eyes were on me. Two niggas got up from tables on opposite sides of the room and approached. I had been prepped by a few niggas when I was in the infirmary so I knew what was about to happen.

"What's good, li'l brah?" One of them nodded. He was tall, dark-skinned, clean shaven with a bald head.

"You folks or people?" the other one asked. He was brown-skinned, his hair braided to the back in cornrows.

"I'ma gangsta," I said.

"That's you, Savage," the one with the braids said before walking away.

"What up, family? I'm Savage," he said, shaking my hand.

"What's good, my nigga. I'm Carl."

He looked me over like he was trying to see if I had heart. I stood strong, chest poked out, chin up.

"Where you from, Carl?"

"Out south. 119th and Hausted."

He smiled. "Oh, you from K-Dog deck?"

"Yeah. That's my nigga."

He turned towards the dayroom. "Ay, Vontay! Where K-Dog at?"

Hearing that somebody I knew from the hood was on the pod made me feel a little better about my situation.

"That nigga still asleep," a tall dark-skinned nigga answered. "Who dat?"

"This Carl. One of the guys from out south on K-Dog deck," he responded before turning to me. "You know some pieces?"

I'd been practicing and memorizing lit while I was in the infirmary. "I'm familiar wit 'em."

"A'ight. Come with me. You gotta holla at Black and then we gon' get you settled in."

I dropped my property off at one of the dayroom tables before being led upstairs to a cell at the end of the tier. Black's name fit him to a tee. He looked like one of them big-ass gorillas off *Planet of the Apes*. I spent thirty minutes in the cell being screened before I got the green light.

"A'ight, family. You good. Holla at Savage and we gon' get you a bed," Black said before shaking my hand.

When I left the cell, I found Savage and was given a cell on the top tier. I grabbed my shit and found my new digs. All the cells looked just alike: brick walls painted some off-white color, a toilet/sink combo, a metal bunk bed bolted to the floor, a small concrete table in the corner, and a little-ass window that we couldn't even see out of. When I walked in, my celly was laying on the bottom bunk listening to a Walkman and reading a Donald Goines book. He was short, brown-skinned with a low haircut.

"K-Dog!" I yelled, happy to see a familiar face.

He took off the headphones and set the book down before standing to greet me. "Carl, what's good, li'l nigga?"

I threw my shit on the top bunk and broke it down. "Nigga, Jewels tried to get down on me. We made a move and he snaked me at the end and hit it with the bag."

K-Dog's eyes grew wide. "Jewels with the white Caddy? On what, he got down on you?"

"On everything I love. He tried to shoot me in the head, my nigga. Bullet grazed me." I said, turning and showing off the wound on the back of my head.

K-Dog looked shocked. "Damn, my nigga. At least you still here. We gon' reach out and get that nigga touched. He a neutron and a lotta niggas been looking for a reason to get on his ass."

"Hell yeah. Tell 'em to get that nigga."

"So, what they knock you for? The shit with Jewels?"

"It was some shit with Jewels, but not the one he fucked me up on. We ended up hittin' a check cashing place. They got my prints out the nigga we kidnapped car. They was white, so I think they finna try to bam a nigga. They already gave me a million dollar bail."

"Damn, my nigga. These racist mu'fuckas definitely gon' try to fuck you over. But fuck it. Go down swinging, my nigga. Never let 'em see you sweat."

***

My time in the county jail was going by smooth. The guards stayed out of our way and the only time they showed their faces on the pods was when something popped off. And when 6-1 came, shit got real and niggas got fucked up. But that wasn't an everyday thing. Like I said, they stayed out of our way. The prisoners ran the pod and we governed ourselves, keeping the peace for the most part. Respect was big in here because a wrong word, look, or action could set off a riot and most niggas didn't want that. We was too busy tryna fight our cases.

My case wasn't looking too good. I talked to my lawyer regularly and he basically told me there wasn't shit he could do. They had my fingerprint, I got picked out of the lineups, and they described the scar on my arm perfectly. He advised me to do a speedy trial and take a plea because he couldn't build a good defense with all the evidence they had against me. Plus, if I went to trial and wasted the court's time and resources, that might make the judge mad and he could give me more time. I was cooked either way it went. So I let my lawyer do his work and waited for my day in court.

"Yo, you see this move right here is called the King's gambit. This a real popular move. A lotta gods use this opening and don't even know what they doing," Supreme explained. Supreme was a

90

nigga from New York that I kicked it with a lot. I liked being around him because he challenged me and made me think.

"How you learn to play chess?" I asked, watching intently as he taught me the basics of the game.

"I learned in school back when I was a li'l pup. Did a bid and became a student of the game while I was learning to be a student of life. It's a lot of similarities between chess and life. In life, as in chess, once a move is made, it stays on the board. It also has a racial theme and shows the struggle between black people and white people. And when you get to another level of thinking, you will recognize the king and queen as wisdom and knowledge."

The last one got my attention. "What that mean? Kings, queens, and knowledge and wisdom?"

He grinned. "I don't think you ready for that yet. Yo' organization teach to think like a soldier. I ain't tryna cause no discord in what y'all got. Its structure up in here and I ain't tryna make no noise."

Supreme was a smart nigga. Everything he said and did had meaning, like a chess game. And he knew that comment would make me want to dig deeper. "How is telling me about kings, queens, wisdom, and knowledge gon' make noise?"

He thought for a moment. "Because it will fuck up everything you been taught yo' whole life. You a part of the eighty-five percent. Everything you know is based on lies and I don't think you ready for the truth."

I stared at him, trying to read between the lines. Somewhere along the way he called me stupid and it pissed me off. I was about to check the fuck out of him when my name was called over the PA system.

"Carlile White, come to the officer station."

All eyes on the pod went to me.

"What the fuck?" I questioned, heading for the officer station. The jail staff was separated from us by an office hidden behind mirrored windows and metal. I walked up to the microphone. "What up?"

"Go out in the hall. The chaplain wants to talk to you," a woman said through the speaker.

"For what?"

"I don't know. Go see."

I left the pod and stepped into the hall. The chaplain was a short older nigga with a gray afro.

"You Carlile White?" He asked.

"Yeah," I nodded. "What's up?"

"I'm sorry to tell you this but your aunty Trisha called and said your grandmother passed..."

I didn't even hear the rest of what the chaplain said. My knees went weak and I stumbled, grabbing the wall to keep from falling. I felt lightheaded, like I was about to pass out.

"You okay?" he asked, grabbing my arm to keep me from falling.

I tried to speak, but no words came out. Only sobs followed by tears.

Chapter 9

The next couple days went by in a blur. I chilled in my cell most of the time drinking hooch. Losing my Nana while I was in jail fucked me up. I was supposed to be there take care of her, and now I couldn't even go to her funeral to say my last goodbye. That shit was fucked up.

"Carl, what's goin' on, god?"

I looked up and seen Supreme standing in the doorway.

"I'm fucked up, my nigga. I ain't never felt this kinda pain," I mumbled, struggling to hold back tears. "It seem like er'body around me dying. Two of my niggas got knocked off right before I got locked up and now my ole girl. This shit crazy."

Supreme walked in the cell and leaned against the sink. "I know it ain't nothin' nobody can say to help you through this, but the one thing that could probably help is to think about something else besides the loss. It's cool to grieve and get it out yo' system, but you don't wanna brood on it too long. Shit can depress you."

"I'm already depressed," I admitted.

Supreme went under his shirt and pulled out a book. "This is a good book," he said, tossing me a hardcover book. "It will open your eyes to some of the truths out there. I read it back when I did my first bid and this is what opened my eyes. Hopefully it will open yours."

I read the title. "The Alchemist."

"It's a book about self-discovery. Check it out. You might discover something about yourself that you didn't know you had," he said before walking away.

I flipped the book over in my hand a couple of times, trying to decide if I wanted to read it or if I wanted to sulk some more and think about my granny.

"What's good, family?" K-Dog asked, walking in the room. "What that weird-ass nigga wanted?"

"Supreme a'ight. He just gave me this book to take my mind off Nana."

K-Dog looked at the book and frowned. "The Alchemist?"

"He said it's about self-discovery."

"Self-discovery? You betta give that shit back 'fore yo' ass fuck around and be standing on a table in the middle of the dayroom talking about the mothership is coming," he cracked. "I don't see how you be fuckin' wit' that nigga. Brah, that nigga crazy. He think he be spittin' izm, but that shit laced with bullshit."

"Supreme ain't that bad," I laughed.

"A'ight. Read that shit and see what happen. But I'm finna go buss Black n'em ass in dominoes. You good?"

"Yeah, I'm good. I'm just laying back."

"A'ight. I'm up."

When K-Dog left, I picked up the book and opened it. I wanted to think about something other than my grandmother dying, so I started reading. After the first couple of pages, I was hooked. The book spoke about purpose, destiny, and fate in a way that I had never heard before. And as I read late into the night, I realized what I had always known and what my Nana tried to tell me: that my purpose in life was bigger than being a jackboy and going in and out of prison. I was destined for greatness, and reading the book opened up something inside of me that I couldn't describe or close. The next morning I found Supreme sitting at a table in the dayroom playing chess by himself. I sat down across from him and placed the book on the table.

"Do you got another book I can read?"

"Hold on, brah. First you gotta tell me what you think about that one. Based on yo' reaction, I can tell you liked it."

I thought about how to describe the effect the book had on me. "Man, I feel like it opened up something inside of me. I always knew that I was capable of doing something great, and reading that last night confirmed what I already knew. Now I wanna know more. What else you got?"

"I don't meet too many young brothas this eager to read that brain food." He chuckled. "You special, Carl. You gotta use this time to grow. You more than a nigga, or a gangsta, or a soldier. You a god."

"What that mean? Why you always callin' niggas gods?"

"Because that's what we are. Gods. What do you know about yo' history?"

"What they taught us in school. That we came from Africa as slaves. Certain niggas like King, Malcolm, Booker T. Washington, and other people fought for our freedom. Now we free."

"You think this free?" he asked, sweeping his arm around the dayroom.

"Not here locked up. I'm talkin' about black people being free. No longer slaves."

He laughed and shook his head. "Let me give you a quick lesson in history, li'l brah. The reason I say we gods is because that's what we are. The white people that run America don't want you to know that, which is why you only hear about black people being niggas and slaves. Black history in America is a joke, brah. They don't let the schools teach the truth, because that would give us too much power. Do you know what would happen to the mind of millions of young black men if they knew they came from royalty? We was Kings and Pharaohs. If they knew that, it wouldn't be no Bloods and Crips and Folks and Vice Lords gangbanging. All of that was created by brothas tryna give other brothas a direction and identity. The truth is, Black Africans came to America before Christopher Columbus 'discovered' this land. Our people was trading with Mexicans before their country was named Mexico. There were Black Gods being worshipped over here. Tezcatlipoca was a Black God worshipped by Aztecs. Navalpilli, the God of jewelers, was a Black God worshipped by Olmecs, or ancient Mexicans. Ek-chu-ah is a trader God, also referred to as Black Christ, and was worshipped by Indians in Central and South America. He is also talked about in Mayan mythology. My dude, Africans been trading in America before Christ was born. They found African images on Terracotta art by Mexicans that date back to 800 B.C."

I listened to Supreme in amazement, shocked by his knowledge of African history. I wanted to know more. "So that's why you say we gods, because of the Black Gods?"

"Yes and no. I call brothas gods because we, like supreme beings, have the power to create. We can speak things into existence.

We can create life with our sperm. We can turn dreams and thoughts into reality. We are the original man. Millions of years ago, when all the continents were all together, it was called Pangaea. Life began in the center of Pangaea, which was Africa. Africa was and is the heart of this planet."

I sat for a moment and tried to digest everything he told me. It was so much information that I couldn't remember of all. And the crazy thing about that was, I still wanted more.

"Can you give me the books that taught you all this?"

He nodded. "I'ma write down a list of books for you to read while you doing this bid. You gotta educate yo'self while you doing this time. Treat it like a college experience. Study yo'self. Study people. And always remember this: education prevents manipulation."

***

Another month went by and I went to court twice. Since my lawyer filed motions for a speedy trial, my court dates were coming fast. At my last court appearance, we set a trial date. It was four months away. Now I was just sitting in jail, waiting for trial. I spent most of the time with Supreme, picking his brain and learning. He was the smartest person I ever met and knew a lot about everything.

We was sitting at the table playing chess when the big lock on the pod gate clanked. Everyone in the dayroom turned their attention to the door. A chubby dark-skinned nigga with a nappy afro walked in. He looked familiar, but I couldn't place the face.

"You know him?" Supreme asked.

"He look familiar, but I don't know where I remember him from."

And then it all came rushing back to me like I was reliving a dream. I remembered leaving The Rink, heading towards Crash's car. I remembered hearing the footsteps and turning around. He was the fat nigga with the pistol. He killed my nigga, Crash!

"Bitch-ass nigga!" I cursed, rising to my feet.

Supreme grabbed my wrist. "Yo, son! What you doing?"

"He killed my nigga. I'm finna get that ass."

Supreme looked towards the door. Savage and Steve were approaching the new nigga to check his affiliation.

"You sure you wanna do this right now?" he asked.

"Hell yeah. He killed my nigga."

Supreme let me go. I walked over as Steve and the fat nigga embraced. The new nigga looked up when I got close. I didn't know if he recognized me or seen the intent in my eyes, but he pushed Steve back and tried to square up. I timed it perfectly. As soon as Steve was out of the way, I threw a haymaker that landed right on the fat nigga's jaw. He stumbled backwards and I rushed, throwing lefts and rights. I only connected one or two punches before he grabbed me and we started wrestling.

"Get'cho boy!" Steve snapped at Savage.

"What you doing, li'l fam?" Savage asked, trying to decide if he should break it up.

"He got down on one of the guys at The Rink," I managed as I tussled with the fat nigga.

"Whoop that ass, fam," Savage cheered. "Whoop that ass!"

Me and the fat nigga continued wrestling, bumping into a table and falling on the floor. I moved faster, climbing on top of him and busting him in his shit repeatedly.

"Get'cho boy," Steve said.

"Fuck that nigga. He killed one of the guys."

Steve didn't like that response and walked over to help his boy. Savage punched him in the back of the head. Niggas had been standing around, unsure what to do, but when Savage and Steve started boxing, the pod went up. Niggas started fighting all over, an all-out riot breaking out.

I was beating the fat nigga's ass when somebody came from behind and busted me in my shit. Next thing I knew, I was on my back, dazed.

"STOP FIGHTING! LOCK IN YOUR CELLS! STOP FIGHTING!" the intercoms blared.

The neutrons and niggas that wasn't in the fight locked in they cells, but the rest of us was in go mode and didn't stop. I crawled to my knees, trying to stand up, when the fat nigga jumped on top of me. I was dazed and he was heavy so I couldn't move him. All I could do was cover up as he started raining down blows. Then the punches stopped. I looked up and seen K-Dog stomping the fat nigga.

"Get up, nigga!" he yelled.

I got up from the ground and joined K-Dog in stomping the fat nigga unconscious. When he stopped moving and was out cold, I looked around and seen niggas in battles all across the dayroom. K-Dog ran to aid another one of the guys and I ran over to help. We whooped the nigga's ass and when he hit the ground, we stomped his ass too.

A loud clang at the door got my attention. I looked up as 6-1 entered the unit. There were about twenty big-ass deputy sheriffs running in the pod dressed in protective riot gear, carrying black batons. They ran around busting niggas' heads and talking shit.

"Break this shit up! Get'cho ass on the ground!" one of them screamed, busting a nigga in the head.

"Y'all wanna gang fight, huh? We the gang in here!" another one said as he swung his stick recklessly.

I didn't know what to do, so I froze. And that was my mistake. A big-ass nigga swung the stick at my head like he was trying to hit a home run. I lifted my arm just in time and took most of the blow on my forearm. Before I could react, he kicked me in the chest and I flew to the ground.

"You think you tough, huh?" he yelled.

I knew he was about to beat my ass, so I curled into a ball, protecting my head. The nigga stomped me, punched me, and beat my ass with the baton. In less than a minute, they broke up the fight and beat all our asses. More sheriffs poured into the unit and a couple captains.

"Which one of them started it?" the captain asked.

"The bubble said it was them," he answered, pointing the baton at me and the nigga that killed Crash.

"Get they asses outta here!" the captain yelled.

Three niggas from the SORT team snatched me up from the floor like I was a rag doll. "Get cho li'l punk ass up!"

They took me and the fat black nigga in the hallway and started whooping our asses.

"Y'all li'l chumps think y'all tough, huh? Y'all ain't nothing but some bitches. This our shit. We the muthafuckin' mob around here!" they yelled while beating my ass.

There were too many of them and they were too big to fight. All I could do was cover up and hope they didn't break shit.

***

After getting the worst ass whoopin' of my life, they put me in the hole for thirty days. I had never experienced solitary confinement before and that shit was crazy. Niggas banged on the doors, walls, and toilet and screamed twenty-four hours a day. It took me a week to adjust to the sounds of the hole before I was able to figure out how to survive. I eventually got used to the noise and learned to tune it out. I spent most of the time in the hole reading everything I could get my hands on. I took Supreme's words to heart and planned to learn. In thirty days, I read sixteen books.

When I got out of the hole, they moved me to another max unit. I didn't have any more fights and three months later, my trial date had arrived. I already talked to my lawyer and the plan was to take a plea in the ninth hour, right before we picked the jury. I was in the holding cell behind the courtroom, waiting for my lawyer to make the deal. I had been waiting for twenty minutes when the sheriff came to get me.

"You ready?" The bailiff asked as he opened the door.

"Let's get it."

"Let me put the cuffs on."

After I was cuffed, the bailiff led me into the courtroom. The judge wasn't in the courtroom yet, just my lawyer, Marty Goldman, at one table and the DA at the other.

"I spoke to the district attorney," my lawyer whispered. "He's not going below thirty years. What do you want to do?"

"Thirty years?" I mugged him, having a hard time wrapping my mind around the length of time.

"It's up to you, Carl. But considering the amount of time you're exposed to, I would take the deal. I don't think we have a strong enough defense to beat these charges. They have your prints and you were picked out of a lineup. If you go to trial and lose, the judge can give you sixty years. I'm sorry, but this is as good as it's going to get. If you take the deal, with good behavior, you can be out in about fifteen years. You're young so you can still get out and live a full life. But it's up to you."

It felt like the room was spinning. Thirty years was a long time. I knew I was going to the joint, but I never imagined the sentence would be that long. And if I didn't accept it, they was gon' blam my ass and probably give me the whole sixty years. I was fucked in the game. Caught between a rock and a hard place. Damn. I looked over at the district attorney. He was a pudgy white mutherfucker with no hair on his face. He stared me in my eyes like he could whoop my ass. I wanted to get up and show him that he couldn't.

The door behind the judge's bench opened and pulled my thoughts away from killing the DA. The honorable Judge Jerry Macintosh walked to his throne and sat down.

"Good morning, gentlemen. I've read over the case and is this right that the defendant wants to switch his plea to guilty?" the judge asked.

The district attorney stood. "Good morning, Your Honor. I was approached by Mr. White's counsel about twenty minutes ago with the impression that he might want to plead guilty. The state has agreed to offer a sentence of thirty years if the defendant pleads guilty."

The judge turned to our table. "Counselor, have you discussed this with your client?"

My lawyer gave me a look. "What do you want to do? It's up to you."

I didn't want to do fifteen years in the joint. But I also didn't want to get maxed out. "Take it," I mumbled.

My lawyer stood. "I've discussed the plea with my client and he doesn't want the family to have to relive the experience or cause the court unnecessary time and energy. Mr. White has agrees to plead guilty to the charges for a thirty year sentence."

The judge peered down his nose at me. "Mr. White, to the charges of kidnapping and robbery, how do you plead?"

"Guilty." When I said the word, I could feel coldness entering my bones.

"The court accepts your plea of guilt and passes sentence. Thirty years in the Illinois Department of Corrections."

J-Blunt

BOOK II: HUSTLE & MOTIVATE

HUSTLE - TO GET OR SELL. A WAY OF MAKING MONEY.

MOTIVATE - TO INCITE OR IMPEL. TO PROVIDE WITH OR AFFECT, AS IN MOTIVE POWER.

WHEN YOU EMBODY AND TAKE TO HEART THE WORDS HUSTLE AND MOTIVATE, YOU WILL REALIZE THAT WITHIN YOU IS AN UNLIMITED POWER FOR GREATNESS.

ALL OF US ARE BORN GREAT, BUT FEW ACHIEVE IT.

THE DECISION TO ACT UPON THAT GREATNESS IS UP TO YOU.

WHEN YOU DEDICATE YOURSELF TO SOMETHING, IT BUILDS AN INFINITE STRENGTH WITHIN THAT CAN BE DRAWN FROM TIME AND TIME AGAIN.

SOMETIMES SUCCESS CAN APPEAR IN A FORM DIFFERENT THAN WE EXPECT.

THAT IS THE TRICK OF OPPORTUNITY.

IT CAN BE DISGUISED AS MISFORTUNE OR DEFEAT.

TO MAINTAIN SUCCESS, YOU MUST FIRST BE PREPARED TO RECEIVE IT. LEBRON JAMES WENT TO THE NBA FINALS SEVERAL TIMES BEFORE HE WON A RING.

DEFEAT TAUGHT HIM HOW TO WIN.

WHEN A HUSTLER IS MOTIVATED, HE WILL STOP AT NOTHING TO OBTAIN HIS BURNING DESIRE.

BUT FIRST, YOU MUST CRAWL BEFORE YOU WALK.

J-Blunt

Chapter 10

May 1st, 2013

Damn it feel good to be free!

That single thought passed through my mind over and over as I rode the Greyhound bus. I had been locked up for nineteen long-ass years and the whole world changed in that time. Went from beepers, to cell phones, to smartphones. Cars went from gas to electric. The music went from tapes, to CDs, to MP3 players. And we had a black president from Chicago in the White House. Shit felt crazy as hell.

As I rode the bus along the interstate, I felt like a kid discovering the world for the first time. Everything looked shiny and new. My eyes were wide, constantly looking around, not wanting to miss anything.

And as I rode that bus, I also knew that I was behind like a motherfucker. I was thirty-seven years old and didn't have a pot to piss in or a window to throw it out of. I had to give up the house that Nana left to me to Aunty Trisha while I was locked up. She turned around and sold it, sending me five thousand, before moving to Madison, Wisconsin. I spent the money while I was locked up and now I was broke, alone, and on my own. It was up to me to make a way for myself. And I knew without a shadow of a doubt that I was going to be successful. I survived almost twenty years in prison and made it out. My mind and body were fully intact and better than they were before I went in. I wasn't just a survivor; I was a conqueror. I had conquered prison. And now I was going to conquer the world.

When the bus pulled into the terminal in Chicago, I grabbed my shit and hopped off the bus. I didn't have much but the jogging suit on my back and the Nike's on my feet. I had another jogging suit in my bag, along with a few pairs of socks and underwear. In another bag were some hygiene products, some paperwork, a couple of books, a TV, and a radio. I could fit everything I owned in three brown paper bags. And that was okay. I had to crawl before I walked.

I made my way through the bus station, looking around at everybody and everything, wanting to take it all in. When I walked out the front doors, I paused to look around. Downtown looked so much different than the last time I had seen it and it bustled with activity. I wasn't able to look too long because of a horn blowing. To my left was a white Chrysler Pacifica van. Behind the wheel was my PO, Daniel Rumpel, and he was waving me over.

"How are you doing, Mr. White?" he asked as I climbed in the van.

"Man, I'm free." I smiled. "I ain't complaining about nothing."

"That's a good attitude to have. How long you do? Twenty years, right?" he asked as he pulled away from the curb.

"Almost nineteen long-ass years," I said, taking in the sights and sounds of the city.

"A lot has changed since you went in. The whole world is different now. Cell phones are smartphones and you can have everything in your life literally in the palm of your hand."

"I seen it all on TV. I'm excited about getting to know everything."

He glanced at me before focusing back on the road. "So, you're going to be living in a temporary living center for ninety days. They're going to help you find a job and get reintegrated back into the world. I'm not one of those parole officers that's going to be all up in your ass. You make your reports and you stay out of trouble and you won't hear from me that much. After we get to the center, I'm going to need you to sign some basic supervision rules. It all boils down to keepin' your ass out of trouble. Got me?"

"I hear you. I'm not the causing trouble type. I just want to enjoy life and my freedom. I'm thirty-seven years old and I don't own a damn thing. I'm focused on building, Daniel. I don't got time for the bullshit."

He glanced at me again. "So, tell me your plans. Where do you want to be in five years and how will you get there?"

I took a moment to recall the plan I'd been reciting in my head almost every day for the last five years. "I'm going to start at the bottom. I worked prison jobs for a couple cents an hour, so I'm willing to do almost anything to provide for myself. My first goal is self-sufficiency. That means gettin' out of this TLP as soon as I can. I also want to build my credit. Can't get nothing in this world without good credit. When my credit is good, I'm going to see if I can get one of those loans for first time homeowners and buy a house. Then I'm going to flip that house, pay off the bank loan, and do it all again. In five years, I want to own at least five houses."

My PO looked blown away by my plans. "Sounds like a good plan, Carl. Hell, you got me thinking about investing in you because I believe you. And that is a rare thing, because I've heard all kinds of bullshit from new releases. But I believe you. I'll do everything to help you get ahead."

The temporary living center turned out to be a boarding house on the West Side with five bedrooms. They housed parolees and newly released men two to a room. The place was run by a husband and wife, Mr. and Mrs. Jackson. After signing the parole rules, my PO left me in the hands of the Jacksons.

"Good morning, Mr. White." Mr. Jackson smiled, inviting me in the house as he shook my hand. He was a short stocky brown-skinned man in his early fifties.

"Good to meet you." I nodded.

"Welcome home, Mr. White!" Mrs. Jackson beamed. She was a few years younger than her husband. She wasn't all that fine, but she had a banging body that she showed off in a snug T-shirt and tight jeans.

"Nice to meet you, Mrs. Jackson."

"Oh no. Call me Janet. Is it okay if we call you Carl?"

"That's fine."

"Have a seat, Carl," Mr. Jackson offered.

I sat down on the couch.

"We're going to go over the basic house rules with you. First of all, there is a nine o'clock curfew, unless you have a job that keeps you out. This is a drug and alcohol free zone. We don't want none of that in here. You also cannot have visitors. You will share a room with another recently released guy. You are expected to clean up after yourself," Mr. Jackson explained.

"We won't be all in your business and we will try to respect your privacy. All we ask is that you follow the rules," Mrs. Jackson added. "You will meet with your caseworker tomorrow. She has an office in the basement and would normally be a part of this orientation, but she had a family emergency. Do you have any questions?"

"Not at the moment, no. Can I see the room I'll be in?"

"You sure can. Follow me," Mr. Jackson said, getting up from the couch as his phone rang. He pulled it out and checked the screen. "Dammit. I gotta get this. Janet, show him to his room."

"Follow me, Carl."

I followed the swaying of Janet's wide hips up a flight of stairs and down a short hall. She stopped at the second door and pulled out keys.

"You'll be rooming with Tyson. He's at work right now," she explained, unlocking the door and holding it open.

I was waiting for her to move so I could pass by, but she stood in the doorway and stared at me as if wondering why I wasn't going in. After an awkward moment, I eased by, our bodies only a few inches apart. I looked around the room and noticed it was split in half. All of Tyson's shit was on one side and there was another bed, dresser, and table on the opposite side.

"I'm going to bring you a key," Mrs. Jackson said, stepping into the room. "The bed is fairly new and has good springs," she said, bending over and pressing her hands into the bed to show it had bounce. Her titties bounced in the T-shirt and her wide ass jiggled in the jeans. My dick started getting hard, so I moved one of the shopping bags in front to cover it. She looked over her shoulder and caught me looking at her ass. Then she looked at the bag I was holding in front of my dick.

"How long did you do?" she asked as she stood.

"Nineteen long-ass years," I said.

"That is a really long time. You must have a lot of pent-up sexual energy?" she asked, closing the distance between us and moving the bag I had in front me.

I stared into her eyes for a moment, trying to figure out what the fuck was going on. I had only been out of the joint for an hour, and already a married chick was flirting with me while her husband was downstairs. And it wasn't just any married chick. She and her husband were in charge of the house I was going to be living in. This shit screamed messy and I wasn't trying to get in trouble.

"What's going on, Janet?" I asked.

"Don't worry. I'll explain everything later. Get situated. I'm going to make lunch around eleven o'clock. Do you need to use the phone to call your family?"

"Yeah. I need to call my brother. He lives in Wisconsin."

She pulled a phone from her back pocket. "Here you go."

I looked at the phone like it was a spaceship. "I got locked up before these came out. Can you dial the number for me?"

"Oh, I'm sorry. I forgot."

After dialing my little brother's number, she handed me the phone. "I'm going downstairs to make lunch. Bring it down when you're done."

"Okay. Thanks."

"What's good?" Chris answered.

"What up, li'l nigga. This Carl."

"Carl! Oh, shit! Where you at, big bro? They let you out yet?"

"Yeah. I'm staying at a temporary living center."

"Hell, yeah, my nigga! Gimme the address. I'm coming to the city tomorrow to see you!"

After kicking it with my little brother, I went downstairs to give Janet her phone back and eat lunch with the few niggas that was in the house. When done, I went back to my room to get situated. I was packing my underwear in the drawer when Janet showed up again. She had clothes and linens in one hand and a shopping bag in the other.

"I wanted to bring you a few things. We give everybody some sheets and a change of clothes. I also got some hygiene products in the bag."

"Thanks," I said, taking the things from her hand.

"I don't know if you can fit the clothes. You want to try them on?"

"Right now?"

"Yeah. If they don't fit, I can run downstairs and change them. Don't tell me you're shy," she smirked.

I recognized the challenge in her eyes.

"You funny," I said, pulling off my shirt. Fuck it. She wanted to see me, I was going to show it. The mandatory workouts had me in the best shape of my life. Arms, chest, shoulders, and abs sculpted like I was an Egyptian God.

I pulled off my jogging pants and stood before her in only my draws, letting her see my dick print through my boxer briefs. She was looking at me like she wanted to fuck. I knew her panties got wet. Then I threw on the Levis and T-shirt she brought.

"You look nice," she said, sticking her finger in her mouth.

I checked myself in the mirror. "Perfect fit."

"Don't think this is over," she said before leaving the room.

My roommate came home around five o'clock. He was a big black-ass nigga in his forties. He was also one of the guys, so we hit it off right away and he explained more about the house rules. He told me he used to be the brick man and was getting money. I had a hard time believing that since he was just as broke as me. But I let him have that. I really wanted to ask him about Janet, but since he never brought her up, I didn't either. He had to go to work the next morning, so we went to sleep around midnight. He woke up around six and was gone by seven o'clock. I lay awake, staring at the ceiling, thinking about how good it felt to be free. I slept good as fuck on the real bed. And Janet was right; the springs was all good.

Light taps at the door got my attention. I was about to climb out of bed when the door opened.

"You awake?" Janet asked, peeking her head into the room.

"Yeah. Good morning," I said, sitting up in bed.

She stepped into the room and closed the door behind her, mischief lighting her eyes. She wore a loose-fitting blue and white sundress. "How did you sleep?"

"Best sleep I had in a long time," I said, trying to gauge what she was on.

"That's good to hear," she said, staring in my eyes as she walked over and stood before me. "Do you have a towel?"

"Yeah. In the drawer," I said, nodding towards the dresser.

She walked over and grabbed the towel before coming back and kneeling between my legs.

"Relax."

I didn't move, just watched with anticipation as she sat the towel on my lap, dug into my boxer briefs and pulled my dick through the pee hole. Then she lowered her head and started sucking. I hadn't gotten head in nineteen years and that shit felt so good that I wanted to pass out.

"Aw shit!" I moaned, closing my eyes as shivers ran through my body.

I wasn't even sure if Janet gave good head, but I was grabbing fistfuls of the sheets and sucking in deep breaths. I tried to hold off my nut, but couldn't. Thirty seconds later, I exploded.

"Oh shiiittt!" I groaned.

Janet moved her head and spit on the towel while jerking my shit. Nut shot out of my dick like a geyser, coating her hand. My toes curled, and I felt lightheaded.

"Damn. That's a lot!" Janet said, her eyes wide as she watched the nut spill.

When I was drained, she threw the towel aside and spun around, lifting the dress up onto her back. She wasn't wearing panties and her ass looked beautiful.

"Stay right there. I got this," she said.

I gripped her fat ass as she sat down on my dick reverse cowgirl. Her insides felt too good. She began riding slowly and I started nutting immediately. She continued riding me and I sucked in sharp breaths as pleasure and pain flooded my body. When the feeling passed, I watched the nut spill down the sides of my dick every time she bounced up and down. My dick stayed hard and she continued riding. I bussed once more before she got hers.

"Damn, that was good," she sighed, standing up to wipe herself with the towel. "Next time I need to see if you know how to work that."

I just stared up at her, wondering where her husband was and how many times she did this.

"Why you looking at me like that?"

"Nothing," I said, shaking my head.

"I don't do this with everybody, if that's what you think. Just the ones I'm attracted to. I know it sounds crazy, but I can read a person's aura. You have good energy. And you're handsome."

"But what about your husband?"

"He's not here yet. He comes around eight o'clock. And he has erectile dysfunction so our sex life ain't really a sex life. I love him and don't want to divorce him over sex. So I do what I can when I can."

"I'm not complaining, but I don't want to get in trouble."

She laughed. "You'll be fine. Get up and get cleaned up. You have to meet with Charlotte. She's your caseworker and she going to help you find a job."

***

After a shower and throwing on a jogging suit, I went to the basement to meet Charlotte. She was a middle-aged light-skinned woman with a short natural fro and freckles on her face. When I walked in the office, she greeted me with a smile.

"Good morning, Mr. White. Welcome home. Have a seat."

"Thank you."

"My name is Charlotte Brown and I'm your caseworker. How does it feel to wake up in a real bed and not a cell?"

I thought about waking up to getting my dick sucked. "Best feeling I ever had."

"That's good. As your caseworker, I'm going to help you get established out here. Get your birth certificate, Social Security card, and ID. You will need all of that before you can get a job. How about we start with some basic information. What is your full name and date of birth?"

I sat in the office with Charlotte for thirty minutes filling out paperwork and answering questions. It would take about a week for my ID and Social Security card to come, so the plan was for me to take a few classes on financial literacy and anger management to keep me busy. When done filling out the paper work, I went back upstairs and ran into Mr. Jackson.

"Good morning, Carl. How are you doing?"

"I'm good. You?"

"It's a good day. You plan on going out?"

"Yeah. I wasn't sure how it worked."

"You're a free man. You can leave for a couple hours a day. Since you don't have a job, you can go out from ten in the morning until five o'clock. Talk to Janet and she'll give you a bus pass."

I looked around the house for Janet and found her in the office, sitting behind the desk.

"You got a minute?" I asked.

"Anything for you, baby," she smiled. "How was your meeting with Charlotte?"

"Good. We trying to get my ID and shit. I seen your husband and he said you had a bus pass for me."

"You going somewhere?"

"Yeah. I wanted to visit my grandmother's gravesite. She died while I was locked up so I didn't get to say goodbye."

She got emotional. "Oh, my goodness. I am so sorry. Do you want a ride? I'll be done with work in about an hour. I could drive you if you want."

"Nah, I'm good," I declined. "I need to get out and figure out these bus routes since I'ma be using them to get to work."

She gave me a look. "That's a good idea. Don't get lost. You have a five o'clock curfew."

After getting the bus pass, I went and ventured around the city. It took about an hour to get to the graveyard on 129th and Hausted. I didn't know where Nana was buried, so I went to the office and asked the woman behind the desk to ask for directions. She looked up the plot on the computer and used a map to show me the spot. It took five minutes to find the pink granite headstone. It said her name, date of birth, and date of death. While in prison, I had gotten in tune spiritually and I could feel my Nana's presence when I walked up to the headstone. I kneeled to run my fingers across the engraved letters.

"Hey, Nana. I can feel your presence and I want you to know that I'm okay. I'ma make something of myself and be somebody. You always told me I was smart and to come up with a plan. I got one and I'ma make you proud. I love you."

I sat at the gravesite for about twenty minutes before heading back to the bus stop. I had one more stop to make. I needed some information to take care of some unfinished business. After getting on the bus, I rode for about ten minutes before getting off in my old stomping grounds, 119th. Nostalgia gripped me as I walked down the blocks I had grown up on. When I got to Nana's old house, I paused to stare up at it. The new owners kept it the same and it felt surreal to be there after so long. Memories of growing up in the house played in my head. When I started feeling sad, I continued down the block and walked upon the porch of a blue and black house and rang the doorbell.

"Who is it?" a woman called from behind the door.

"Carl. Is K-Dog here?"

The door opened and a pretty brown-skinned woman with hazel brown eyes appeared. "Who is you?"

I looked her from head to toe. She wore a T-shirt, jeans, and Jordan's. The tight denims showed off a slim thick frame.

"I'm Carl," I said, trying to recall who she was. She looked so familiar.

She gave me the same look. "Carl? Did you used to stay down the street?"

"Yeah. I know you, don't I?"

"Yeah, nigga. It's me. Kianna. K-Dog's cousin."

I remembered her instantly. Back then she was a cute twelve or thirteen-year-old and now she was a fine-ass woman.

"Kianna, what's up, shorty. Damn, you all grown up and shit."

She struck a girly pose. "You know. Milk do a body good. But look at you all buff and shit. You just got out?"

"Hell yeah. Just did nineteen long-ass years."

Her eyes popped. "On what?"

"For real. I was locked up with K-Dog. Where that nigga at?"

"That nigga outta town right now. How long you been out?"

"Shit, I just got out yesterday. I'm stayin at a li'l rooming house right now. You got his number?"

"Yeah. Come in and say hi to the family and I'ma call him for you."

I went in the house and spoke to a few of K-Dog's family members before Kianna was able to get him on the phone.

"Carl, what's good, nigga? Welcome home, family!"

"I appreciate it, brah. When you coming back to the crib? I need to holla at you."

"Uh, prolly like a week, my nigga. Where you at?"

"I'm stayin' at a rooming house until I get on my feet. I ain't got no phone yet, but I'ma prolly get one tomorrow."

"Okay. This the number. Get at me."

"Fa sho'. Love, fool," I said, ending the call and giving Kianna back her phone. "Good looking. I gotta move out."

"Okay," she said, looking me up and down. "You don't gotta be a stranger, Carl. I'm grown now."

I gave a smile before saying bye to everybody and leaving.

***

After leaving K-Dog's crib, I went back to the TLP. I was about to walk onto the porch when the driver's door of a light blue Ford Escape opened. My little brother hopped out wearing a big-ass smile.

"Carl, what it do, nigga!"

"Chris, what's up, li'l brah?" I laughed as me and my brother shared a hug. I stepped back to look him over. I hadn't seen him in person since he was ten years old. Like most niggas in prison, I didn't get visits and had to watch him grow up in pictures. "Look at you, li'l nigga. Got a mustache and shit," I cracked.

"Stop, playin', bro. I'm having my way out here. I told you that. Get yo' parole transferred to Wisconsin and come fuck with me. I'm in Madison fuckin' it up."

"Nah, li'l bro. I'ma stay at the crib and build my shit here. Only thing I know about Wisconsin is the Green Bay Packers, and I hate them muthafuckas."

"It ain't that bad, brah. You can get money and don't gotta worry about whose deck it is. It's wide open, fam."

"I hear you, li'l brah. But I'ma stay here. How Aunty Trisha doing?"

"She good. Working at the hospital. I really don't see her that much. I live with my white bitch," he said, nodding towards the truck.

I looked closer and seen a white girl with blonde hair sitting in the passenger seat. "You fucking with them snow bunnies?"

"If it ain't snowing, I ain't going," he laughed. "They let niggas have they way. I'm tellin you, brah, you gotta come to The Town. Shit is sweet."

"I'm not coming to that redneck-ass state and fucking with no white girls, nigga," I laughed.

"A'ight. So how long you gotta be here?" he asked, nodding towards the house.

"Ninety days. I'ma get a job and get my shit together. Do the right thing, you know. What you doing? How you taking care of yo'self?"

He pulled out a wad of cash. "I'm hustling, brah. I told you it's sweet in Wisconsin. Here you go," he said, handing me five hundred dollars.

"Good looking out, brah. I'ma get it back to you."

"Yeah, right. Cartier Chris don't need nothing back. That's you."

I looked at him for a moment. "Cartier Chris? Fuck is that?"

"That's my name, nigga. Come get in the truck with me and let me take you to the mall. And I want you to meet Megan."

I kicked it with my brother and his girl for the rest of my out time before they dropped me back off at the TLP.

J-Blunt

Chapter 11

It took a couple weeks, but after getting my birth certificate and Social Security card, I went to the DMV to get my ID and begin a job search. Charlotte hooked me up with a temp service and I was able to get a job right away at Ferrari Candy. It was the first real job I ever had and the work was hard, but I was cool with that. I worked prison jobs that only paid a few cents an hour. $11.75 was a major raise compared to working in a prison kitchen. I was currently working on the conveyer belt and at 11:30, I took a fifteen-minute break. Once in the break room, I grabbed my phone to check messages and seen a missed call from K-Dog.

"What up, family?" he answered.

"Working. What's going on? I seen that I missed yo' call."

"I got a line on that chump you was looking for."

Even though he didn't say a name, I immediately knew who he was talking about. "You got word on Jewels?"

"Yeah. He ain't in the city no more, but he be poppin' in and out. They say he own a bar called Motown."

Hearing about Jewels had me so flustered that I couldn't think straight. I had been wanting to get even with his ass for nineteen years. "Okay. Good looking, family. I'ma definitely see that nigga."

"You need some AA? You know I'm down to ride."

"Let me think on that. I'm at work right now. What you doing after five?"

"I don't know. Just hit me."

"Fa sho'. Love."

After ending the call, I walked to the vending machine to buy a snack and chill. The only thing I could think about was getting my hundred G's and putting a bullet in Jewel's head.

I got off work at five o'clock and called K-Dog for a ride. He showed up in a white Lexus with Kianna in the passenger seat.

"Carl, what it do, nigga?" he greeted.

"Hey, Carl," Kianna waved.

"What's good with y'all?"

"Shit. Givin' li'l cuz a ride. I was about to drop her off, but she wanted to see you."

"Damn, nigga," Kianna mugged K-Dog. "You didn't have to put me on the spot."

"It's all good," I laughed. "I been meaning to holla at you, but I been focused on tryna get my shit together and get the fuck out this TLP."

"That's good. I like that you focused. Don't see too many niggas out here really on they shit. Most niggas tryna get a bitch pregnant and live off her."

"That's 'cause they don't know they potential. When a nigga get locked in a box for twenty years, you get forced to get real with yo'self. I know what I want and I'm gettin' that shit, and I ain't gon' let nothing stop me. I wanna be great."

"Talk that shit then, nigga." Kianna nodded.

"You think about what I said about Jewels?" K-Dog asked, meeting my eyes through the rearview mirror. "You need that aid and assistance?"

I glanced quickly at Kianna, letting him know I didn't want to talk in front of her.

"Li'l cuz valid, my nigga. She know how we do."

Kianna spun in the seat, defiance showing in her hazel brown eyes. "I know you don't think I'm some punk-ass bitch that don't get down?"

I looked in her eyes for a moment. She was ready.

"You was a shorty when I left. I don't know what you capable of."

"I'm more than capable, Carl. Try me and find out," she smirked.

It was my turn to laugh. "Okay. I respect yo' gangsta. I wanna hit that bar and see if Jewels in there before I go in."

"You mean Jewels that had that white car back in the day?" Kianna asked.

"Yeah. Him. I need to know where he live."

"Why?"

I touched the scar on the back of my head. "He gave me this scar and I wanna return the favor."

"You want me to see if he in there?"

"Nah. I ain't tryna get you in my shit."

"I think you should let her in," K-Dog spoke up. "She a female and could go places we can't go."

I thought about what he said. Nigga had a point. "A'ight. Go in there and see what you can find out."

When K-Dog pulled up outside the bar, Kianna got out and went inside.

"You sure she know what she doin'?" I asked.

"My li'l cousin certified, Carl. She got more heart than a lot of these niggas out here. She got a pretty face, but she got savage in her blood."

Hearing K-Dog's high praise made me relax. She came out fifteen minutes later wearing a smile.

"He not here today," she said, climbing in the passenger seat. "The bartender gave me a free drink and damn near told me his life story. Jewels only show up a couple times a month and it's only on Fridays."

K-Dog gave me an "I told you so" look.

"Okay. Good lookin', shorty. Drop me back off at the crib."

***

A couple days later, I was back at the TLP, taking a shower and getting ready for work. I had just finished drying off, about to head to my room to get dressed. I opened the bathroom door and Janet appeared. She pushed me into the bathroom and started kissing me.

"Fuck is you doing, Janet?" I panicked.

"C'mon, Carl. Fuck me real quick," she moaned, pulling me between her legs as she climbed on the sink.

I knew this was a bad idea. This wasn't my bedroom and people were up and moving around. "Chill, Janet. You gon' get us caught. Get outta here."

She grabbed my towel. "I don't care. Fuck me hard."

Just because she didn't care doesn't mean I didn't. "Janet, you tripping and this shit reckless. Yo husband-"

Knock, knock, knock!

We both froze when someone knocked on the door.

"I'm in here," I called.

"I gotta piss. How much longer you finna be?"

I looked into Janet's wide eyes and seen terror. "Tell him to use the bathroom downstairs," she whispered

"I just got in here. Use the bathroom downstairs."

We sat in the stillness, listening to see if he left.

"I'm so scared," Janet panicked, looking like she was about to cry.

I went to the door and peeked out. The hallway was empty. "Hurry up and get out," I said angrily.

Lust and mischief shone in Janet's eyes as she walked past me and into the hall. "This ain't over with. My pussy is so fuckin' wet right now! Damn, you do something to me."

When Janet was gone, I shook my head and headed to my room to get dressed. She was always horny, wanting to fuck all the time, and we had almost been caught together a couple of times, this one being the closest call. I knew that I wasn't going to last long in this house dealing with her, so I would have to find a backup plan soon.

After getting dressed, I left the house and headed to work. When I was finished putting in my eight hours, I called K-Dog. Today was Friday and Jewels was supposed to show up at the bar. When K-Dog didn't answer, I sent a text. Ten minutes later I called him again and still didn't get an answer. All out of options, I called Kianna.

"Hey, Carl."

"What's good, shorty. You heard from K-Dog?"

"You haven't heard?"

I could tell by the sound of her voice that she was about to give me some bad news. "Heard what? What happened?"

"K-Dog got caught up in a sweep last night. He in jail."

I hung my head and let out a breath. "Fuck."

"What's going on? You need me to help you with something?"

I was quiet for a few moments, trying to gather my thoughts. Jewels was going to be showing up to that bar and I didn't want to miss the opportunity to get even. "K-Dog was supposed to take me to the bar. He was my ride."

"I can take you. Where you at?"

"I'm at work. You got a car?"

"Nah, but I can get one. I'ma call you when I'm on my way."

I waited for Kianna outside the factory for thirty minutes before giving up and heading for the bus stop. I was devastated that I had missed the opportunity to get Jewels. But I knew it wouldn't be my last shot. Sometimes defeat happens before a victory.

I had just got to the bus stop when my phone started ringing. It was Kianna.

"What's up, shorty?"

"I'm pulling up to your job right now. Where you at?"

Elation flooded my body as I looked towards the factory. "I'm down the street at the bus stop. I didn't think you was gon' make it."

She laughed. "I'm in the blue Firebird."

A few moments later she pulled up to the bus stop.

"You gon' learn to stop doubting me." She grinned.

"I won't do it no more," I said, sitting in the passenger seat. "You keep surprising me."

"Good. Now what's the plan? You want me to go in again?"

"Nah, not this time. I don't want him to see you. We gon' sit outside and wait. I need to know where he live."

"How much time do you got? Don't you got a curfew?"

The clock on the dash read 5:43. "I got like three hours."

When she pulled up to the bar, she parked across the street and we sat to wait.

"So, we just gon' sit here and watch the bar?" she asked.

"Yeah. You said he was coming Friday, right?"

"That's what the bartender said."

"Then we wait."

We was quiet for a few moments before she broke the silence. "You don't got a girlfriend, huh?"

I looked into those pretty hazel brown eyes. "Nah. I don't got my shit together and the last thing I need to be tryna do is be booed up. What about you? You gotta nigga?"

"If I did, I wouldn't be here with you."

"Whose car is this?"

She smiled, something glowing in her eyes. "A friend's."

"This friend is a him, huh?"

She nodded. "He is. But it's not like that. He helps me out when I need it."

I wasn't going to get too deep in her business. "That's the best kind of friend to have."

"True. So, you haven't had none since you been out?"

I looked in her eyes again trying to see if she was trying to fuck or just being curious. "Why you wanna know?"

"I'm just curious. Nineteen years is a long time. You been out for a couple weeks and I know if I did that much time, I would need some."

"I took care of that the first day out."

"So, you do got somebody?"

"Not exactly. It's the lady that runs the TLP. She got a husband that works with her but his shit don't work."

She busted out laughing. "Oh my God, Carl! That is too crazy."

"I know. But I ain't really trippin. It ain't nothing serious. Like I said, I ain't looking for a girl."

"So, if you was looking for a woman, what would she be like? Do you have a type?"

I gave Kianna a once over. She was girl next door fine. Hair pulled into a ponytail. Milk chocolate complexion. Those pretty eyes. A nice smile. And a body that had me wanting to pop that hood and check her temperature.

"I don't know if I really got a type. Obviously, I want somebody that looks good, but that ain't everything. I think it's about the compatibility of our personalities. Do we laugh at the same things? Do we want the same things in life? Do she got my back? Can I trust her? What about you?"

"I feel like you, for the most part. I want somebody that wants something out of life. I'm tired of dealing with niggas that expect me to provide. I work at a clothing store and I don't make enough to be taking care of no nigga. I want a man with a vision. A man that knows what he wants. And I want to help him build that. I want a nigga that I can be great with."

"Somebody you can be great with," I repeated. "That's good. I like that."

"You said you wanna be great. What you mean by that?"

"Before my Nana died, she always told me to be somebody. I promised her that I was gon' be somebody great. While I was locked up, I came up with a plan. Now I'm finna get to it."

A moment of silence passed between us.

"I believe you, Carl. And I want to help you be great."

I turned to stare in those hazel browns and got lost in the moment. To do what I needed to do, I needed a partner. Somebody that believed in me and would help me. I was about to tell her that when someone leaving the bar caught my eye. He was about average height with a stocky build and looked to be in his late forties or early fifties. He was bald with a salt and pepper goatee and walked with a slight limp.

"That's him!"

Kianna looked to the bar. "You sure? He looks old."

"Yeah, I'm sure. I'll never forget that nigga's face. Follow him."

Jewels walked to a black Benz and pulled off. Kianna followed in the Firebird. We ended up following him all the way to a house in Peoria, a Chicago suburb.

"So what now?" Kianna asked.

"Now I'ma pay his ass back. I got what I need. Take me back to the crib."

"You still got an hour before you gotta be back. You wanna kick it with me for a li'l while?" Kianna asked as she drove away.

She wanted to fuck. Normally I would be down, but we was cutting it close on time. I had a curfew and I couldn't be late. "As much as I want to kick it with you some more, I can't be late on this curfew. So let's not move too fast. We don't wanna rush greatness."

***

"I need some extended time out tonight. I wanna get in some over time," I told Janet.

"Okay. Did you tell Frank?" she asked, sliding her panties back on.

"Nah. I'm telling you so you can clear it with your husband."

She stood and slid into her jeans. "Why don't you tell him yourself?"

I walked over and grabbed a fist full of her hair. "Because I just told you. Now take care of that or else."

A challenge showing in her eyes. "Or else what?"

It was seven o'clock in the morning and we were at a hotel. Janet hooked it up so I could get out of the house early to meet her. We'd been fucking since about five-thirty and it was time for me to get ready for work and for her to head to the TLP.

"You lucky I gotta get ready for work. Or else I would have you make the neighbors know my name."

She stood up and gave me an aggressive tongue kiss. "I'll take care of it. Just make sure you keep taking care of me."

After leaving the hotel, I headed for work. For the entire day, all I could think about was getting back at Jewels. I trusted that nigga and all the while he was grooming me to kill me. I couldn't wait to see the look on his face right before I put a bullet through his mug.

When my shift was over, I sent Kianna a text for her to come get me. She texted back immediately saying she was already outside. I stepped into the parking lot and seen her waiting in the blue Firebird.

"Just so you know, I never doubted that you would be here," I said as I climbed in the passenger seat.

"I know you didn't." She smiled. "And I got the other stuff you asked for. It's in the bag."

I looked in the backseat and seen a duffel bag. Inside was a black hoodie, gloves, and a Glock. "You a beast, shorty."

"I got your back. You ready to get this nigga?"

"I been waiting on this for nineteen years."

We drove to Jewels's bar and Kianna parked across the street. His car wasn't in the parking lot, so we would have to wait. I threw on the hoodie and gloves and we began the wait. It took about an hour for the Benz to show up.

"There he go. He owe me a hunnit thousand so I need you to follow us," I told Kianna.

"I got you, baby. Go get his ass."

When he walked in the bar, Kianna pulled the Firebird in the parking lot and parked on the driver's side of the Benz. I gripped the Glock, anticipation filling my body as we waited. Ten minutes later, Jewels walked out the bar. I turned to face Kianna so he wouldn't see my face.

"Let me know when he open the door," I told her.

"He just walked over. Okay. He opening the door right now."

I moved quickly, hopping out the passenger seat with the Glock. Jewels turned at my quick movement, but it was too late for him to react. My Glock was already pointed in his chest. Recognition immediately flashed in his eyes, and then fear. Like he had seen a ghost.

"Don't do nothing stupid or I'ma wet cho ass up in this parking lot. Get in the car."

"Okay, young blood. Be cool," he said, remaining calm as he climbed behind the steering wheel.

I got in the backseat. "Where my cut?"

He met my eyes in the rearview mirror. "That was a long time ago and I thought you was dead."

"I'm not. I was in jail, nigga. Where my shit?"

"Listen, Carl. It's not easy to come up with that kind of money. I need some time."

"Check this out, Jewels," I said, pressing the pistol into the back of the headrest. "The only reason you still alive right now is because I want my money. If you telling me you can't pay me, we done talking."

"Wait!" he yelled. "I can get you something. But I need yo' word that you not gon' shoot me."

"You got my word."

We had a stare-off in the mirror.

"Let's go, Jewels. Take me to my shit."

He started the Benz and pulled out the lot. "I'm sorry, man. I really mean that. I did a lot of bullshit during my life and betraying yo' trust was really fucked up. I'm sorry for that. I thought you died and that shit was heavy on my heart because I had real love for you."

I didn't respond. No words were necessary.

"Things didn't go like I wanted, Carl. After I took that money, I went to Saint Louis and lived good for a li'l while. I think some kinda karma happened to my ass because I fucked around and fell in love with a dopefiend and got hooked on that boy. Did so much shit in East Saint Louis and Indiana that I got niggas looking for me everywhere. They ended up catching up to me. That's why I got this limp. They killed my girl, but I got away. I had to come back to the city and try to put my life back together. I'm telling you this because I'm not the same person I used to be. Losing my wife and everything I owned changed me. It humbled me. I was at the bottom and I knew the only way I was going to get back up was to turn my life around. So I did. I accepted Jesus and I been clean and sober for three years. The old me, the man you know as Jewels, is dead and gone. I'm a new man because of Jesus Christ. And my name is Gregory."

I stayed silent, thinking about everything that he told me. I didn't want what he said to have an effect on me, but it did.

"You know, I pictured this moment being a lot different when I was sitting in that cell. I wanted to walk up to you and squeeze off in yo' face like you did me. But after hearing everything that you been through, I feel sorry for you a little bit."

"That's because you held onto your humanity, Carl. Despite everything you've been through, there is still good in you. That is a blessing."

I thought on his words. I had killed six people and I wasn't a deranged maniac. "I think you right, Gregory. In fact, I actually prefer not to kill. While locked up, I became a fan of diplomacy. War and bloodshed should be a final result after an attempt at peace."

"Those are wise words, Carl. You sound like you educated yourself while you were inside."

"I did. Read everything I could get my hands on. But I gotta be honest, man. The best lessons I ever learned came from you."

Sadness washed over his face. "You don't know how sorry I am for that. One day I hope you can find it in your heart to forgive me."

I talked to Gregory during the entire ride to his house, and it wasn't about bullshit. The conversations were deep and enriching. When we pulled into his driveway and got out of the car, I didn't even have my gun out. He let me in the house and I immediately noticed the Bible on the front table and the twelve-inch gold crucifix on the wall.

"I'm going to be honest, Carl. I don't have one hundred thousand dollars. But I have something for you. A down payment."

I nodded. "That's cool."

We walked to his bedroom and he pulled a safe from the closet. Inside was fifteen thousand dollars.

"I'll get you some more when the bank opens on Monday," he promised.

I stuffed the money in my pocket. "That won't be necessary, brah. This is good."

He looked confused. "You don't want no more money?"

I shook my head. "Being in prison taught me there are things in this life more valuable than money. Like time. And life."

I watched the realization of my words light his eyes right before I shot him in the face. Then I stood over him and watched him die.

Chapter 12

I left Gregory's house and walked calmly to the Firebird. It felt good to kill his ass after all those years. A line from Tupac's song crossed my mind. "Revenge is like the sweetest joy next to getting pussy". Damn, that shit was true.

"What happened? You good?" Kianna asked, her eyes wide with curiosity.

"I'm good," I said calmly, hopping in the passenger seat. "Let's go."

She sped away from the scene. "Did you kill him?"

I thought about the look in his eyes before he died. He didn't look scared. More like relieved. "Yeah. Slow down. You don't gotta drive reckless. We good."

"I don't know what to do. Where should I go?" she asked, a little flustered. "And why are you so calm?"

I reached for the steering wheel and grabbed her hand in mine. "Because we don't got no reason to panic. We good. Relax. I don't gotta be back at the house until midnight. We can go wherever you wanna go."

She snuck a glance at me. "You wanna come back to my house?"

"Don't you live with yo' mama?"

"Yeah."

"Let's go to a hotel. I want to be alone with you," I said, bringing her hand to my lips and kissing her palm.

When we got in the hotel room, no words were needed. As soon as the door closed, our lips found each other's like there were magnets in them. We fell onto the bed with me on top. She opened her legs and I began grinding against her while we continued to make out. When her hands went under my shirt and started rubbing my back, I paused to take it off. She also took off hers, revealing a black bra underneath. I lifted the bra to see those titties. They were perfect handfuls, firm with big black areolas. I lowered my head and sucked the right nipple in my mouth.

"Ssss!" she hissed, arching her back and rubbing my head.

I continued sucking until it was hard as a rock before moving to the other.

"Oh, Carl!" she moaned, grinding her pelvis against mine.

I knew what that meant. She wanted me to give that pussy some attention. I sat up and started pulling her pants off aggressively. She wasn't wearing panties. I lowered my head between her legs and licked my tongue from the top to the bottom of her slit.

"Oh, yeah!" she moaned, grabbing the back of my head.

I gave her more tongue, licking circles around the labia and vulva.

"Damn, Carl! Ssss! That shit feel good."

After a few minutes of teasing, I finally went to her clit. I spread the lips apart and started flipping my tongue rapidly across the tender ball of flesh.

"Mmmm! Yeah, baby! Mmmhhh!"

I went from licking her clit to sucking it and Kianna went crazy.

"Oh, shit, Carl! Oh shit! Oh shit!" she screamed over and over, smashing my face into her womb. "Suck it harder, baby! Suck harder!"

I gave her what she wanted and then some. I listened to her moans and paid attention to how her body reacted to my pleasure. When she was near her orgasm, I slicked my pinkie with her juice and pushed it in her ass.

"Ohh ahhh! Oh God! Oh my God!" she screamed as the orgasm vibrated through her body. It seemed like she came for a full minute. "Damn, Carl. What did you just do to me?" she whined.

"Nothing yet," I said, standing to take off my jeans. When I was naked, I climbed between her legs and entered her slowly. "Damn, gurl!" I groaned, loving the feel of her insides. She was wet and hot.

"Oh, Carl!" she moaned, digging her nails into my back.

I dove in deep, pausing when our pelvises were touching. I looked down to see her ecstasy face. Her mouth was slightly open, hazel eyes glowing. She looked so sexy that I bent down and started kissing her. She began moaning in my mouth when I started stroking. I began slow, picking up speed with every thrust. A few moments later, I had her legs spread as far apart as they would go, drilling that pussy.

"Oh, Carl! Oh, Carl! Yeah, baby!" she screamed over and over.

Sweat dripped down my body like we was in a sauna. I could feel my nut getting close, but I held it off. I couldn't get mine until she got hers. To speed up her orgasm, I pressed my thumb against her clit, continuing to deliver the D.

"Oh, shit, baby! I'm finna cum again," she warned.

That shit was music to my ears. I hit it harder and began wiggling my thumb.

"Oh God! Oh shit!" she screamed as her body went stiff.

While she came, I hit that pussy even harder. Her walls were spasming, gripping my dick. Shit felt too good and I let go.

"Aw shit! Damn, Kianna! Shit!" I groaned.

I fell on top of her and we both lay there collecting our breath.

"Damn, Carl. Oh my God, that shit was so good," she moaned.

"Yo' pussy was my motivation," I managed between breaths, rolling onto my back.

"What do it feel like to kill somebody?" she asked.

I looked over at her, surprised by the question. "That's not a normal question somebody asks after we fuck."

She turned her head to look at me. "I don't care. People die around me all the time, but I never talked to somebody right after they did it. I wanna know what it feel like."

I thought for a moment. "It depends why you do it. With Jewels, it was about revenge, so it felt like getting pussy."

Something shone in her eyes. It looked like she wanted to kill.

"Why you ask me that?"

She looked towards the ceiling. "Because I want to kill somebody, but I'm scared."

Her words troubled me a little. "Who do you want to kill? Why?"

She took her time answering. "For revenge."

I completely understood. "What did they do?"

"I don't want to talk about it right now," she said, going quiet.

I respected that.

She rolled over and kissed me on the cheek. "I like you, Carl. For real. I want to help you be great. I mean that."

I stared into those hazel browns and seen nothing but the truth reflecting. "Okay. We can be great together."

She smiled and kissed me again. "Okay."

Her hands started rubbing my body, stopping at the scar on my chest. "What happened?"

I thought about Carla. "The same thing that happened to my head. Trust."

"Jewels did both?"

"Nah. Somebody else."

"An ex-girlfriend?"

"My mother tried to kill me when I was like ten. She was schizophrenic and bipolar. Heard voices. I walked in the bathroom right after she killed one of my twin brothers. She was about to kill Chris when I tried to stop her. She stabbed him and then stabbed me. Killed our daddy and the lady next door before she killed herself."

She looked horrified. "Damn, Carl! That's fucked up."

"I know. The people you trust hurt you the worst."

We went quiet again.

"I know what you mean," she said, sniffling.

I looked over and seen tears rolling down her face. "You good? What's going on?"

She wiped the tears, trying to be strong. "My uncle used to rape me when I was little. That's who I want to kill."

I took a moment to gather the right words. "Whenever you need me, I'ma be there for you. I mean that."

She smiled. "Thank you."

I sat up and grabbed my pants from the floor and pulled out the money.

"What is that?" she asked.

"Jewels gave it to me. It was all he had. This is how we gon' start our journey to greatness. I need you to get an apartment. Somewhere we can be alone at. I also need you to buy a car so we can get around. How much you think you need?"

"Depends on what kind of car."

"Just something to get us around in. Nothing too fancy."

"I can probably get us a nice car from an auction for two or three thousand. And an apartment might cost six or seven hundred a month. Gotta pay the security deposit too."

I peeled off seven thousand. "Take care of everything. And get some furniture too."

"Are you living there too?"

"Nah. That's for you so we have a place to chill."

Disappointment flashed in her eyes but she didn't speak on it. "Okay."

"I need to flip this. I heard the city changed and we can get a li'l money on our own now. You know where I can buy some work?"

"I can ask around. K-Dog's guys hustle."

"See what you can find out. I'ma work on finding some buyers."

"I got you. You can trust me."

I didn't have a response for that. She had seen my scars.

"I get it," she nodded. "But I'ma show you. We are going to be great."

***

When I talked to Kianna the next day, she told me she found a plug and that she was working on getting the car and apartment. Now that we had the plug, I needed to work on getting clientele, and I knew just the person to holler at. When I got off of work, I went home and waited on Tyson. I was chilling in the room watching porn on my phone when he walked in.

"What's good, family?" I asked.

"Shit, my nigga. Tired as fuck," he said, flopping down on his bed. "They had a nigga slanging boxes all fuckin' day. My back is killing me."

"You need some Tylenol?" I offered.

He looked at me like I just told him I had the cure for cancer. "Hell yeah!"

I went in my drawer and threw him the bottle. "Check it out. I'm finna get my feet wet with this hustling, but I ain't got no clientele. You know somebody I can build with?"

Tyson popped a pill in his mouth and gave me a long stare. "You serious, fam?"

"Yeah. I can't do this nine-to-five shit forever. I need to get to it. I ain't finna be in this boarding house forever. I gotta make a move."

"But you just did twenty years, my nigga. You finna take a chance and play with yo' freedom like that?"

"I just need to make about a hundred thousand and I'm out. Six month run and buy a house and fall back. The plan I had when I got out didn't work. Nigga owed me and he didn't have it when I went to collect. Now I gotta get it on my own and I gotta get it fast."

"Walking away from getting money ain't that easy, Carl. Especially if you touching them books. That shit come fast and you spend it as soon as you get it."

"Not me. I got a plan and I'm sticking to it. I'm damn near forty and I ain't never had shit. Been in the joint since I was nineteen. All my twenties I was locked in a cell. You don't know what that feel like 'cause you had yo' run. You know what it feels like to have it. I don't. And now I'm ready to take my shot."

I could see that he felt my words. "Yeah, you right. They took yo' best years. But this game is risky, boss. Cutthroat. You sure you wanna get in this?"

"One hundred percent."

"Okay. My uncle is a head. He helped me when I was on my way up. We can ride down on him after we get off work tomorrow. You got a ride?"

The next day I had Kianna pick us up from the TLP. Tyson's uncle lived on the West Side. It was springtime and sixty degrees outside, so the block was alive with action. We followed Tyson up on the porch of a white house that was in desperate need of a paint job. He banged on the door like he was the police.

"Who the fuck banging on my door like that?" someone called from inside.

"Its Big T!" Tyson called.

Locks clicked and the door opened a few moments later. A frail and old dark-skinned nigga with no teeth stepped onto the porch. He was bald on the top with nappy graying hair around the sides.

"Big T! What's going on, nephew?" He smiled, showing pink and purple gums.

"What's good, Unc?"

"You looking good. When you get out, boy?" he asked, looking Tyson from head to toe.

"About two months ago. I'm staying at a rooming house until I get my shit together."

The old man frowned. "A rooming house? You not working?"

"Nah, Unc. I'm done with that shit. But I wanna introduce you to my nigga, Carl, and his girl, Kianna. Ay y'all, this my uncle Cotton."

We exchanged nods.

"My boy want yo' help. Let us in so we can talk."

The house was a mess with all kinds of junk, paper, and garbage everywhere. I found a spot on the couch and sat down. Kianna didn't want to sit on the furniture, so she sat on my lap.

"What you need my help with, young man?" Cotton asked after we sat down.

"I'm a rookie and I'm tryna get in the game. I need a good coach."

Cotton smiled so wide that it looked like the comers of his mouth touched his nostrils. "I like the sound of that. What you tryna sell?"

"Whatever you think can make the most money."

"Well, if you going for the money, than you want that boy. Them people go crazy for that shit. This is the hood, so rocks sell too. That's my shit."

"A'ight. Let's do that boy. You bring 'em in and I'ma bless you real good."

Cotton licked his dry lips. "Do you got somethin for me right now?"

"I don't. But I got some money," I said, pulling out a twenty.

Cotton's smile grew wider, showing all gums. "I like you, Carl. Yeah. We gon' get along good."

Me and Kianna laughed.

"Listen, I'ma get some shit and let you know when I'm ready."

"Make sure you get the good shit, nephew. Some of that shit round here be stepped on so much that when you recook it, you don't got shit left. If you got that good shit, you guaranteed to make yo' money. Guaranteed!"

"Say no more, Unc. I'ma see you in a minute.

***

It only took a month for our line to start rolling. Shit was going so good that Kianna had to quit her job to get money full time. And it was worth it. I invested five thousand into the product and we already had double that in the safe. My plan was to get a hundred thousand, buy a house, and call it quits. Flip that house and grow. I wasn't going to be greedy and try to get it all at once. But I needed a good start, and a house was a damn good first investment.

"Why don't you leave the TLP and move in with me, Carl? I don't understand why you still living there when you don't have to. It's temporary until you get your own house. We got that."

I sat in the passenger seat listening to the same questions she had been asking since she got the apartment. Truth was, I didn't want to live with Kianna because I didn't want to be in a relationship. She was already falling in love and I knew that if I moved in, shit was gon' get real deep real fast. I didn't want that. I wanted to be single. Do what I wanted. And I still wasn't sure how to tell her that.

"I told you my PO wants me to stay at the TLP until my ninety days is up. I can't tell him what to do. He my PO."

"I don't believe you, Carl. That don't make no sense. Why do he want you to stay? You supposed to be getting independent."

"I don't know. That's just what he want."

She took her eyes off the road to mug me. "I don't believe you. Gimme his number and let me talk to him. What's the number?"

"C'mon, man. You tripping. You ain't finna talk to my PO. You don't trust me?"

"You know I trust you, Carl. Do you trust me?"

I deflected the question. "C'mon, Kianna. I just got off work and I wanna chill. Why we always gotta do this?"

"Is it that old bitch? Is that why you staying? You fell in love with the married lady?"

"C'mon, Ki-Ki. I'm not in love with her. I told you my PO wants me there."

"I know you lying to me, Carl. I just don't know why."

I massaged my temples and took a couple deep breaths. "I'm tired of hearing this shit. Drop me off at the TLP."

She mugged me. "You don't gotta be back til nine o'clock. You coming home with me."

"No, I'm not. I'm tired of arguing with you. Take me to the crib."

She was quiet for a moment. "That's how it is, for real?"

"Yeah. I'm not finna go through this every day. I'm tired and I wanna chill."

We didn't talk for the rest of the ride. She pulled in front of the TLP, parked, and turned to face me. "What is we doing, Carl?"

"What you mean? I'm finna go in here and chill. Come get me to take me to work in the morning."

"I'm not talking about that. I'm talking about me and you. What is this?"

I let out an exhausted breath. "C'mon, Ki-Ki. Why you doing this?"

"Because I wanna know where yo' head at. What is we doing?"

"We friends, Kianna. I told you that."

"That's it? Just friends?"

I grabbed the door handle. "Let's talk about this some other time. I'ma call you later," I said before getting out of the car.

"Carl! Carl!" Kianna called.

"I'ma call you later," I said before walking in the house. I checked the window to make sure she didn't follow me. When the Monte Carlo drove away, I fell on the couch and sighed. I was going to eventually have to tell her how I felt, and I wasn't looking forward to it.

"What are you doing here so early?"

I looked up and seen Janet standing in the doorway to the front office.

"I'm tired. It's been a long day."

She walked over to lock the door before kneeling between my legs. "You want me to make you feel better?"

"What is you doing? Get up before somebody sees you!" I panicked.

She started unbuckling my pants. "Nobody is in the house but me and you. And Frank is gone for the rest of the day."

That changed everything. "You sure you wanna do this right here?"

"You're right. Come in the office and let me suck your dick while you sit behind my husband's desk."

I followed her into the office and sat behind Frank's desk in the plush leather office chair. Janet locked the door before crawling under the desk and in between my legs. A devilish grin shown on her face before she unleashed my meat and started sucking. I closed my eyes and enjoyed the head, listening to her mouth making slurping noises. About ten minutes into the blow job, I thought I heard the front door close. I grabbed her head to stop her from sucking me.

"I think somebody just came in the house."

"The door is locked. Nobody has a key but me and Frank," she said before getting back to the head.

When I heard the key being inserted into the office door, my heart sank. I looked down at Janet and seen her life crumbling in her eyes. Before we could move, the door opened.

"The hell you doing in my office?" Frank grumbled.

I didn't have the words so I started stuttering. "I...um, shit. Uh."

"Get the hell out of my chair! Where is my wife?" he snapped before looking down the hallway. "Janet! Janet!"

I looked between my legs and seen tears along with the fear of God in her eyes.

"You can't hear, boy! Get the hell out my office!" Frank yelled, stepping further into the room.

I got up and started buttoning my pants. He looked down at what I was doing and then back into my eyes. In his eyes, I seen the same look that I seen in Janet's.

"Where the hell is my wife?" he yelled, rushing over to look under the desk. "Janet, what the——! Oh my God! How could you do this to me?"

"Frank, baby, I'm sorry. It's not what you think," Janet cried.

"You mean you wasn't just sucking Carl's dick in my office?" he shrieked.

"I was, but I love you, Frank!" she said, grabbing hold of him.

"Get'cho damn hands off me!" He shoved her away. "I can't believe you did this."

"Please, Frank. Just hear me out. I love you. You can't have sex and I was just doing this to get some. But I don't want him. I want you."

Frank didn't respond to her. He turned all of his anger on me. "Get the hell out of my house, right now! I'm calling——" he was yelling, but then stopped and grabbed his chest. "Ahh! Call 911! I think I'm having a heart attack!"

J-Blunt

Chapter 13

I sat in the passenger seat of the Monte Carlo, expecting Kianna to snap out at any moment. After I told her Frank caught his wife sucking my dick, she mugged the shit out of me and didn't say another word. Now we rode in silence. When we got to the apartment, she went to the room and slammed the door. I flopped down on the couch and drowned in my misery.

I had fucked up and let some pussy jeopardize my freedom and livelihood. Now Frank was laid up in the hospital and I was going to have to explain to my PO why I got kicked out of the TLP. I didn't know if fucking a staff member at the house would be considered a violation. If it was, I was fucked. And it also looked like Kianna was about to get her way because I was going to have to move in. Shit was fucked up all the way around the board.

The bedroom door opened and pulled me from my thoughts. Kianna's hazel eyes burned gold with anger as she stormed into the living room.

"How the fuck you gon' go fuck that bitch after you just argued with me? Huh? You's a dirty muthafucka, Carl. That's why yo' ass don't wanna live with me, because you wanted to keep fucking both of us, ain't it?"

I was about to respond, but she wasn't done.

"I can't believe yo' ass gon' give that bitch my time. Yo' ass was supposed to be with me til nine o'clock. That's why you started the argument, so you had a reason to leave and go fuck yo' old bitch. That's why y'all got caught, because God don't like ugly. And y'all gave her husband a heart attack. Why the fuck is you fuckin' her when you could fuck me whenever you want? I'm not enough for you? My pussy ain't good enough? You don't——"

"Is you gon' let me talk, or is you just got keep talking shit?" I cut in. "You knew about Janet out the gate. I didn't lie about shit. You was cool with me fuckin' both of y'all. Matter of fact, I was fuckin' her first. Now all of a sudden you acting like I played you. Ain't nobody play you. You knew what you was getting into. Stop actin' like you the victim."

"I'm not acting like I'm a victim. I'm mad because right after you argued with me and cut our time short, you go right and fuck her. You know that shit is bogus."

"It wasn't like that."

She gave me that "nigga, please" look.

"I mean, I did let her suck my dick, but it wasn't like that. She didn't mean shit. Janet was just something to do."

"So what about me? Am I just something to do too?"

"C'mon, Kianna. You know it ain't like that."

"Well, tell me what it's like then, Carl," she said, rolling her neck and placing a hand on her hip. "You can't run to the old bitch's house this time. Explain to me what it's like."

I closed my eyes and lay my head against the head rest for a moment. I had to be real with her. When I opened my eyes, I gave her what she wanted. "A'ight. You wanna know what it's like? Well, it's like this. I don't wanna be in a relationship or fall in love, Kianna. Love makes people weak and that shit ain't for me. I know you catching feelings and if I move in, shit gon' get deeper. I don't want that. I wanna be able to do me. I don't want nothing between us to change. I don't want us to fall in love and I don't want us to break apart. I wanna keep everything like it is right now and focus on getting this money. That's what I want."

She stared at me for a moment. Her face was blank so I couldn't guess what her reaction would be. Then she laughed.

"You know what, Carl? You ain't shit. So, you wanna fuck who you wanna fuck, and that's that?"

"I just did nineteen years in the pen. What the fuck you expect?"

"I expect you to show love to the people that's showing love to you. I expect you to be a man. But you wanna be a boy. Okay, Peter Pan. Fuck you and all yo li'l Tinkerbells," she said before walking back into the room and slamming the door.

I closed my eyes and lay back again. Kianna was blowing me and all her emotional shit was getting on my nerves. But I told her how I felt. Now it was on her to accept it or reject it.

144

I continued chilling on the couch and about thirty minutes later, somebody rang the doorbell. We didn't get visitors so I was surprised.

"Who is it?" I asked, getting up from the couch.

"BJ."

I checked the peephole and seen a tall chubby brown-skinned nigga at the door. I had never seen him before.

"Who you looking for?" I asked, opening the door.

"I'm looking for Kianna."

The bedroom door opened and Kianna stepped out of the room wearing one of my t-shirts. "That's for me. I got it. Come in, BJ."

"Excuse me, brah," the nigga said, stepping past me and wrapping Kianna in a hug. "Hey, baby girl. I was wondering when I was gon' hear from you again."

"I was getting myself situated. You see I got an apartment. This is my roommate, Carl."

"Sup, brah?" He nodded.

I didn't acknowledge the nod. I just stood, holding the door opened, shocked by what I was seeing. Kianna had actually invited a nigga in my shit.

"Come to the room with me, BJ. Let's let Carl have his privacy."

BJ followed Kianna to the room and closed the door.

I closed the front door and tried to get my thoughts in order. I had so many feelings and emotions flooding my body that I found it hard to think straight. I was pissed off that she had the audacity to bring a nigga to our spot. I knew she was probably trying to make me jealous because of what I said, and that shit was working. There was a burning in my chest that I'd never felt before and I couldn't stop my top lip from twitching. My hands were shaking and my whole body was warm. And the final thought that stayed in my mind was whether or not Kianna was fucking him.

I walked into her room without knocking. Kianna and BJ were sitting on the bed.

"What is you doing, Carl?" Kianna asked.

I opened the drawer, pulling out the Glock I used to kill Jewels and pointing it in BJ's face. "Get the fuck out my house right now, nigga!"

His hands shot in the air. "Okay, brah. Chill."

"Carl, what the fuck are you doing?" Kianna shrieked.

I turned the gun on her. "Shut the fuck up, bitch! You done lost yo' muthafuckin mind inviting this nigga where I lay my head at?"

She didn't look scared. "You said that we friends. You don't wanna be in a relationship or fall in love, so why is you tripping? You can do what you want, but I can't?"

I thought about putting a bullet in her face. But then I would have to kill BJ too, and I didn't want to go back to jail over some pussy. So I turned back to BJ. "Why you still in my shit?"

"Okay. I'm gone," he said before taking off from the room.

I followed him to the door and locked it. When I turned around, Kianna was walking towards me.

"Why you tri——"

I grabbed her by the throat and put the gun to her head. "You wanna play these li'l stupid-ass games? I ain't no fuckin' toy. You want me to kill yo' ass?"

There was no fear on her face and she didn't try to stop me from choking her. "Why are you so mad? You don't love me, right? Why can't I do me?"

"Because I said you can't."

She looked turned on. "Because you jealous?"

"Because you mine."

"No, I'm not."

I squeezed her throat harder. "Don't make me fuck you up."

"Do it," she challenged.

We stared in each other's eyes for a moment. She was waiting to see what I would do. The look in her eyes got my dick hard.

"I know what you want," I said, pushing her onto the couch and stripping out of my clothes.

She watched me with lust-filled eyes, opening her legs, revealing that she wasn't wearing panties. "Don't touch me, Carl," she said, making no motion to get up.

146

When I was naked, I walked over and tried to climb on top of her.

She lifted her legs and threw a kick. "Don't fuckin' touch me!"

"Oh, it's like that?"

Challenge shone in her eyes. "Yeah. It's like that. You don't own me. Fuck you."

I don't know why, but her defiance and fight turned me on even more. I wanted to dominate her. I wanted to make her submit.

"You is mine," I said before rushing her.

She tried kicking me again, but I caught her foot and threw it aside before jumping on top of her. She put up a fight and I had to pin her arms down.

"Stop, Carl. Get the fuck off me. I hate you. Leave me alone."

I reached a hand up to her throat and started choking her while my other hand began tearing the shirt from her body. "Well, hate me then. I don't give a fuck. I hate yo' ass too."

She started fighting me again and I had to pin her down with my body. Then I was between her legs and without even trying, my dick slipped right into her pussy.

"Stop, Carl," she whispered. "I hate you. Stop."

Her weak cries turned me on like a mutherfucker. I pressed my body into her some more, going deeper in her guts. "I hate yo' ass, too. And I'm not stopping. This is my pussy. You hear me? This pussy is mine!"

One of her hands got loose and she started choking me. I returned the gesture and started choking her ass back while thrusting my hips.

"Oh, Carl! Oh, shit!" she moaned, opening her legs so I could go deeper.

I gained leverage and started fucking her like I hated her. "Yeah, muthafucka. Talk that shit now! Talk that shit now!"

"Fuck you, nigga. Oh, shit! I still hate yo' ass," she moaned.

I hit it even harder, our pelvises slapping violently every time I thrust forward. "I don't give a fuck. Hate me. But this is my pussy, ain't it? Tell me it's my pussy."

"No...oh shit! No, it ain't yours. Fuck you!"

Her words added fuel to my fire and I continued to hit it hard. I paid attention to her body and I knew she was getting close to cumming. "Say it, nigga. Tell me it's mine. Say it!"

She tried to hold out, but I was winning the pleasure battle. I was fucking her good and the orgasm was close.

"Tell me it's my pussy. Say it right now! Say it!"

"Oh, Carl! It's yours! It's yours! Oooh!" she screamed as an orgasm rocked her body.

I kept on hitting it until I finally busted my nut and fell on top of her. We lay there for a moment catching our breath. I needed to make sure she understood me so I rested on my elbows to look in her eyes.

"I ain't playin', Kianna. This is my pussy. This world ain't big enough for you to fuck nobody else but me. I don't wanna ever see a nigga in my house again."

All the defiance was gone from her eyes. "Okay, baby. It's yours. I'm yours," she said before lifting her head and kissing me.

***

I got a call from my PO the next day telling me to come to his office. I thought about going on the run, but didn't. And it was good I went to see him, because he only wanted to talk about what happened at the TLP and see if I had somewhere to stay. After explaining that I did fuck Janet a couple of times and that she did it because Frank was impotent, my PO started laughing. Since there were no rules about fucking TLP staff, he said he wasn't tripping. I gave him the apartment address and told him that's where I was staying and he let me leave.

Things between me and Kianna got serious once I moved in. I didn't want her fucking nobody else, so she became my woman. A few weeks later, shit was going smooth. I had a crib, a job, a hustle, and a down-ass bitch. Life was good.

"Cotton sent a text. He wants us to come over," Kianna said after checking her phone.

"Let's get it," I said, getting up from the couch and helping her up.

She grabbed the car keys and I went to get the work from the bedroom. We were down to our last twenty grams and I planned to re-up tomorrow. After getting in the Monte Carlo, Kianna drove to Cotton's house.

"Hey, Nephew!" The addict smiled, showing pink and purple gums.

"What up, Unc? Tell me something good," I said as me and Kianna walked in the house.

"You know you got the best hand. I need five grams," he said, going into his pocket and pulling out three hundred fifty dollars.

I pulled out the work and a small digital scale to weigh up the heroin. "There you go, Unc. You need anything else?"

"Nah, that's all for now. You go——"

Boom!

A loud crash scared the shit out of me, making me jump. I turned towards the front door as it came crashing open. Four Chicago police officers rushed in with their guns drawn.

"Get on the fucking ground!" They yelled.

My life and freedom flashed before my eyes. I thought about running, but Chicago Police was notorious for shooting niggas in the back. Instead of being the next poster child for a protest about police brutality, I got on the floor.

"Oh yeah! Look at this!" a tall dark-skinned cop with a long scar on his cheek whistled. He was checking out the scale with five grams on it.

"What's going on, Cotton? You gotta operation going on that I don't know about?" another cop asked. He was short and light-skinned with green eyes.

"Aw, c'mon, Friendly," Cotton whined. "I was just trying to get in my groove."

They searched us roughly, setting my money and drugs on the table before slamming us onto the couch.

"You been doing more than grooving around here. Y'all got people talking. Who is your boy?" Officer Friendly asked, stopping to stand in front of me.

"That's my nephew. He good."

"What's yo' name?" he asked me, staring into my eyes like he was trying to judge my character.

"Carl."

"And who is this fine brown-skinned thing sitting next to you?" Officer Friendly asked, tapping Kianna's titty.

"Watch yo' hand," she mugged him.

He looked amused by her defiance. Then he reached back and backhanded her across the face before grabbing her by the jaws and squeezing. "You think yo' punk ass is tough? This is my city, bitch. You in my streets. The only reason you still breathing is because I'm allowing it. Don't you ever forget that!" he cursed before muffing her into the couch.

Seeing him manhandle my girl pissed me the fuck off, but there was nothing I could do. If I bucked, they would beat my ass and probably kill me.

"Now, back to you, Carl. The old man didn't tell you that this is my deck?"

"I didn't know," I said.

He turned to Cotton. "What's going on, Cotton? You didn't tell yo' nephew that he was stepping on my toes? Did you think you was gon' get over on me and my boys again? We already went through this with yo' other nephew, Big T."

"C'mon, Friendly. It was a mistake. It won't happen again," Cotton said, the disdain evident in his voice.

"I know it won't. And you know why it won't?" The cop asked, slipping on a pair of brass knuckles. "Because I'm about to hand out some lessons."

He punched the old man in the face, splitting his eye. But he didn't stop. He held Cotton by the collar and punched him five or six more times. The old man's face gushed blood and he was knocked unconscious, his head leaning to the side like it was about to fall off. The cop dropped the old man onto the floor, wiping the blood from his brass knuckles onto Cotton's shirt. Then he walked to stand in front of me.

"You from Chicago, Carl?"

I nodded. "Yeah."

"You must not be from the West side. Because if you was, you would know that you trespassing."

"I just got out, man. I didn't know this was yo' deck."

He looked surprised. "Oh, you been up state? Where?"

"I just did nineteen in Joliet."

His eyes grew wide and he looked to his boys. "We gotta real one here, boys," he said before turning back to me. "What you go up for? Caught a body?"

"Nah. Robbed a check cashing place."

"So, you did nineteen years up north and yo' dumb ass decided that since you got knocked for robbery, you would try selling dope in my neck of the woods?"

I didn't answer.

He pulled out his gun and pointed it in my chest. "When I ask you a question, I expect an answer."

"I didn't know this was yo' deck," I repeated.

He looked thoughtful. "I guess you didn't, considering you just came home. So, because I'm fair, I'ma give you the opportunity to walk away without you and yo' bitch getting fucked up. Either I'ma take you and yo' girl down and book y'all ass for this dog food, or you can take me to yo stash and give it to me. I want it all. How much is yo' freedom worth?"

I looked in his green eyes and seen his soul. This nigga was pure evil and not to be fucked with. I had fifteen thousand dollars in my stash and he wanted it all. And I didn't have no choice but to give it.

"I got fifteen G's at home."

His eyes lit up. "You a smart nigga, Carl. 'Cause I'ma be honest, I was looking forward to beating yo' ass, so help me God. But that money got you a pass. You gon' take a ride with me and my boys gon' stay here with yo' girl. Let's go."

151

I took the cop to my apartment and gave him the money. He drove me back to Cotton's house and left me with a final warning.

"Don't let me catch you back on my deck, Carl. Next time it'll be worse. Take yo' girlfriend and get the fuck outta here."

Chapter 14

The next couple of days was rough for me and Kianna. Not only did we lose all of our money and dope, but we were both violated. She got slapped around while her man sat there and didn't do shit. We both know that I wasn't supposed to try to fight Officer Friendly for hitting her and that I was supposed to give up the money, but accepting it was hard.

"I'ma kill him," I mumbled.

"What you say?"

"I'ma kill Officer Friendly. I put that on everythang I love."

"No, Carl. This is one that we gon' have to let go. He got a squad. And if you kill a police, you not gon' be able to stay in Chicago. The whole city gon' be hot. I know it's hard, baby, but you gotta let it go."

"I can't. I feel violated. He took everything. All we got is my work check. And he put his hands on you and it wasn't shit I could do. That's how the slave owners did our ancestors. They fucked yo' wife and got her pregnant and it wasn't nothing you could do about it because they would lynch yo' ass. They took them niggas' manhood. Officer Friendly violated me. I can't let it go."

Kianna sat up on her elbows and looked into my eyes. "Carl, don't do this. I'm down with you one hundred percent, but this is not a fight we can win. Its suicide. I know it's hard, but you have to let it go."

I stared into her eyes and seen a mix of emotions. Fear was the primary one.

"Do you believe in me?" I asked.

"You know I do. I never met a nigga like you. Which is why I want to keep you with me. Let it go."

"Do you trust me?"

"Yes, baby. You know I do."

"Will you ride for me?"

"I will. I told you I want to be great with you."

"I'm destined for greatness, baby. I can feel it in my soul. And I need you with me to reach that level. I need you to trust that I'ma take care of us. Do you believe that?"

She searched my eyes like she was looking for something to hold on to. Then she found it.

"Yes. I believe that, Carl."

"I won't let us down. I promise," I said before kissing her lips. "What do you know about Wisconsin?"

"Not that much. But my sister lives in Milwaukee. Why?"

"Because that's where we going."

She looked confused. "How? And why?"

"Because after I burn this city up, we gon' have to leave. Get dressed. We about to take a ride."

After we got dressed, I called Big T and told him I was coming over to talk. When Kianna pulled up to the TLP, he was waiting on the porch. I waved him over and he climbed in the back seat.

"Carl, what it do, family?"

"You got it, my nigga. How yo' uncle doing?"

"He making it. Officer Friendly's bitch ass fucked him up. I hate that bitch-ass fag."

"Do you know what station he at? I wanna file a complaint on yo' uncle's behalf."

He gave me a worried look. "I don't think you should put yo' name on nothing like that. Officer Friendly plugged in. If he find out you tryna get at him, he gon' come for you."

"I don't give a fuck 'bout that. Somebody gotta start a paper trail. That's the only way to get him out the way."

"A'ight. It's yo' life. He at 11th District, over on Harrison and Kedize. And his name ain't Officer Friendly. It's Sergeant Kenneth Sherman."

"Okay. Good looking. How shit going in the house? Frank good?"

Tyson laughed. "I ain't seen him or Janet. You a fool, dog. You came and turned this mu'fucka out." He laughed again.

Kianna grunted, mugging me and Tyson.

"A'ight, Tyson. We gotta get outta here."

"Okay, fam. Be safe," he said before getting out of the car.

"You had to ask about yo' old bitch, huh?" Kianna asked as she drove away.

"It wasn't like that. I was just seeing how the old man was doing. But fuck them. We got what we needed. I need you to do yo' thing and see what you can find out about this nigga on social media. Now let's get over to this check cashing place so we can work on getting some more money."

***

Three days later I was chilling in bed with Kianna when she got my attention.

"Baby, look," she said, showing me her phone screen. It was Officer Friendly's Facebook page.

"What am I supposed to be looking for?"

"Look at the truck. We can use it to find him. Go to the precinct and see if it's in the lot and follow him home like we did Jewels and the check cashing place manager."

"That's good shit, baby," I smiled. "But we can't be parked outside a police station waiting for this nigga. We might get spotted. We need a way to track this nigga without being seen."

Kianna thought for a moment. "Oh! I know," she said, her brown eyes lighting up. "One of my friends bought a little tracking device and put it in her man's car to keep track of him. You can buy one that looks like a little bug or something and put it on his truck."

I loved the way her mind worked. "Damn, you good. I'm glad you on my side. Get up. Let's get to it."

We left the house and drove to a spy shop. They had all kinds of shit in there to spy on people with. I bought a little tracking device that looked like a fly before heading to 11th district. It didn't take long to find the black Ford 150. It was parked in the parking lot on the side of the precinct. The problem was, I wasn't going to be able to plant the tracking device during the day.

So we went back home and waited until it was dark outside before heading back to the police station. When all the traffic around the precinct slowed down, I made my move. I was nervous as fuck as I walked through the lot. When I got to the truck, I acted like I dropped my keys and stuck the tracking device under the rear wheel well. After it was secure, I got the fuck outta there. Part one was done. I stayed up all night watching the tracking device's monitor. Around midnight the dot on the screen started moving. Thirty minutes later it stopped.

"Got'cho bitch ass." I laughed before setting the monitor down and going to sleep.

The next day I went to work and treated the day like a normal day. When I got off work, Kianna was waiting for me in the parking lot.

"Hey, baby," she greeted me with a kiss.

"What's good? Did you get the van?"

Excitement shown in her eyes. "I did."

"Let's get to it."

Kianna drove for about twenty minutes and then parked behind a silver Dodge minivan. Before getting out of the Monte Carlo, we changed into blue jumpsuits, work boots, and plain black ball caps. I made sure to cover my arms with a long sleeved shirt and put on a pair of gloves. No way I was making the same mistakes that landed me in prison. When we were dressed in our disguises, she drove to Waukegan, a suburb on the outskirts of the city. She parked in front of a gray and blue house and turned to me. Fear and uncertainty swirled in her eyes.

"You can do this, baby. It's easy. You got this," I said, giving her a pep talk.

She took a deep breath, trying to calm herself. "Okay. I got your back."

"That's what I'm talkin' about. Grab that clipboard and let's get this money!"

I grabbed the small plastic toolbox and led the way up the walkway. When we were upon the porch, I rang the doorbell.

"Who is it?" a woman called from inside.

"I'm Richard from Direct TV."

The door opened and a middle-aged white woman looked at us quizzically. "Hi, guys. What's going on?"

"We're here to fix the satellite connection," I said.

She frowned. "We don't have a problem with our satellite."

Kianna looked at the clipboard. "Are you Mrs. Wentworth?"

"Yes. That's me."

"Your husband called us and told us to come over. Should we at least take a look? If it's nothing, we will leave. I mean, since we're here, we might as well take a look, right?"

I watched the woman reason with herself. "Okay. Guess it can't hurt to look," she said before allowing us in.

I gave Kianna a wink as we stepped into the house.

"This is a nice house," Kianna commented.

"Oh, thank you. The television is right here," she said, pointing to a 60" screen on the wall.

I sat the toolbox down and pulled out the Glock. "A'ight, lady. I'ma need you to have a seat. How many people in the house?"

"What's going on? Who are you?" she asked, terror showing on her face.

"We work for DirectTV. Now sit yo' ass down," I said forcefully. "I don't wanna hurt you, but I need you to do what I say."

"What do you want?" she asked as she sat on the couch.

"We're not here for you. What time does your husband get home?"

"At eight o'clock. What do you want with my husband?"

"We just want to talk. Tie her up, baby."

Kianna grabbed zip ties from the toolbox and a sleep mask. After tying the woman's hands and feet, she put the mask over her eyes. Then we waited for her husband to come home. He showed up a little after eight and found us waiting in the living room.

"What the fuck is going on? Who are you?" he demanded.

I pointed the gun at his wife. "Have a seat, Mike, or I'ma kill her."

His face flushed as he sat down next to his wife. "What do you want?"

I threw him a sleep mask. "For you to put this on."

He didn't want to cover his eyes, so I lifted the gun to his wife's head for motivation. After mugging me, he begrudgingly covered his eyes.

I looked to Kianna. "Tie him up."

While she put the zip ties around his ankles and wrist, I explained what we wanted.

"Tomorrow morning, you gon' take me to yo' job and give me the money. I don't wanna hurt you or yo' wife, but I will kill both of y'all if you make me. We just want the money."

I sat with the husband and wife until ten o'clock. The plan was for me to leave to kill Officer Friendly and come back. I knew it was a risky move, but I had to take the shot. After kissing Kianna, I hopped in the van and drove to the 11th precinct. I parked a block away and waited in the van for the truck to leave. Ended up waiting for an hour and a half. Since I had him on the tracking device, I didn't have to follow close. Thirty minutes later the truck stopped. When I turned onto the block, Officer Friendly was getting out of the truck. I rolled down the passenger window as I pulled alongside him.

"Hey, Ken!"

He turned to look in the van and right down the barrel of the Glock.

Pop, pop, pop, pop, pop!

When Officer Friendly fell to the ground, I threw the van in park and hopped out. I ran up on him and shot him three more times in the face before grabbing the tracking device from his truck and hopping in the van. I continuously checked the mirrors as I drove away. My adrenaline rushed and it felt like my heart was beating in my ears. Killing the cop gave me feelings similar to when I killed Jewels. I felt relieved and avenged.

When I got back to the check cashing manager's house, everything was still good.

"How did it go?" Kianna asked.

The smile on my face and in my eyes answered for me. "I got his ass."

She let out a relieved breath. "Whew."

"It'll all be over in the morning."

When the morning came, I untied the husband and gave him a final warning.

"I'm only gon' tell you this one time. I'm keeping my partner at the house with yo' wife. If I don't call in exactly thirty minutes, she is going to kill your wife and I am going to kill you. Don't try to be a hero, Mike. It ain't worth it."

"Let's just get this over with so you can get the hell out of my life," he said angrily.

We jumped in his car and drove to the check cashing place. He let me inside and emptied the safe. I walked out with twenty-seven thousand dollars cash money. When I was safe in Mike's car, I sent Kianna a text.

I got it. Meet me at the spot.

I drove to the Monte Carlo to wait. Kianna pulled up in the van ten minutes later. I grabbed the baby wipes and we wiped down the minivan before hopping in the Monte Carlo.

"Oh my God! I can't believe we did it, baby!" Kianna yelled, grabbing my face and kissing me.

"I told you it would be easy. I told you we can do it."

"I just feel so geeked up that I don't know what to do with myself!" She laughed.

"For now, let's go home and get our shit and get the fuck outta this city. It's about to get hot around here."

"Okay. I'm ready to go," she said, calming a little. "Wait. Before we leave, can we just do one more thing?"

"What you got in mind?"

Her eyes burned a golden-brown fire. "I wanna get revenge."

***

We stayed in the house and slept until the sun went down. Around nine o'clock, we packed our bags in the trunk of the Monte Carlo and drove to the South side. Kianna parked on Wabash Street and cut the engine. I waited to see what she would do.

"You sure you want to do this?" I asked when she didn't move.

She looked at me with tears in her eyes. "I can't let him get away with doing that to me."

"Whatever you wanna do, I'm with you, baby."

She took a couple of deep breaths. "Okay. I'm ready. Give it to me."

I handed her the Glock. She stared at it for a moment before tucking it in her waist and getting out of the car. I followed her onto the porch of a black and white house and she rang the doorbell.

"Who is it?" a man called from inside.

"It's Kianna."

Locks clicked and the door swung open. A dark-skinned older nigga stood in the doorway. He was short, fat, and bald. He also didn't have any facial hair or eyebrows. Looked like a poster man for the definition of a rapist.

"Hey, Kianna. What you doing over here?" he asked, surprised to see her.

"I need to talk to you. Can I come in?"

He glanced at me before stepping aside. "Yeah. Come in. Who is he?"

"My boyfriend. Where is Michelle?"

"She's at work. What did you wanna holla at me about?" he asked, locking the door.

"I need some closure."

He stared at her for a moment. I could see the realization of the moment dawn in his eyes. He knew why she had come.

"Closure? Closure from what?" he asked, beads of sweat popping onto his forehead.

Kianna pulled the gun but kept it at her side. When she spoke, tears began rolling down her face. "How could you do that to me? I trusted you."

"Put the gun down, Kianna. Let's talk about this," he said, lifting his hand up, palms out.

Kianna lifted the gun to his face. "Talk. Tell me why you took advantage of me. Tell me why you raped me."

"C'mon, Kianna. Don't do this. You wanted it just like I did. You said it was okay."

After hearing his explanation, I wanted to shoot his bitch ass.

"What!" Kianna screamed. "How the fuck could you say that? I didn't want to be raped. I was ten years old."

"C'mon, Kianna. Please, put the gun down," he begged on the verge of tears.

"First tell me why you did it. Tell me the truth."

I could see him weighing the options in his head.

"Because you was a pretty little girl. I couldn't help myself from wanting you. I think something is wrong with me. I'm sorry. I——"

Pop!

I flinched when she pulled the trigger.

The pedophile fell to the ground and started shaking as blood began spilling from his right eye. I looked to Kianna. She was still holding the gun up, tears spilling down her face.

"You okay?"

"No," she mumbled before falling to the ground.

"Shit! Kianna!" I called, rushing to her side. Her eyes were closed. "Kianna!" I yelled again. She didn't answer, so I slapped her. "Kianna!"

Her eyes opened slowly like she was waking up from sleep.

"C'mon, baby. We gotta go. Get up."

"What happened?" She asked groggily, struggling to stand.

"I don't know. You fainted. But we can't stay here. C'mon."

I helped her to the car and put her in the passenger seat before running around to the driver's side.

"Is he dead?" Kianna whispered.

"Yeah. He gone," I said, driving away.

"It didn't make me feel better. It feels like I did something bad," she whined.

"You didn't do nothing wrong. Sometimes the first body is hard. But you didn't do nothing wrong. That nasty muthafucka deserved to die."

J-Blunt

Chapter 15

I pulled into Madison, Wisconsin at three o'clock in the morning. Instead of waking my little brother, I followed the highway signs to a Comfort Inn hotel on East Washington Street and rented a room for the night. I knew the murder was fucking with Kianna, so I held her while she slept. She jerked around a little in her sleep. I tried to watch over her, but I was tired as fuck and sleep eventually took me under. I don't know how long I was out, but when I opened my eyes, Kianna was sitting in bed Indian-style watching me. That shit was creepy as fuck.

"What you doing?" I asked.

"Watching you sleep. I always do this."

"Well, I'ma need you to stop that shit. What time is it?"

She grabbed the phone. "Almost nine o'clock."

We both began staring at each other.

"How did you sleep?" I asked.

"I dreamed about him. Is that normal?"

"Yeah. I dreamed about the first nigga I killed too."

"Who was he? What happened?"

"I didn't know the nigga. We was robbin' they house and he ran. I shot him in the back."

"How many people have you killed?"

I didn't want to tell her the number. "A few. Gimme the phone so I can call my brother. Let's see what kinda connections he got."

"What up, brah?" Chris answered, sounding wide awake.

"What up, Chris? You woke?"

"Hell, yeah. The grind don't stop. Early bird gets the first worm."

Jewels's words popped into my head. "The second mouse gets the cheese," I said.

"What?" Chris asked.

"Nothing. I need to holla at you. I'm in Madison. At the Comfort Inn."

Chris sounded surprised. "You in Madison? On what?"

"I'm for real. I came last night. I'm in room four. Come holla at me."

"Say less, my nigga. I'm on the way."

Fifteen minutes later, there was a knock on the door. When I opened it, Chris was standing in the hallway with a tall brown-skinned nigga with a dying front tooth.

"Carl, what's good, nigga!" Chris said, wrapping me in a hug and jumping up and down.

"Chill, li'l nigga. Damn," I laughed, pushing him off me and locking the door.

He stepped in the room and looked at me like he couldn't believe I was standing in front of him. "Damn, brah. I can't believe you here. Why you ain't tell me you was coming, nigga?"

"Because it was short notice. I had to move quick and this was the closest spot."

He looked concerned. "What happened? You good?"

"Yeah," I said, looking to his guy. "Who is he?"

"Oh, this my nigga Donovan. He one of the guys. Donovan, this big brah."

I shook his hand. "What's good, fam?"

"Same shit, different asshole, my nigga," he said.

"Who is she?" Chris asked, nodding at Kianna.

"That's my girl, Kianna."

"'Sup, shorty?" Chris nodded, licking his lips like a ladies' man.

"Hey, Chris," Kianna smiled. "Yo' brother told me a lot about you."

"He sho' didn't tell me nothing about you. Where yo' sisters at?"

"Leave my girl alone, nigga," I cut in.

"C'mon, brah. She bad. I want one too," Chris said.

"I don't got no sisters," Kianna said. "I got some cousins back in the city. Next time we in the Chi, I can hook you up."

Chris mugged me and went over to give Kianna some daps. "That's what I'm talkin' 'bout, Kianna. Yeah, I like you."

I blew off their little moment. "Check it out, brah. I need to know what the city like. You said it's sweet and we can get money. I'm ready to eat."

Chris nodded, dollar signs showing in his eyes. "That's what I'm talking about, nigga. Yeah! Check it out. We fuck with that girl. Got some white heads that keep niggas runnin' up a check. The Town is open. You get money anywhere you want. Find some heads, get 'em on line and run it up. It's that easy," he explained.

"So, what you working with? Can I shop with you?"

"Nah, I ain't holdin' like that. But I got a plug."

"I thought you was having yo' way, Chris? What you coppin'?"

He looked bashful. "C'mon, brah. You can't be all in a nigga pocket like that. But I'm good. I got some money."

Chris's reaction told me what I suspected. "What you buyin'? Like an ounce or two?"

He wiggled a little bit. "Yeah. Something like that."

"Okay. I mean, you gotta start somewhere," I said, not wanting to belittle him. "But I'm talking big shit. At least a half a book. Maybe the whole thang if it's a good number."

Chris looked at me skeptically. "You want a whole book? Thirty-six zips?"

"Yeah, if the price is right."

He stared at me again, trying to see if I was serious. "What happened back home?"

I met and held his stare. "Don't worry about that. Just know that I'm here to stay and I'm not fucking around. I'm ready to eat. You wanna plate, or you wanna keep eating Happy Meals?"

He laughed and sat on the bed. "What's the play, brah? What kinda moves you tryna make?"

I sat next to him. "I'm not tryna play around, Chris. I'm ready to get to it. I'm destined for greatness, and this is where I'm finna put it down at. We all got the potential to be great, but a lotta niggas don't understand that or recognize they own potential. We gods, li'l brah. The first muthafuckas that walked this earth was black. Once you start thinking like that, you won't be satisfied until you become great."

My little brother and Donovan looked at me like I just quoted the Bible from cover to cover.

"Damn, fam. That was real shit," Donovan nodded.

"I see y'all potential and I wanna maximize that. I need to know if y'all tryna fuck with me on that level. I'ma buy the shit and we can work y'all lines and make 'em grow. No more Fords and Monte Carlos. I got Maybach dreams. What y'all wanna be doin'?"

Chris grabbed my hand and shook it vigorously. "We ready to eat, nigga! Eat, eat, eat!"

After making a few calls, Chris's plug agreed to meet. I took ten thousand just to test the water. I wanted to start up a business relationship and see what the nigga was about before I bought heavy. His name was Miko, a nigga from Minneapolis that discovered how good the set-up was in Wisconsin and never returned home. He met us in a McDonald's parking lot.

"Don! Cartier! What's good, my niggas?" Miko greeted, hopping in the back seat of Chris's Ford escape.

"You got, it my nigga. This my brother, Carl, I was telling you about," Chris introduced.

"What's good, family?" Miko nodded.

"You got it. Li'l brah say you the man. I'm tryna cop like a 9 piece. What that number look like?"

"Hard or soft?" he asked.

"Soft."

"It ain't cheap, my nigga. I need ten stickers. It's scale though. One thing I don't do is step on my shit. I give it to niggas how I get it. Drop."

I looked to my little brother to see if Miko was keeping it real.

"Valid," Chris nodded.

"Yeah, let me get it."

"A'ight. I'ma go grab it and meet you back here in thirty minutes. From now on, you can just send me a text with a number for how many zips you want so we won't have to go back and forth like this. Don't put nothing else in the text but the number."

"A'ight. Say no more."

Thirty minutes later we exchanged money for product and went our separate ways. Chris took us to his house so me and Kianna could meet Megan. After the pleasantries, he called me to the kitchen.

"Gimme that work so I can put my whip on it," he said.

"Brah, you bet' not fuck up my shit," I warned.

He looked at me like I said something disrespectful. "After you see me in action, don't ever say no shit to me like that again. Gimme the work."

I watched as he put on a pair of dishwashing gloves and poured the cocaine in a metal spaghetti strainer. He used his hand to move the dope around. It broke down and poured from the holes into a cake pan. After flattening it, he ground up kelp, the fish food, and poured it on top of the dope and began mixing. When done, he poured two cups of 151 vodka into the mix and stirred it into a paste. After that, he spooned the dope into a pair of pantyhose and began squeezing it to pull out the excess liquor and mold the dope into a brick. When done, he took the brick and sat it on the table then looked at me.

"I learned that from my Columbian triple beam niggas. Turned yo' nine into twelve and it's still flake. Thank me later."

***

A month later, I felt like a genius.

The decision to come to Wisconsin and hustle with my little brother was one of the best decisions I had made in a long time. Chris and Donovan's lines were doing numbers. I fronted them ounces for fourteen hundred a pop and they moved them like bottled water during a heatwave. I was able to get me and Kianna a house, furnish it, and upgrade the ride to a 2003 Lexus. Things was going good for me. I had a bad bitch by my side and I was getting money. Life was good. The only way things could get better was if I found a better plug and was able to get dope cheaper and make more money. The prices in Madison were expensive. But since I was making a profit, I really didn't give finding a new plug much thought.

"Why you smiling like that?" Kianna asked, walking in the bedroom wearing a red silk nightgown.

"I was just thinking about how good the decision to leave Chicago turned out to be. I was taking stock of everything we been through and it seem like this is where we about to make our mark. This is where we become great."

Kianna crawled in bed and straddled my lap. "I like when you talk like that. Tell me some more."

"I want to take us to the top, baby. Mansions, Benzes, jewelry, trips to islands. Get you yo' own walk-in closet to fill with Gucci, Prada, and Louis Vuitton. I want us to look back on this moment five years from now and smile at how we came from nothing to the top of the world."

Kianna stared in my eyes as I spoke, swallowing the words as they left my mouth. She believed in me like the twelve disciples believed in Jesus.

"I love you, Carl."

I couldn't believe she said it. I didn't know how to react. This was exactly what I didn't want. She seen the struggle in my eyes.

"It's okay, Carl. You don't have to say it back. I just wanted you to know how I felt. I believe that you love me in your own way and you can tell me when you're ready. Okay?"

I stared at her for a moment to see if there was some kind of catch, but she looked normal.

"Okay," I mumbled.

"Why are you looking like that?" She laughed.

"Like what?"

"Like I'm about to torture you. Does talking about love make you that uncomfortable?"

"I don't know. I guess. I never been in love before so I'm not sure what it's supposed to feel like."

She leaned forward to kiss me. "It feels like getting jealous when you see me with another man."

I thought about BJ and laughed. "Can I tell you what I really love?"

Her eyes grew bright. "Tell me, baby."

I rubbed my hands up her smooth chocolate thighs. "I love when you wrap these legs around me when I'm fucking you."

168

She laughed and bit her bottom lip. "What else?"

"I love the way you scream my name when you about to cum."

She started grinding on my lap. "Tell me some more."

"I love watching you suck my dick."

She leaned down and started kissing my chest. From my chest to my stomach. From my stomach to my waist, pulling my dick through the hole in my boxers. "Do you wanna see how I look sucking it?"

"Yeah, baby. Suck my dick. Suck it."

We maintained eye contact as she slowly sucked my dick into her mouth. I watched without blinking as she gave me head in slow motion, looking me in the eyes the entire time. Then my phone rang. I didn't want to answer it, but now that I was hustling, every call meant money. I grabbed the phone and checked the screen. It was my PO.

"Damn," I cursed.

Kianna stopped sucking. "What is it?"

"It's my PO," I grumbled before answering the phone. "What's up, Daniel?"

"Carl, what's going on, man? How are you?"

"Everything is good? What's up with you?"

"I need to see you. I'm going on vacation for a few weeks and I want to see all my high risk guys a little early. What time can you get to my office?"

"You mean today?" I asked, sitting up in bed.

"Yeah. Is that a problem? You're no longer working, right?"

"Uh, nah. It's not a problem. I'm just in Peoria right now and it would take me a minute to get to you."

"Okay. I'll tell you what. How about you come see me first thing in the morning. Say, eight o'clock. How does that sound?"

It sounded terrible, but I couldn't tell him that. "It sounds like I'ma be in yo' office in the morning."

"You have to see your PO tomorrow?" Kianna asked after I hung up the phone.

"Yeah. At eight o'clock in the morning."

"I thought he only wanted to see you every three months?"

"He going out of town and wanna see me early. This is fucked up. I don't even wanna step foot in that city again."

Kianna watched me for a moment. "So what do you want to do?"

"Ain't shit I can do. I gotta see my PO in the morning."

Chapter 16

By the summer of 2013, I was having my way. The city of Madison was my bitch and I was fucking her good. Me and my niggas was moving two kilos a month and the money was rolling in. I had eighty thousand dollars cash in my stash and bought another car, this one an old school. The wet paint on my sky blue 1977 Chevelle on 26's made the bitches stop and stare and niggas jealous on sight. And I wasn't faking it like most niggas that buy a piece of shit and paint it and put rims on it. The whole car was restored. The engine alone was worth twenty G's. I drove through the city in the donk with Kianna in the passenger seat looking like a bag of money. The more money we got, the better she looked. Manicures and pedicures was a must. Her hair stayed whipped. And any time we went to the mall, she knew to just throw it in the bag.

I pulled the Chevelle into the parking lot of Silky's, a brand new strip club that was opening tonight. Chris was following me in his Jaguar with his girl Megan. Donovan brought up the rear in a Porsche. We pulled up shining like we were stars. People in the parking lot or in line outside Silky's rubbernecked to see who was getting out of the expensive rides. I opened the suicide door and stepped out rocking a blue Rockstar 'fit with Giuseppe shoes. Kianna climbed out of the passenger side matching me in a blue Giuseppe dress and Giuseppe heels. After being joined by my niggas, we by-passed the long line and mobbed to the door.

"Y'all gotta wait in line," one of the buff-ass security guards said.

I went in my locket and pulled out a bankroll. "We don't do lines, my nigga. Say a number."

He laughed. "C'mon, man. Just fall back."

"You said three hundred. Here you go," I said, peeling off three hundred dollar bills and holding them out.

The big man looked stuck. I could tell he wanted to take the money, but he was wrestling with his integrity.

"Oh, that ain't enough. Here go two more," I said, holding out five hundred dollars.

The big man smiled. "C'mon in, brah."

I led my family into the club like I belonged in it. The lights were dim and several small sparkling disco balls bounced rainbow colors all over the club. There were small tables spread throughout the place along with little poles on platforms. Strippers of all races with nice bodies danced on the platforms or walked around in thongs and bras.

"I like this spot, baby," Kianna said, looking around as we took a table.

"Bring some of that ass over here!" Donovan sang, dancing in his seat and snapping his fingers.

"Good evening, guys! Would you like to order drinks?"

I looked to my right and locked eyes with a fine-ass white chick with blue hair. She wore a snug halter top, tight pussy-cutting shorts, and heels.

"Yeah, we want drinks. What y'all got?"

"Fuck a drink," Donovan cut in. "I want a lap dance!"

She smiled, curling her hair around her finger. "I'm not one of the dancers. I'm a bottle girl. I don't do lap dances."

"Aw, that's some bullshit," Donovan sulked.

"What about those drinks?" I asked.

"We have bottom shelf and top shelf. Champagne, vodka, cognac. All the top brands."

I looked around to see if anybody at my table knew what she was talking about. They all looked like they were waiting for me.

"Surprise me, baby girl. Bring me what you think we should drink. And I ain't one of them cheap niggas either."

A few moments later, I noticed sparklers going off and seen the white bottle girl and a friend walking to our table carrying five bottles of Ace of Spades with sparklers.

"When you buy bottles of Ace of Spades, we put on a show for you." She smiled.

The tab was $2,500 and I threw it like it was nothing. I also bought a brick, one thousand singles, so me and my people could have some spending money. For the next couple of hours we drank and partied like bosses. It was the first time I had fun spending money. When "Make It Rain" by li'l Wayne and Fat Joe came on, I grabbed handfuls of money and started throwing it in the air. The strippers flocked to us like pigeons around birdseed and I felt like I was on top of the world.

"Shout out to my people over there making it rain! I see y'all! Got the sparkly bottles going! Do it big then!" the DJ called.

I lifted a bottle of Ace of Spades to the DJ and nodded. When I seen the bottle girl, I had her take him a liter of Hennessey.

"Shot out to my nigga over there doing his thang! Good looking on the bottle. One of y'all come over here and tell me who y'all is."

Me and Kianna shared a look.

"Let's go, baby!" I said, grabbing her arm.

We walked and stumbled over to the DJ booth.

"Thanks for the bottle, my nigga," the DJ said, shaking my hand. "I'm Ren. What they call you?"

"I'm Carl and this my baby, Kianna."

"I like the way y'all kickin' it. Like real players. What's up with yo' squad? Y'all gotta name?"

I thought for a moment and said the first thing that came to mind. "Yeah. We the Triple Beam Team! We doing big things in Mad Town!"

"Shot out to Triple Beam Team!" The DJ laughed.

After kicking it with the DJ, we went back to our section.

"I like that name, baby." Kianna said.

Happy to have her approval, I turned to Donovan and Chris. "Ay, check it out. Lemme holla at you niggas real quick on some serious shit. From now on, we finna be known as the Triple Beam Team. We a team and we gettin' money. Loyalty over royalty."

Chris nodded. "You know I love that shit since it was really my idea."

"It's a Triple Beam Team take over!" Donovan yelled.

We continued to party hard and when Kianna was good and drunk, she started to get freaky. A fine-ass light-skinned dancer named Larena was dancing in front of us when Kianna started getting touchy feely.

"Give my girl a lap dance," I said, wanting to see how Kianna would react.

Larena turned and straddled Kianna's lap and started gyrating. Kianna grabbed handfuls of the stripper's ass and squeezed. Then both of their hands got very touchy feely. They were looking into each other's eyes like they wanted to fuck. All they needed was some encouraging.

"Kiss her, baby," I said.

Kianna looked unsure, but Larena dove right in. The kiss looked a little awkward at first. Then slowly, Kianna started getting into it. A few moments later, they looked like they were fucking. My dick was hard as fuck watching them.

"Get it, girl!" Megan yelled and whistled.

Kianna snapped out of her zone and looked at me. It was like she forgot where she was and when she realized she made out with another female, she looked embarrassed.

"It's okay, baby," I said, reassuring her.

Kianna looked into my eyes for reassurance so I leaned forward and kissed her. Then I kissed Larena. Then we all shared a three-way kiss. That's when I knew I was about to have my first three-some with Kianna.

"She coming home with us tonight," I told Kianna. Then I turned to Larena. "You leaving when we leave."

"Okay," she agreed.

We all left the club at two in the morning. Me, Kianna, and Larena hopped in the Chevelle. I drove while they freaked in the back seat. I watched through the rearview mirror as they kissed and groped one another. Then Larena's head disappeared and I could no longer see her. But I could see Kianna's face.

"Oh, shit! Oh shit! Damn, girl!" Kianna moaned, looking like she was experiencing pure bliss.

Watching my girl's fuck faces in the rearview mirror and hearing her moans turned me the fuck on! I wanted to park the car and hop in the backseat with them, but we was almost to the crib.

"Oh, baby! Carl! Carl!" Kianna called, reaching in the front seat and grabbing my shirt. "Carl, she finna make me cum, baby! Ahhh shhhiiittt!"

When we got to the crib, I ran to unlock the door and let us in. After locking the door we started stripping out our clothes. I had just snatched off my pants when Kianna knelt in front of me and started giving me head. Larena knelt next to her and they both took turns sucking my dick. Shit felt too good. Then while Kianna was sucking me, Larena went underneath me and started sucking and humming on my balls. That shit was too much and I busted my nut.

Next I was on my back with Larena riding my face and Kianna riding my dick. A few minutes later we switched positions again and Larena was sitting on the couch, her legs spread with me digging in her guts while Kianna was standing over her getting her pussy ate. The threesome was cracking so hard that I said fuck it and leaned forward and started licking Kianna's ass. She went crazy. That night was one of the best nights I had in my whole life.

I woke up the next morning to the sound of my phone ringing. I was tired and hung over so I ended the call and rolled back over. My phone started ringing again. Shit was irritating as fuck. I snatched it up and seen that it was Donovan.

"What, man?" I answered.

"I just got robbed!"

That shit woke me up instantly. "What?"

"Some niggas just robbed me. Ran in my house and put bangers in my face and took my shit?"

I sat up. "What they take?"

"Couple zips and some money. Damn, I can't believe them bitch-ass niggas did that shit."

"Okay, my nigga. Say no more. Call Chris and let him know what's up and to meet me at yo' crib."

I hopped out of bed a little upset that I had to leave the warmth of Kianna and Larena's bodies, but my nigga got robbed and I had to take care of that. After throwing on some clothes, I hopped in the Lexus, wishing I had a pistol. I threw the Glock that I used to kill Officer Friendly in the river when I got to Madison and now I was kicking myself in the ass.

When I got to Donovan's house, he was standing on the porch.

"How them niggas get in?" I asked.

"They had some li'l bitch knock on the door. When I opened it, them niggas ran in."

"Did you see who it was?"

"Yeah. It was Draymon n'em. They didn't wear no masks."

"You talkin bout Draymon off Allied?" I asked, surprised that niggas we knew would get down like that.

"Yeah. Him and Vince's bitch ass."

I paused for a moment trying to think of a reason they would rob my nigga and not wear a mask. "That shit sounds crazy. Why the fuck would they rob you without a mask? They don't think we gon' hit 'em back or somethin'?"

"That's exactly what them niggas think. They got down on Guapo n'em right before you came to the town and them niggas didn't do shit. Draymon and Vince think it's sweet."

Hearing they thought we were a lick pissed me off. "We gon have to show 'em it ain't."

When Chris pulled up, we explained the situation to him. He said the same thing, Vince n'em thought it was sweet.

"A'ight. We gon' fuck them niggas up. Y'all got some fire, right?"

"Nah. I never needed one," Donovan said.

I looked to Chris. "You got somethin', right?"

He shook his head. "I know er'body. I didn't think they would do no shit like this."

"You been gettin' money all this time and you never got a banger?" I asked.

Both of them wore stupid faces.

"Listen, my nigga. Y'all gettin' money and that shit gon' breed all kind of jealousy and envy. Niggas hate to see niggas shining. Getting money make you have enemies. More money, more problems. You always need a thumper when you gettin' to it."

They shrugged.

Seeing the stupid-ass looks on their faces pissed me off. "Do y'all at least know where we can get some burners from?"

"Yeah," Chris spoke up. "Nigga named Trav be having them shits."

"A'ight. Call that nigga and tell him we need to holla."

Chris pulled out his phone and made some calls. He was able to track down Trav at a car shop. We piled in the Lexus and drove over. When I pulled into the lot, a dark-skinned nigga with a bald head walked over. He was tall and skinny, eyes sunken in like a skeleton.

"Trav, what's good, fooly?" Chris said as we climbed from the Lex.

"What's up, Cartier?" he asked, his voice deep and booming.

"We need some tools. Bitch-ass niggas just hit up my nigga this morning," Chris said, nodding to Donovan.

Trav looked all of us over, stopping to stare a Donovan before coming back to me. He had them crazy nigga eyes. Pupils so dark that they looked black. They were the eyes of a killer. No doubt about it. "I know Don. Who is he?"

"This my brother, Carl."

I nodded. "What's good?"

He sucked the back of his teeth. "You got it, chief. Y'all know who did it?"

"Yeah. Vince n'em hoe asses," Donovan spat.

Trav laughed. "They still testing niggas, huh?"

"They fucked with the wrong ones this time," I said.

Trav looked at me and smiled. "What you tryna get?"

"Whatever you got. But I need it ASAP."

He nodded. "I get off work at five. I'ma get wit' my people and call y'all later."

We got the call from Trav around eight o'clock. He showed up to Chris's house carrying a duffle bag.

"'Sup, fellas?" He nodded, laying the bag on the table. "These all I could come up with on short notice."

"We don't got shit, so whatever in that bag, I want," I said.

Trav showed us the hardware. "I got a AR-15 with a thirty shot clip. A .44 Bulldog. A ten shot 380 Smith and Wesson. Glock 21 with a twenty-one shot clip. All of 'em come loaded. The serial numbers already removed and they clean."

Chris and Donovan picked up pistols and fingered them. I picked up the AR and fell in love with that bitch instantly.

"We want all of 'em," I said.

"I need twenty five hunnit," Trav said.

I paid him quickly.

"Happy hunting!" Trav smiled before leaving.

***

Vince and Draymon weren't hard to find. Them niggas carried on like they didn't have a care in the world. Me and Chris tracked them for two days, learning their habits, where they lived, and where they kicked it. I decided to hit them where they lived, just like they did Donovan. We waited until the sun went down to get to work. We split into teams. Me and Kianna would hit Draymon. Chris and Donovan would get Vince. I stole a car and parked down the street from Draymon's house. We ended up waiting for almost three hours.

"That's his car, baby," I said, watching the red Camaro pull up.

Kianna grabbed the 380. "I'm ready."

I grabbed the AR-15 and we hopped out of the car. I kept the chopper at my side as I speed walked. Kianna was right behind me. Two niggas got out of the car and walked up on the porch. When I was two houses away, I got their attention.

"Ay, Draymon?"

The niggas paused to see who I was. I lifted the AR and let it ride.

Pop, pop, pop, pop, pop, pop!

Kianna joined me a second later with the 380.

Clap, clap, clap, clap, clap!

Draymon's friend was closest to us and caught most of the bullets. He fell on the porch. Draymon collapsed against the door and fell into the house. I ran towards the house, knowing I had to end that nigga. I couldn't let him live. When I got to the porch, I seen the door was partially open. I ran up the stairs, ready to run in the house. Draymon was trying to drag himself away from the door, but he had a pistol in one hand, pointing it outside. As soon as I stepped on the porch, he started shooting.

Boom, boom, boom, boom!

"Shit!" I cursed, ducking out of the way just in time and tripping over his nigga's body. I could hear the bullets whizzing past me as I fell. I knew I wasn't going to be able to get through that front door, and we had to get the fuck out of there before people started coming outside.

I looked back to see where Kianna was. She didn't walk up the stairs, but climbed the porch from the side and looked through the window. Then she lifted the 380 and started shooting.

Clap, clap, clap, clap, clap!

"I got him, baby!"

I almost didn't believe her. "On what? For real?"

"Look," she pointed.

I crept to the front door and peeked into the house. Draymon lay on the floor, blood leaking from his body. I wanted to kiss her.

"Let's go, baby!" I said, taking off running to the getaway car.

J-Blunt

Chapter 17

"Killing is easy," Kianna mumbled. She was lying on my chest, drawing circles in the palm of my hand with her finger.

"I told you it gets easier. And I'm proud of you, baby. You did yo' thang and came through for me. I didn't know how I was gon' get that nigga. And he damn near got my ass," I said, blowing out a cloud of weed smoke and reliving last night's killing in my head.

"I wasn't even scared. I mean, I was a little, but not like it was with my uncle. Last night, I wanted to get Draymon. Especially when I seen you almost get shot. When I looked through the window and seen him, the only thing I thought was 'I got his ass'." Then her face twisted and eyes grew wide. "What am I saying? I can't believe I said I wanted to kill somebody!"

"I think you just saying how you really feel," I said, passing her the blunt. "When you do certain shit, especially something you didn't think you could do, it empowers you. It gives you confidence and you feel bolder. You speaking how you really feel. You wanted to kill that nigga."

She was silent for a moment.

"Is that what this is?"

"That's how it was for me."

"Does this mean we crazy?"

I seen the questions glowing in her eyes.

"No. It means that we reached a level that not too many people can reach. We are gods, baby. We have power. We can take like and make life. When you realize what you are capable of, you are closer to being a god."

"I think this some good-ass weed!" She laughed and took a hit from the blunt.

Ringing from my phone pulled me from our moment. I grabbed the phone from the table and checked the screen. It was Miko.

"What's good, my dude?"

"It's all bad, Carl." He sighed.

Hearing the stress in his voice made me sit up. "What up, my nigga? Something happened?"

"Who is it, baby?" Kianna asked, reading the stress on my face. I lifted a finger, signaling to hold on.

"My cousin got killed last night. Shit fucked me up a li'l bit."

Coldness entered my bones. What were the chances that he was kin to them niggas?

"Who is yo' cousin? Where it happen at?"

"Happened in Madison. Vince is - or was - my cousin. Damn, that shit so fucked up."

I looked at Kianna, devastation washing over me. "His cousin Vince died last night," I told her.

Her eyes bucked.

"Damn, my nigga. That shit fucked up. Who they say did it?" I asked.

"Lotta names floating around. That's why I called you. Yo' man Donovan's name came up. They saying Vince robbed him a couple days ago."

I thought fast. One thing I couldn't do was deny the robbery. "Yeah, Donovan told me about that. But that wasn't us. He took some light shit and we charged that to the game."

"Okay, I hear you. Man, I don't know what to believe. That nigga did so much bullshit that it ain't no telling who did it. I just wanted to holla at you and see if you heard something."

"Nah, I ain't heard nothing. Shit, I didn't even know he was dead until just now."

"I gotta give it to you, Carl. You a good liar, my nigga."

I looked at Kianna again, my eyes growing wide.

"What happened?" she asked, barely able to contain herself.

I focused on the call. "What you talkin' 'bout, Miko. That wasn't me."

"Brah, yo' niggas posted a video on Facebook a couple hours ago holding pistols and bragging. I just wanted to see what you was gon' say. And I also wanna tell you this. I ain't with that gunplay shit. I get money. But my cousins coming from Minneapolis and they 'bout that drama. If I was you, I would leave Madison because they coming to fuck it up."

After he hung up, I dropped the phone and pinched the bridge of my nose.

"What happened, Carl?" Kianna asked.

"That was Miko. Vince is his mu'fuckin' cousin and he know we had something to do with him getting killed. They got some more cousins coming from Minneapolis to get at us."

Kianna's eyes grew wide. "How the fuck he find out that fast?"

"Chris and Donovan bragging about the shit on Facebook. Get dressed. I'm finna go whoop them niggas' asses."

After we were dressed, I called Chris.

"What up, brah?"

I checked my anger. "Where you at?"

"At the crib. What up?"

"Donovan with you?"

"Yeah, he right here."

"Stay there. I'm on my way."

By the time I got to Chris's house, I was even madder than I was when I talked to him on the phone. Not only did these stupid-ass niggas bring us beef, but they also fucked up my money.

When Megan answered the door, I pushed past her and into the house. Donovan and Chris were sitting on the couch. I walked right up to Donovan and started busting him in his shit.

"Chill, brah!" Donovan yelled, trying to get away.

"Carl, what you doing?" Chris yelled, grabbing me.

I turned my anger on him and started whooping his ass too. Chris folded onto the couch, covering his face and head. I started banging his ribs.

"Man, what the fuck!" I heard Donovan scream.

I turned my head just in time to see Kianna point the 380 at him.

"You bet not touch him or I'ma buss yo' ass!"

I stood up and started snapping. "What the fuck is wrong with you niggas positing videos on Facebook talking about killing niggas? How fuckin stupid is you dumb muthafuckas?"

"We didn't say who we killed," Chris whined.

I wanted to beat his ass again. "You li'l stupid-ass nigga, Madison don't got no high-ass murder rate. Two muthafuckas died last night. Do you think the rest of the people in the world as stupid as you niggas? Vince was Miko's cousin. He called me this morning because he seen y'all li'l stupid-ass video. And they got some niggas coming from Minnesota to see about us. Congratulations on being the world's dumbest criminals."

Donovan and Chris gave stupid looks.

"And y'all fucked off our money. Miko is the mu'fuckin' plug, you stupid-ass bitch-ass niggas. I should pop both y'all ass."

"My bad, Carl. I didn't know," Donovan said weakly.

When I seen the stupid ass look on his face, I had to talk myself out of killing him because I wanted to blow his brains out so fucking bad.

"If either one of you niggas ever do some stupid-ass shit like this again, Chris, I'ma forget that we brothers and I'ma smoke yo' bitch ass. And Donovan..." I didn't even need to finish talking. If I threatened kill my brother, he knew what I would do to him.

I left Chris's house and hopped in the Lexus. Kianna drove.

"What you wanna do, baby?"

"I don't even know. I put all my eggs in this one basket. Madison is so sweet and I don't wanna leave. We eating good, baby. But I also don't wanna go to war. These white people around here aren't ready for that shit. If innocent people start getting killed, the police coming hard and we ain't gon' be able to do shit. Not to mention we don't even got a mu'fuckin plug. You don't know how bad I wanna kill them stupid-ass niggas."

"We should just lay low for a li'l while. See what happens, you know? Play it by ear," Kianna said.

"Shit, that's about all we can do," I mumbled.

Rumbling noises from the car made me forget about the money and drama.

"What the fuck is that?" I asked Kianna.

"I don't know. It's the engine I think."

"Just what the fuck we need. More muthafuckin' problems. Pull over."

When she pulled over, I looked under the hood. Smoke and oil was everywhere. I walked to the driver's side.

"It's fucked up. Move over. I'ma drive us over to Trav and see if he can fix it."

The Lexus sputtered to the car shop and cut off in the parking lot. Me and Kianna walked in the front office. There was a short buff dark-skinned nigga at the front desk wearing a little-ass tank top.

"What happened?" he asked, his voice high-pitched and feminine.

I was startled by the built-ass nigga's voice but I maintained my composure.

"Car broke down. Is Trav here?"

He pointed to the garage. "He's in there."

Kianna snickered as we walked away. "He gay!"

"Quit," I whispered. Wasn't no way I was fighting that nigga over her bullshit. We stepped in the garage and seen Trav jacking a truck on the lift.

"Trav!"

He looked in my direction. When he recognized me, he stopped what he was doing and walked over. "Carl, what going on, my brotha?"

"Man, my car just broke down in the parking lot. Can you look at it?"

"Yeah," he said, looking to Kianna and fucking her with his eyes. "And who is this?"

"This my girl, Kianna."

He licked his lips. "My, my, my!"

I felt a little disrespected that he was checking out my girl, but I didn't sweat because I didn't want to look jealous and I needed him to fix the car. "She taken, brah. The car outside."

"My bad," he said, picking up on my tone.

We walked outside and he looked under the hood of the Lexus. "Damn, Carl. This is bad, my brotha. The engine is fucked. You gon' have to buy a new car unless you got good insurance."

I shook my head.

"We don't got insurance," Kianna said.

He whistled. "I would sell the body to a junkyard or something. This car done."

"Damn, that shit stupid as fuck," I cursed.

He watched me for a moment. "I see y'all was busy last night."

I looked up and seen excitement dancing in his eyes. "What you know?"

"Just what the news said. But I hear they got some people on the way to Mad town. You need anything?"

"Yeah. Some vests," I said sarcastically.

"I might be able to get you a few of them. We don't want nothing happening to you or yo' girl," he said, looking Kianna over again.

"You can get some vests, for real?"

He wore a smug smile. "I can get a lot of shit."

"Well, I need like four vests. Can you get that?"

"I'll see what I can do. I'll give you a call when I get off work."

"A'ight. Get at me," I said, about to get in the Lexus when I realized it didn't work. I turned to Trav. "Can we get a ride?"

When we got home, me and Kianna sat around and tried to come up with plans for what we would do if shit got too rough in Madison. We came up with two options. Go back to Chicago, which neither one of us wanted to do. Or go to Milwaukee and stay with her sister until we could figure our next move.

Around eight o'clock, I got call from Trav. He said he had something for us and told us go come by his house. I had never been to Trav's house and I wasn't too familiar with Madison, so he had to guide me over the phone. He lived on the outskirts of Madison in a country-ass town called Bellville. And he didn't live on a regular block, but right off the highway on a dark-ass back street. There were no houses next to Trav's for at least two city blocks. His house was covered in vines and trees lined the front. There was a cornfield across the street that stretched as far as I could see, which wasn't far because it was dark as fuck. Me and Kianna hopped out the donk and looked around.

"This is some scary shit, baby," Kianna said as we walked toward the house.

"Nah, this some *Chainsaw Massacre* shit," I said, looking behind us when a car turned onto the road.

Movement near a tree made me reach for my shit.

"Chill out," Trav said, appearing from behind the tree.

"Man, don't be doing that shit! Can't be scaring muthafuckas and shit!" I snapped.

"My bad," he said, looking at the car that was slowing down. "I think y'all got followed. Hurry up and come with me."

We followed Trav to the side of the house and hid behind bushes. Sure enough, a car pulled up alongside my Chevelle. It was too dark to see what the people inside the car were doing. Then it pulled a little ways down the road and pulled over.

"Y'all stay here," Trav said before creeping away.

"What the fuck is going on?" Kianna whispered, her eyes wide with terror.

"I don't know. But if he gets on some bullshit, I'm shooting his ass."

The leaves in the grass shuffled a few moments later. I pointed the pistol, ready to bust.

"Stop pointing that damn thang!" Trav whispered.

I lowered the gun.

"I think them the niggas from out of town. Go in the cellar and I'ma take care of this," he said, a crazy and deranged look in his eyes.

Wasn't no way I was gettin in this creepy-ass nigga's cellar. "Hell, nah. We ain't gettin' in no cellars."

"Okay. But don't move. They coming."

He disappeared again. A few moments, later we heard screams and a gunshot. Then silence. Trav came back breathing hard. "Hurry up and come in. I got the vests."

"What happened to them niggas?" I asked, following him into the house.

He turned to look at me, his eyes wide, smiling like the devil. "I'm going to feed my plants."

I looked him over, trying to figure out what he meant, and noticed the blood on his hands and shirt. "You bleeding."

187

He didn't even look at the blood. "It ain't mines. I'ma need to rush this sale. I gotta do some clean up. Two G's for four vests."

I pulled the money out and hurried up and gave it to him.

"Let me know if you need anything else," he said, rushing us from the house.

Me and Kianna hopped in the Chevelle and didn't speak until we was far from Trav's house.

"That nigga scare the shit outta me," Kianna said. "I think he a serial killer."

"Or a vampire," I added.

When we got home, I took the vests in the house and looked them over. I was about to call Chris when my phone rang. It was my brother.

"What's up?"

"THEY KILLED MEGAN!" Chris screamed. "Them niggas killed Megan!"

"Hold on, brah. What is you talking about? Who killed her?"

"I don't know. Some niggas ran in my house and started shooting. They killed my bitch," Chris sobbed.

"Where they at now? Is the niggas still there?"

"Nah, they gone. Damn, Carl. Them niggas killed my bitch."

"A'ight, chill. I'm on my way."

I grabbed Kianna and we hopped in the Chevelle and raced to Chris's house. When I turned onto the block, the shit looked like the entire Madison emergency unit was there. Several fire trucks and police cars had their lights on, lighting up the whole block. I thought about leaving, but I didn't want to leave my little brother on stuck, so me and Kianna hopped out the car and walked down the block.

We had just made it to the house when they brought a body out on the stretcher. Several police were using crime scene tape to block off entry into the house. I tried to find someone to ask about my little brother and seen a light skinned black woman. Me and Kianna walked over.

"Excuse me, Officer. My little brother, Chris, lives here. Do you know where he is?"

She pointed to the unmarked blue car parked across the street. "He's talking to the detectives."

I waited around for Chris to finish talking to the police. He got out of the car and ran into my arms like a little kid. It felt like he was ten years old again and we was back at Nana's house in Chicago.

"They killed my girl, Carl. They killed her," he cried.

I held him and tried to comfort him. "You gon' be okay, man. You gon' be okay."

I made the decision to leave Madison while I was standing there holding my little brother. We had two close calls in one night and I didn't want there to be a third. We went home and packed some clothes, guns, and money and got the fuck out of Madison.

J-Blunt

Chapter 18

I felt like shit.

I was lying in bed in the hotel room staring up at the ceiling trying to figure out where I went wrong. Madison was sweet. That was where I was supposed to become great. Shit was going good. And evidently it was all too good to be true. Leaving was one of the hardest things I ever did. But we had to. It was too dangerous. We didn't know who our enemies were and they proved they knew who we were. They tried to get me and Chris at the same time like we did Vince and Draymon. If it wasn't for Trav's weird ass, ain't no telling what would've happened to me and Kianna. I didn't know how Chris got away, but I was thankful that he did. And even though we escaped with our lives and I had almost a hundred G's, I still felt like shit.

When I got out of Joliet, my goal had been to get a hundred thousand, buy a house, and start a business. Now that I had touched that hundred, I knew that wasn't enough to do what I planned. In all my plan making, I never considered how much it would cost to live the life I had become accustomed to. And that's when I thought about what Tyson told me about the game. He said it was addictive. We always wanted more. Damn, that nigga was right, because now that I had reached my goal, I realized it wasn't enough. I wanted more. Way more. And I felt like shit because I had no idea how I was going to get it.

"You woke?" Kianna asked.

"Yeah. I can't sleep."

She rolled over and kissed me on the cheek. "What's wrong?"

"Everything, baby. Everything was going so good in Madison. We was eating, baby. We was supposed to become great. Then them stupid-ass niggas had to rob Donovan. Now I don't know what the fuck to do."

"If we did it once, we can do it again, Carl. I believe in you like I believe in my next breath. You the smartest and most driven nigga I ever met. Once you set your mind to something, you make it happen. That's what I love about you. You remind me of the Jeezy song

'Amazing'. You an amazing nigga, Carl. And I believe we can be great anywhere as long as we got each other."

I wasn't one of them super sentimental-ass niggas, but Kianna's words touched me and I felt what she was saying in my heart. I could see the truth behind her words in her eyes. That's when I realized I had fallen in love with her. She was my rock. With her by my side, I could do anything.

"I love you, Ki-Ki."

Her eyes grew wide as full moons. "What you say?"

I felt unsure. "I don't know. What did I say?"

She up in bed, tears filling her eyes. "You said you loved me."

Seeing her emotions fucked with me a little bit, so I kept it real. "That's right. I love you for real, baby. And I know that as long as I got you with me, I can do anything. I love yo' ass, girl," I said, reaching up and kissing her.

That kiss turned into a make-out session. We was laying on top of the covers with all of our clothes on, but they started coming off with the quickness. We slipped under the sheets and I removed my boxers. Kianna was just about to take off her panties when Chris stirred on the bed next to us.

"Man, what time is it?" he asked.

I wanted to tell him it was time for him to get his own room because I wanted some pussy, but since his girl died last night, I took it easy. "It's early. How you feeling?"

"Man, I don't even know," he said, letting out a long breath and shaking his head. "What we doing in Milwaukee? When we going back to Madison?"

"We not going back. We burnt it up. It's too hot."

He mugged me. "So, we finna let them niggas run us out the city?"

"We don't got no choice. Vince's niggas coming for us."

"So what? Fuck them niggas. Let's grab our shit and hit back. I ain't no bitch-ass nigga. I don't run from no niggas. Them niggas killed my bitch. I ain't finna run."

I understood Chris's anger, but knew I made the best decision. "So, what we supposed to do, Chris? We don't know who them niggas is or where they from. How we supposed to get back at 'em?"

"I don't know. Wait for them niggas to come back."

"Why? So they can get another chance to knock us off? I ain't finna play with my life like that. Y'all fucked up posting that video. Them niggas know who we is and can get at us whenever they want. We need to stay outta Madison til shit cool down."

"Man, I ain't tryna hear that scary-ass shit," Chris said, pulling out his phone.

I watched him, listening to his call.

"Donovan, I need you to come pick me up, brah. I'm in Milwaukee. Yeah, I'm good. They got my bitch, but I'm straight." He listened for a moment, then his eyes grew wide. "On what? Damn, brah! They shot up yo' mama house?" He listened again. "So where you stayin at?" He paused. "Damn, that's crazy. We stayin' in a hotel. Carl right here," he said before tossing the phone to me. "He wanna holla at you."

"What up, Don?"

"This shit crazy, Carl. Niggas shot up my mama house last night and she won't let me back in the house."

"Damn, that's fucked up. The fam good?"

"Yeah. These niggas fuckin' the city up and got me spooked. I'm tryna see what y'all doin'. I got some cousins that live in Milwaukee. That's where y'all stayin'?"

"For now, yeah. We don't know who them niggas is and I ain't finna get caught slippin' like that. Madison might be burnt up. If I can, I wanna see what it's like in Milwaukee. Maybe we can start Triple Beam Team back up here."

"Yeah, I was thinkin' the same shit. I'm tryna see if I can lay low with y'all. I know the city a li'l bit and might be able to help get shit started again."

I didn't know how I was going to do it, but I was going to use Donovan's knowledge of the city and his relationships to build Triple Beam Team bigger and better.

"Yeah. You always gon' be part of the team. We stayin' at the Best Western. Room 6."

After hanging up, I tossed Chris the phone. "He on his way. He wanna get down with us in Milwaukee. You still wanna go to Madison by yo'self? You see them niggas ain't stopping?"

Chris mugged me, getting out of bed. "Let me see the keys to the Chevelle so I can go get something to drink."

I nodded towards my pants on the floor. "They in my pocket."

After grabbing the keys, he left the room. As soon as the door closed, Kianna rolled on top of me.

"Tell me how much you love me while I ride this muthafucka."

***

Later that afternoon, I dropped Kianna off at her sister's house. The plan was for them to look for a house. Since her sister was familiar with the city, she could show Kianna good locations. Me, Chris, and Donovan went to meet his cousins, Brandon and Tony. I needed to add some niggas to team that had hustle and knew the city. Donovan swore that his cousins would be good additions. They lived with their mother in a house on the corner of 66th and Marion. When I pulled up, they were in the backyard.

"What's good, cuz? See you finally got tired of Madison and came back home, huh?" Tony cracked as he embraced Donovan. He was average height, dark-skinned, with brushed waves and a husky build.

"Man, it wasn't even like that," Donovan said, waving them off.

"I know. We heard them Madison niggas ran you up out that bitch!" Brandon laughed. He was taller and skinnier than his brother. "How you get aunty house shot up, my nigga?"

"Niggas robbed me and I got down. They came back and shot up OG crib. Now she talkin' 'bout don't come back."

"You know who them niggas is?" Tony asked.

"Nah. Niggas from Minnesota or some shit. But fuck them niggas. I'm back in the Mil now. This my nigga Cartier Chris and his brother Carl."

We exchanged nods and handshakes.

"My nigga, Carl, tryna find a plug."

"What you lookin' for?" Brandon asked, looking me over.

"Whatever you can get yo' hands on."

"We fuckin' wit' that boy."

"That's cool. What can you grab?"

The brothers shared a look. Tony answered. "We fuck with this nigga Mikel, but his shit ain't all the way a hunnit. And the nigga be on bullshit. Sometimes I gotta chase the nigga down to get my shit right. If I knew a better plug, I woulda been stop fuckin' with this nigga."

"That don't sound like a plug at all. That sound like a nigga that love playin' games."

"That's exactly what the nigga is," Brandon cut in. "But sometimes he be having that flake. Right now he good, so if you was gon' cop, this would be the right time."

"What's the numbers?"

"Depends what you want. We buy twenty grams a pop and he bless us for seventy a grit."

"And what's the come back off that? Is it worth it?"

Tony looked at me funny. "What you mean? How much we make off twenty grams?"

"Yeah."

"You don't fuck with boy?"

"Yeah. I wanna know what the scene like in Milwaukee."

"The shit he got right now is flake, so you can whip it to twenty-eight or thirty. Depends on what yo' heads pay. I got white clientele and they give me anywhere from eighty to a buck a grit. Depends on where they from. The further from up north they come, the more I whack em for."

"Shit, I had a bitch come from Fond Du Lac payin' one twenty five a grit." Brandon laughed.

I nodded. "How y'all feel about doing something with me? I don't know shit about Milwaukee, but I got a few dollars. Donovan say y'all good and I need to put together a team."

"Nah, I'm good," Tony declined. "I'm doing my own thing.

"What kinda move you talking 'bout making?" Brandon asked.

"Really some front shit. Y'all lines already slappin' so I would front y'all some work for a li'l cheaper than y'all payin' right now. I was having my way in Madison til this shit happened with them niggas from Minnesota. Now I'm moving my operation to Milwaukee. I got the money. I just need the team."

I could see the wheels turning in Brandon's mind. "How much you fronting twenty grits for? Right now I'm payin' seventy a gram."

I did the math. "Depending on what I can get 'em for. I'm thinkin' like sixty-five. Maybe cheaper."

Brandon looked to Tony. "Sixty five a gram, brah."

Tony smiled. "If you give it to me for sixty-five a grit, I'ma fuck with you all day."

"Call yo' boy and set up a meeting."

Mikel agreed to meet me at a strip club called Phoenix later that night. Kianna rode with me. Brandon and Tony met us in the parking lot. We walked in and found a table to have drinks and wait for Mikel. A slim Latin woman was at our table as soon as our asses hit the chairs.

"Hola, guys. You want me to dance for you?"

Brandon pulled out money. "Hell yeah! Let me see you shake that muthafucka!"

The entertainment was okay, but I wasn't too concerned with the dancers. I wanted to meet with Mikel and talk money. An hour later, he still hadn't showed up.

"What's up with yo' boy?" I asked Tony.

"I just texted the nigga. I don't know."

"This what we was talkin' 'bout. Nigga be on fuck shit," Brandon said.

Feeling like I wasted my time, I looked to Kianna. "Let's get the fuck outta here, baby."

We were walking to the Chevelle when I heard a woman screaming for help.

"You hear that?" Kianna asked.

"Yeah. Sound like somebody's screaming," I said, never breaking my stride to the car.

"Look, baby! That girl needs help!" Kianna pointed.

I looked to where she pointed and seen a man and woman struggling near the side of the building. "That ain't got nothing to do with us. Let's go."

The women's scream got louder.

"What if he tryna rape her? We can't just let her get killed," Kianna said.

I opened the driver's door. "I'm not finna be a witness or the Good Samaritan that get killed. We got other shit to worry about."

Kianna mugged me before heading towards the struggle.

"Ki-Ki, we got——"

"I'm not finna let her get raped," she said.

"Stupid-ass shit!" I cursed following Kianna.

The Latin stripper that danced for Brandon was in a struggle with some weird-looking white dude.

"Let her go!" Kianna screamed, running over and busting him in his shit.

He took a step backward and grabbed his jaw. Then a crazy look flashed in his eyes right before he rushed Kianna.

"Sit cho bitch-ass down!" I yelled, pulling the Glock.

When he seen the gun, he stopped in his tracks. "I wasn't going to do anything!"

"Sonofabitch tried to rape me!" the Latina woman screamed before kicking the white man in the balls.

"Ahhh!" he screamed, doubling over in pain.

"C'mon. Come with us," Kianna said, helping the woman to our car.

"Thank you so much, mama. You are an angel," the woman said as she climbed in the back seat.

"What the fuck was that about?" I asked.

"The mutherfucker said he would give me a ride. I was going to pay him, but he wanted me to suck him while he drove. I didn't want to do it, so he tried to rape me. Nasty mutherfucker."

"We can give you a ride. Where are you going?"

I looked at Kianna. How the fuck she offering rides when we didn't even know our way around the city?

"On 76th and Florist. Thank you so much."

"You gonna have to tell me where that is. We not from here," I said, mugging Kianna.

"Oh. That's cool. Where you guys from?"

"We're from Chicago," Kianna said. "We just moved here yesterday and we're still learning the city."

"Well, Milwaukee is nice in the summer and cold as fuck in the winter."

"Just like Chicago," Kianna laughed. "My name is Kianna. This is my man, Carl. What's your name?"

"I'm Marielle. It's nice to meet you guys."

I minded my business and followed Marielle's directions while the women kicked it like they knew each other they whole life.

"Do you guys party?" Marielle asked.

That got my attention.

"What do you mean?" Kianna asked.

Marielle pulled out a little baggie with white powder from her purse. "Coke?"

"Oh, no. We don't mess around," Kianna said.

"Well, do you mind if I take a line?"

"Nah, baby. Do yo' thang," I spoke up. "But it would be nice if you let me know where you got that from."

"My cousin, Diego, has tons of this shit," she said, digging her pinky into the bag and scooping some powder onto her nail before snorting it.

Me and Kianna looked at each other at the same time.

"You think you could introduce us to Diego?" Kianna asked, reading my mind.

Marielle shoved a pinky nail full of dope into her nose again and sniffed. "Yeah. Sure. You guys saved my ass and I owe you."

She directed me to the south side, on Oklahoma and Superior. I could smell the water from Lake Michigan and see the property values increase as I drove past big-ass houses and mini mansions. Diego's house looked like a castle, sitting on a big ass plot of land. The lake was in his backyard.

"I'll be right back," Marielle said before hopping out of the car.

"Damn, these some nice-ass houses!" Kianna said, rubber necking at all the expensive properties.

"Whoever this Diego nigga is, he must be holding! I think we might've came up on something good," I said, feeling butterflies in my stomach.

"Now ain't you glad I helped her?" Kianna said, rubbing it in my face.

I gave her props. "That was a good call, baby."

Diego's front door opened and five Latino niggas walked out, heading towards my car. I looked at their faces and body language and they didn't look friendly. And they was strapped!

"Shit! What the fuck this bitch got us into?" I said, clutching my Glock.

"Drive, baby!" Kianna yelled, panic in her voice.

I put the key back in the ignition, when one of them walked in front of the car with an AK-47.

"Get out the car!" he demanded.

I looked around and seen that all of them was pointing choppers at us. Fuck! If I acted like I wanted to drive away, they would light the Chevelle up like a Christmas tree.

"We gotta get out, baby," I told Kianna, dropping the Glock on the seat and opening the door. "Okay. Chill. We coming out. What's going on?"

"Stop talking. Don't say shit," the nigga that was standing in front of the car said, pointing the gun at me. "Omar, search 'em."

One of them stepped forward and gave us rough pat downs. "They clean."

"Follow Omar towards to the garage," the nigga with the AK ordered.

I kept my hands where they could see them and followed the one that pat searched us. On the side of the house was a big-ass three car garage. Inside was a silver Range Rover and a red Corvette.

"Stop right here," the AK-47 holder said.

I looked at the niggas, trying to guess if they were going to kill us. They all wore blank faces and kept their guns pointed at us. A few moments later, the side door opened and Marielle walked in with a husky light-skinned nigga. He was a little taller than me with dark eyes and long wavy hair pulled into a ponytail. He stood in front of me and Kianna and just stared at us. I held his eye contact. Even though he had all the power, I wasn't going to fold.

"Who you?" he asked, his accent thick.

"I'm Carl," I answered.

"Why you come to mi casa, Carlito?"

Marielle spoke up. "I brought them——"

"Shhh! I no talking to you, Marielle. I talking to Carlito. Why you come to mi casa?" he asked again.

"I wanted to do business."

"What business you talk about? I don't know you. Why I want to do business with strangers?"

I looked to Marielle for a sign of what I should say, but she wouldn't even look at me. She was staring at the floor.

"I just wanted to buy some cocaine, man. I wasn't tryna cause no trouble. I didn't know it was gon' be like this. I just want some money, man."

Diego mugged me. "Oh, you come for my money, eh? You want to take my money?"

"Nah, man. I got my own money. I wanna buy some dope and make my own money. I'm a hustler. I sell dope. I need a connection."

He studied me for a few seconds. "I kill strangers that come to me asking for cocaine. I don't know you. You could be policia."

"I'm not the police. Ask your cousin. I just wanted to buy some shit."

"I don't care what she have to say. You tell me why I shouldn't have you killed right now?"

I looked at Kianna and seen the fear of death in her eyes. I couldn't let us go out like this. I had to figure out a way to save us.

"Because I want to make you some money, Diego. And I can make a lot of it. I got a lot of people that want drugs, but I don't got a connection. If you plug with me, I can get money all over Wisconsin. I can take over all this shit if you help me. We can get so much money that we could build money houses. I'm a real hustler,

Diego. I can sell snow to a polar bear. Let me show you what I can do."

He cocked his head to the side and stared at me again. "Marielle tell me what you did." He nodded. "You saved her from being defiled. Gracias, Carlito. You saved her from great shame. I will do business with you because you save my cousin. But on one condition."

"What?"

"You must eat the worm," he smiled.

I didn't know what the fuck he was talking about, but if it would save our lives and get him to do business, I was going to do it. "Okay. Get the worm."

He turned to his boys and waved his hand. They lowered the guns." Omar, go get the worm for Carlito."

Omar smiled as he ran out of the garage. I looked at the faces of everyone around us and they all wore the same smile. I wasn't sure what the fuck I got myself into, but it seemed like they was all about to be entertained by it.

A few moments later, Omar came back with a fifth of tequila. The worm inside of that looked big enough to be a garden snake.

"Drink the bottle and eat the worm." Diego smiled.

J-Blunt

BOOK III: POWER

POWER - VIGOR. FORCE. STRENGTH. THE ABILITY TO DO, ACT, OR PRODUCE.

WHEN A MAN IS IN CONSTANT CONTACT WITH SUCCESS, THEY BECOME ACCUSTOMED TO IT.

AND IF THEY BECOME ACCUSTOMED TO IT LONG ENOUGH, THEY BECOME INFLUENCED BY IT.

THE INFLUENCE OF SUCCESS PRODUCES POWER.

A WEAKNESS OF MAN IS BELIEVING THE WORD IMPOSSIBLE EXISTS.

KNOWING WHAT CANNOT BE DONE IS DAMAGING TO THE SIGHT OF A VISIONARY.

POWER COMES TO THOSE THAT KNOW IMPOSSIBLE IS NOTHING BUT A WORD.

LIKE CAN'T.

TO SOMEONE WHO IS SEEKING OR HAS EXPERIENCED POWER, THERE ARE NO SUCH THINGS AS CAN'T OR IMPOSSIBLE.

THESE WORDS ARE CRUTCHES AND EXCUSES USED BY MEN TO JUSTIFY THEIR QUITTING OR GIVING UP.

ACHIEVING POWER IS NOT EASY.

YOU WILL CERTAINLY BE IN THE MOST DIFFICULT FIGHT OF YOUR LIFE.

AND THAT IS A BLESSING, BECAUSE A GOOD FIGHT WILL PROVE HOW BAD YOU WANT SOMETHING.

POWER REQUIRES NO APOLOGY, EXPLANATION, OR REASON.

IT JUST IS.

J-Blunt

Chapter 19

June 3rd, 2018

If somebody would've told me that I would have a million dollars by my fortieth birthday, I would've told them they were lying. Then I would have corrected them and told them that I would have two.

As it stood, I was forty years old and I had two million dollars. Most of it was in cash, hidden in the trunk of my sky blue 1977 Chevelle and in a storage closet. I had so much money that I didn't know what to do with it. I didn't have nowhere to put it. I couldn't just go to the bank with my money and say hold this. If I did some stupid-ass shit like that, the Feds woulda been up my ass like a doctor giving a colonoscopy. I bought a few houses and owned a couple businesses, but nothing was in my name. And the dope money rolled in so fast that I couldn't clean the money with the little businesses that I owned, so I stashed it in the Chevelle.

The decision to save Marielle's ass outside that strip club was the best decision I ever made. Hooking up with Diego was truly a gift from God. With his product, I was able to take over all of Milwaukee and I also worked my way into Madison. Next on my agenda was locking up the drug trade in the entire state of Wisconsin. I was destined for greatness!

"I want some now. I want to suck it too!"

Marisol's whining pulled me from my thoughts. I opened my eyes and looked down. Marielle had my dick in her mouth, sucking me like she was trying to win a prize. Mary was sucking my balls with the same vigor. Marisol lay next to them, feeling left out.

"What's wrong, baby?" I asked.

"I want to taste your dick, but Marielle won't let me." She pouted.

"Don't worry, baby. You gon' get yo' turn. When I bust my nut, I'ma let you swallow it, okay?"

Marisol smiled like she guessed the Final Jeopardy question. "Okay, daddy!"

After taking care of the problem, I closed my eyes again, enjoying the mouth service of the women while collecting my thoughts. I, Carlile White, was a boss. My organization, Triple Beam Team, TBT for short, was well known and well respected in the Midwest. My niggas controlled the dope game in Milwaukee. Not wanting to shit in my own backyard, I moved back to Chicago and enjoyed the fruits of my labor. One of my favorite fruits was my condominium. It was the same one Jewels invited me to over twenty years ago, where I had my first threesome with them fine-ass sisters, Valerie and Glenda. I had enough money to do what I wanted when I wanted. I didn't have a care in the world. There was no problem I couldn't solve.

"What the fuck I tell you about this shit, Carl!"

I opened my eyes and seen Kianna standing in the master bedroom's doorway. She wore an all-white business skirt, blouse, and heels. Her arms were filled with bags from designer stores, which she threw down angrily. Her hazel eyes blazed her true emotions. When my girls seen Kianna and her attitude, they tried to crawl away.

"Wait. Don't go," I stopped them.

"Get the fuck outta my house, right now!" Kianna threatened.

The women looked unsure of what to do next.

"Get what you came for, Marisol. I told you, you can swallow it."

The Latin beauty grabbed my dick and started sucking it again.

"Oh, you bitches think I'm playin'!" Kianna screamed, going for the walk-in closet.

Marielle and Mary knew what time it was and grabbed their clothes and ran out of the room. Marisol was determined to swallow my seed and continued giving head.

Pop!

The gunshot scared the fuck out of me. I looked over and seen Kianna holding a pistol.

"Bitch, get the fuck out of my house or the next bullet going in yo' head!" Kianna promised.

Marisol took off from the room like she had super powers.

"Why you have to do that, Kianna? I was almost there," I said, sliding off the bed and walking over.

"Because I told you about fucking other bitches. What the fuck, Carl? I'm tired of you cheating on me."

I walked over to her, unfazed by the gun in her hand or anger blazing in her eyes. "We talked about this already, Ki-Ki. You said I could fuck other bitches."

"I said you can fuck them with me and have a threesome. Not have threesomes and foursomes in our house and in our bed."

I took the gun from her hand. "Baby, you know those bitches don't mean shit to me. I love you. You my queen. My rock. You helped me become great. Nobody can replace you. But I like fucking other bitches. You know that."

"But that don't mean you rub the shit in my face. I don't want to come home and see a bunch of bitches in my bed. And why it have to be Marielle? She's like my friend."

"Baby, she don't mean shit to me or you. I'm yo' friend. Fuck them. Now, since you ran them away, can you finish what they started?" I asked, grabbing her hand and pulling it to my dick.

She pushed me away. "Stop playing, with me, Carl. I'm not touching you after you was fucking those nasty-ass bitches. And I don't want you bringing no more bitches to my house or I swear to God I'ma kill they asses."

I blew her off and left the room. She wasn't sucking my dick, so fuck her.

"Carl, put some clothes on before you go out there! My sister and her friend in the living room!" Kianna called.

It was too late. I had already left the room and Kianna's sister and her friend's eyes went right to my semi-hard dick. I acted like it wasn't shit. Walked right into the living room with my dick swinging.

"What's good, Shawn? Who yo' friend?"

"Uh, h-hey, Carl," Shawn stuttered. "This is Dion."

I looked Dion over. She was light-skinned and skinny with some big-ass lips. I pictured those lips around my dick. "What's up, Dion. You got some nice lips. You know what to do with them?"

She looked down at my dick and then back up at me.

"Carl, what the fuck I just tell you!" Kianna screamed, walking over and getting in my face. "Stop fucking disrespecting me, nigga. Go put on some clothes!"

I normally didn't let nobody talk to me like that, but Kianna was my one and only love, so I let her get away with it. Plus, I was going too far with her sister and friend seeing me naked. "I'm sorry, baby. For real. I'ma go get dressed."

On my way to the room, I looked back and seen them all watching me. "Tonight is the grand opening of my club, Triple Time. I hope to see y'all there!"

***

Later that night, I was standing in the middle of Triple Time, looking around the empty club. The grand opening was in thirty minutes and I was feeling a little nervous. I wanted everything to be perfect. The bar was fully stocked with top and bottom shelf liquor. My fine-ass bartenders, Marisol and Mary, were behind the bar looking good in their halter tops and spandex shorts. My security, Fantasia and Trav, were at the front door looking like soldiers. Pool tables clean with the balls already racked. Dance floor looked freshly buffed and waxed. Everything looked ready. There was only one thing missing. Icy Mike. He was the hottest rapper in the city and I gave him twenty G's to host my grand opening.

"Hey, baby," Kianna sang, walking up behind me. "You ready?"

"I was going over everything. I can't believe I did it. This feel so crazy."

She smiled up at me like I was Future and she was my biggest fan. "I knew you could do it. I seen greatness in you the first time I seen you at my aunty house when you got out of prison. Congratulations, baby!" she said before planting one on my lips.

"Thank you, baby," I said, wrapping her in my arms. "I couldn't have did none of this without you, you know that, right?"

"I know."

My brother came from the back of the club and interrupted our moment. "Carl, why the fuck you ain't open them doors yet, nigga? Let the hoes in so I can see who I'm taking to the crib tonight!"

"We still got thirty minutes, Chris. Gotta make sure everything good."

He looked around. "Everything is good. Let's get this shit crackin'. The line damn near around the block."

"Slow down, Cartier," Kianna laughed. "You gon' have plenty of nasty-ass girls to take home. Eight o'clock is when the doors open."

He waved us off and walked towards the bar.

When the doors opened, Chicagoans filled the club and partied like there was no tomorrow. Icy Mike showed up at nine o'clock and the party really turned up. I did meet and greets all night, making sure everybody was having a good time. Around midnight, Marisol laid on the bar with a lemon in her mouth and people started doing body shots off her. I joined in the fun and when I grabbed the lemon from Marisol's mouth, she started kissing me. Kianna walked over with an attitude.

"Really, Carl? You gon' kiss this bitch in front of everybody and disrespect me like that?"

"C'mon, baby. You tripping. We having a good time. Fall back," I said, blowing her off. I continued partying, not giving a second thought to what Kianna was talking about. This was my club's opening and I was going to show the people a good time and have a good time.

When I got a call, I stepped in my office to answer. I was about to go back on the floor when Trav stepped in the office. I had hired the crazy nigga to do security for me and now he was TBT. He used to be in the military, some kind of Special Forces, and kept us strapped nasty! Nigga could get any kind of gun we needed.

"Carl, lemme holla at you for a minute."

"I always got time for my nigga. What's going on, Trav?"

"It's about that raise. Me and my team take the most risks. When my boys get jammed, I cover that tab. It's starting to add up and we need a li'l bit bigger piece of the pie."

"C'mon, Trav. We talked about this already. I'm taking care of a team, baby. Er'body gotta eat. If I start breaking off more of the pie to you, other niggas might get mad and come at me the same way. I'm fair, my nigga."

"But they don't take the risks like we do. Me and the hit squad put our life on the line every night. Them other niggas hustling and making money. They don't do the dirty work like we do."

I didn't have time to discuss some shit that I wasn't going to change. "Listen, man. Right now ain't a good time to get into this. It's too much going on out of the floor. We gon' talk about this at a later date."

Trav held eye contact longer than necessary. "You the boss."

"Right, right. Now let's get back out here and enjoy this party. I think I might have an orgy tonight," I said, opening the door

"What about Ki-Ki? You don't think you going too far?"

I stopped to look back at him. "Why you worried about Kianna? You know that's my bitch, right?"

"That wasn't never in question, Carl. She seemed a li'l upset and I just wanted to bring it to yo' attention."

I searched Trav's face for a moment. It wasn't no secret that he was attracted to Kianna. He was always watching her. They had even become something like friends.

"Let me worry 'bout my girl, a'ight? You stay focused on keeping me safe. Cool?"

He nodded. "As ice."

After leaving the office, I went back out on the floor to so some more mingling and entertaining and ran into Alderman Bishop Gains. He was a celebrity in Chicago and worshipped by everyone on the South side.

"Carl! What's going on, brotha? Congratulations on a poppin' grand opening!"

"I appreciate it, alderman. Are you enjoying yourself?"

"I am. Like I said, this is a hell of an opening. When you get some time, not tonight, since you're busy, I want to talk to you about some business plans. Here's my card. Give me a call tomorrow."

I pocketed the card. "I'll be in touch, alderman. Have a great night."

After speaking with the politician, I slid behind the bar to mingle and mix drinks. I was making a Long Island Iced Tea when Marisol walked over and started whispering in my ear.

"Do you know how to make a *Hot Sex on the Beach*?"

"Nah, but I know how to have hot sex on the beach." I laughed.

"When am I going to get to finish getting my dessert? Your girl came and ruined it this morning."

I looked across the club, locking eyes with Kianna. She still looked mad. And Marisol whispering in my ear didn't make it no better.

"I don't know. I'll have to see when I can get some time alone with you again."

"What if we didn't need to be alone? What if I tasted it right now?"

While I was trying to figure out what she was talking about, Marisol got on her knees, unzipping my pants as she crawled under the bar.

"Get up, Marisol. We can't - oh shit!" I moaned, gripping the bar as she swallowed my dick. I looked around for Kianna and spotted her talking to her sister, not paying me any attention. I gave the customer their drink and leaned against the bar while Marisol tried her best to make me skeet down her throat. I closed my eyes and nodded my head, acting like I was listening to the music but I was really enjoying the head. When I opened them again, Kianna was headed in my direction. She was too close for me to tell Marisol to get up so I continued letting her blow me.

"Where yo' little slut go?" Kianna asked as she sat on the barstool.

"I don't know. Running around here somewhere," I said, struggling to keep a straight face. Marisol had pulled my dick from her mouth and started sucking my balls. That shit had me wanting to moan.

Kianna gave me a funny stare before nodding. "Besides that kissing shit, tonight has been a good night. Everybody is enjoying they self. I think we about to be Chicago's number one spot for a while."

"Yeah. That would be the - oh shit! I mean, the shit," I corrected, trying to keep my composure as Marisol continued to do work.

"You good?" Kianna asked.

"Yeah. I just got a cramp or something," I said, leaning forward with my elbows on the bar.

I could feel beads of sweat popping onto my forehead as I continued to try and keep my face straight. Kianna stared in my eyes for a moment before looking towards my waist. I was hidden by the bar, but my body rocked a little bit from Marisol's BJ.

"Muthafucka!" Kianna cursed, pushing me.

I stumbled backwards, my dick slipping from Marisol's mouth as I fell against the shelf of liquor behind me. When Kianna seen my dick, her eyes turned gold, blazing with anger.

"Really, Carl! You gon' let this bitch give you some head under the fucking bar while you talking to me?"

People at the bar watched in shock as I slipped my shit back in my pants. "Ki-Ki, the shit just happened, baby. I wasn't tryna disrespect you. You know how it is," I tried to explain.

I think all of my words went in one of her ears and out the other because she wasn't hearing shit. And then Marisol decided to stand up. Kianna reached out, grabbing her by the hair and slamming her head on the bar.

"Punk-ass bitch, didn't I tell you to stay the fuck away from my nigga!" she screamed, punching Marisol in the face a couple of times.

"Kianna, stop!" I yelled, grabbing her.

"Oh, so you wanna protect the bitch, too?" she screamed, snatching away from me.

"It ain't like that. You fuckin' up the club opening." Why did I say that?

"I'm fucking up the opening?" Kianna screamed, looking at me like she couldn't believe I just said that. Then she grabbed a customer's drink off the bar and threw it at me. "Yo' punk ass keep on disrespecting me with these punk-ass bitches is what's fucking up the opening."

I dodged the glass as she picked up another drink.

"Ay! You bet' not throw nothing else at me!"

She gave me a 'what the fuck you gon do' look right before she threw it at me. "Fuck you, Carl, you punk-ass muthafucka!"

I dodged the drink. When she tried to pick up another one, I grabbed her arms and tried to pull her over the bar. "Stop this shit right now, Kianna!"

All the people around and near the bar moved out of the way and watched us wrestle. A few moments later, Trav and his brother came over.

"Y'all chill!" Trav said, grabbing Kianna.

"Get that bitch outta my club right now!" I snapped.

"Fuck you and yo' bitch-ass club, Carl! I hope this muthafucka burn down with you in it!" Kianna screamed as Trav carried her towards the back office.

I turned to look towards the crowd. "Okay, y'all! Keep on partying. That was just a little misunderstanding. Let's get back to it. Matter of fact, next round of drinks is on me!"

That got the crowd back into the party.

"You good, Carl?" Fantasia asked. He was Trav's musclebound gay brother.

"Yeah. Yeah. Let's just get the people back focused on the party."

"You might've went too far with that one," he warned.

"I'm good, man. Go back to doing what you was doing. And Marisol, clean yo'self up. Mary, get a broom and sweep this glass up. C'mon, y'all, let's get back to the party."

J-Blunt

Chapter 20

I was awakened by the sound of my phone ringing. I opened my eyes and seen that I was on the couch in my living room and still had all my clothes on. I reached for the phone, answering the call on speaker. It was Tony.

"What's goin on, brah?"

"You got it, Carl. Just wondering when you was coming through the city? Niggas need them refreshments."

I looked at the time in the upper corner of the phone. It was a couple minutes after nine o'clock. "Gimme a couple hours. I should be at you no later than five o'clock."

"Okay. Bet. I see Triple Time was poppin' last night. Niggas posted plenty of videos and pictures."

"Yeah, brah. You missed a good one. That was one of the best nights of my life. Icy Mike was there. It was live."

"I bet. I'ma come through there soon."

"Fa sho'. You know all TBT got VIP."

"No doubt. Holla at me when you get in the city."

After hanging up the phone, I lay back and thought about last night. The club was a success. Triple Time was the hottest thing in the city. And the fight with Kianna didn't hurt the image at all. In fact, it helped. Gave people something to talk about. I was destined to be great.

I got up from the couch, heading for my bedroom. I needed to shower and get dressed. The team needed more food so I had to get up with Diego.

When I walked in the room, I locked eyes with Kianna. She was sitting up in bed messing with her phone.

"What up?"

She rolled her eyes. "Don't what up me, muthafucka."

I stopped near the foot of the bed. "C'mon, Ki-Ki. Let's leave last night where it's at. That's the past. We can't dwell on that. I had fun and the club is a hit. What more can we ask for?"

"I asked you to stop disrespecting me, but you can't stop doing that. Then you got the bitch sucking yo' dick under the bar while I'm talking to you. Fuck you, Carl. Get the fuck out of my face."

Her angry outburst didn't affect me in the least. I sat on the bed next to her and placed my hand on her thigh.

"Don't touch me, Carl! Get away from me!" she yelled, trying to push me away.

"C'mon, Ki-Ki. You know how I am, baby. Them hoes don't mean shit to me. I love you."

"If you love me, why won't you stop disrespecting me? I told you we can fuck bitches together. But nah, you wanna do what you want when you want and say fuck me. Nah, nigga, fuck you. That ain't love."

"See, the problem is you thinking about this too emotionally. Can't nobody fuck with what we got. I need you to be secure in that. I'm a God, baby. I can't be treated like regular niggas. I'm great, and great people are magnets. People want to be around me. They want to be in my presence. Bitches wanna suck my dick and gimme the pussy. It's my responsibility to share me with the people."

Kianna looked at me like I lost my mind. "Listen to yo'self, Carl. You sound crazy. Like you lost yo' fucking mind. You are not a god and it is not your responsibility to share yourself with people. You doing way too fuckin' much. Your ego is way too big. You are letting the money and success go to your head."

I shook my head. "You wrong, baby. I'm not crazy and this ain't about my ego. The success didn't go to my head. The success completed me. I reached a higher level than I coulda ever imagined. I wish you could understand me. We can do anything we want. We can have people worship us. Why don't you want that?"

She looked at me like I was a stranger. "Just get away from me, Carl. I don't want to talk to you right now. Leave me alone."

I stared at her for a moment before getting up and going into the master bathroom. After a shower and changing my clothes, I took the elevator to the garage and hopped in my Bentley GT. After picking up Chris, I hit the highway for Milwaukee. During the drive, I texted Diego to let him know I needed to see him. He sent a text and told me to meet him at his club.

When I got to Milwaukee, I met with Tony to pick up the money. He gave me two bags. Each contained three hundred thousand dollars. One was for Diego, and I was taking the other one home. After getting the money, I headed to Diego's club. LAVA was a popping-ass Latin nightclub on the south side. When I walked in, Diego was standing at the bar talking to a fine-ass bartender.

"Carlito!" He smiled, opening his arms.

"What's up, big man?" I asked, setting the bag of money on the bar before embracing the Columbian like we were brothers.

"Things are good. I was just telling Christina about the yacht I'm about to buy. Five million dollar floating condo. You have to sail with me one day, Carlito. It will be the best time of your life. Sun, tequila, and fine señoritas!"

"Count me in! Name the date and I'ma be there."

"We gon' be there!" Chris jumped in.

"That's what I'm talking about, Carlito. And there is room for you too, Chris. But enough about me. Have a drink. Christina, get us a bottle of tequila and some glasses. Tell me about your club. How was the opening?"

I couldn't wipe the smile from my face as I relived last night. "It was live, man. One of the best nights of my life."

"That's good to hear. How's business?"

I patted the bag of money. "A-1 like the steak sauce."

Christina came back with a bottle of tequila and three shot glasses. Diego started pouring drinks. "Good. Good. Salud!" He said, holding the shot glass in the air for a toast.

"Salud!" Me and Chris echoed before downing the shots.

"Christina, take care of that for me," he said, giving her the bag. "What do you need, Carlito?"

"The usual ten kilos."

"Okay. I will have Omar drop it to you at the tattoo shop. How's it going with cleaning the money?"

"It's still hard. I'm making more money than my businesses can clean. I got millions in storage."

"Yeah, that is the problem with making money in America. It is hard to clean. You will need to find an investor. Someone who knows how to handle money."

"Easier said than done, big man."

"You smart guy. I'm sure you will figure it out. If not, well, nothing beats cash," he cracked.

"For sure. I'ma get out of here. Make sure you let me know when you get that yacht. I wanna get out on that ocean and catch a great white!"

After leaving the club, I went to the first business I bought to clean my money, Body Art tattoo shop. My money eventually outgrew the tattoo shop, but I still used it to clean a little money, have meetings, and pick up from Omar. The manager was a crazy white dude with a bunch of tattoos named Keith Bump.

"Hey, buddy," Keith greeted as soon as I walked in the front door.

"'Sup, brah?"

"I'm awesome, bro. Fucking awesome. Did a bachelorette party last night that was a fucking rager. Hot-ass black chicks. Pool party. I'm the only white boy. Had a fucking ball! You hear me? A fucking ball!"

"Got you some black pussy last night, Keith?" Chris laughed.

"Hell nah, bro. I didn't get some black pussy. I got dipped in chocolate. Invited to the Motherland! I was swimming in black pussy all night. Now I finally get the saying, the blacker the berry, the sweeter the juice."

I busted out laughing. "Man, you crazy as fuck, Keith. Did Donovan get here yet?"

"Yeah, he's in back. Make sure you leave me something to get right with. 'Bout time for my evening dose."

"You got it, Keith," I said before heading to the back room.

Donovan was waiting for me. "Carl, what it do, boi? I see you had Triple Time shaking last night!"

"What's good, boi? You know how we do. Anytime TBT in the building, we gon' be turned all the way up!"

"I'ma be in the city next weekend. Coming in Triple Time and turning all the way up."

"You know we got you. All TBT get VIP. How everything going in the street?"

"Streets is TBT, you know that. I'm getting short on work. Hopefully you already talked to Diego."

"You already knew that. Omar on the way right now. You pick that up and do what you need to do. I gotta get back to the city and take care of some things. Do y'all need anything while I'm here?"

"Nah, we good. I got it from here, brah," Chris said.

After showing my niggas some love, I left the back room heading for the exit. I was almost to the door when I seen the finest white bitch I ever saw in my life. She had blonde hair, blue eyes, and a nice-ass figure. She was about to sit in one of the tattoo artist's chair, but I stopped her.

"Wait a minute. Don't sit right there."

She looked confused. "What's wrong?"

"You deserve nothin' but the best," I said before looking to the manager. "Keith, hook her up with that VIP treatment."

"No problem, boss man," Keith said, cleaning up his ink table to make room for her to sit down.

"Wow. Thanks, guys." She blushed. "I didn't know you had VIP treatment in here."

"We don't. We make exceptions for people that look important. My name is Carl. I'm the owner," I introduced, extending my hand.

She shook it real lady like. "I'm Lace. Nice to meet you, Carl."

"Same here. So, what are you looking to get done?"

"I was hoping to get a cover up," she said, lifting her sleeve and showing the name Joe written in a heart. "I have my ex's name on my arm and I'm tired of looking at it. Today is the day that I'm deciding to do something about it."

"Whoever Joe is, he is an asshole for letting you get away," I said. "Whatever you want is on the house. All part of the VIP package."

She smiled at me with her lips and eyes. "Thank you, Carl, but I prefer to pay my way. I'm a hedge fund manager, so I can afford it."

Hearing her job title set off a charge of excited energy through my body. "That's crazy that you just walked into my shop because I've been thinking about doing some investing. This must be a sign. Do you have a card?"

"Not with me, but you can take down my number. I'll be happy to meet with you and discuss a financial plan."

I left the shop with an extra pep in my step. I didn't know how, but Lace was going to help me clean my money. And I would be seeing her ass again soon. Real soon.

I hit the highway and drove back to Chicago. My first stop was at the storage. After parking, I grabbed the bag of money and went to my storage container. I unlocked the door and stepped inside. I used to key to pop the trunk of the Chevelle. It was almost completely filled with hundred dollar bills. There was over two million dollars inside and I was running out of space to put the money. I needed to think of something quick. Lace's face popped into my head. I had to figure out a way to get her on board.

After leaving the storage, I got a call from Marisol.

"What's up, baby?"

"Hey, papi. I'm at Triple Time. There's a guy named Bishop here that said he needs to meet with you and it's important."

I had forgotten all about the politician. "Okay. Tell him to chill. I'm on my way."

It took ten minutes to get to the club. When I walked in, I spotted the alderman at the bar laughing with Marisol.

"Bishop! What's going on, brotha?"

He turned at the sound of my voice. "Carl! Hey, brotha! Your bartender is as pretty as she is funny."

"I know. That's why I hired her. Having her behind the bar makes my job easy."

Marisol blushed. "Oh, stop Carl."

"You got a winner right there," Bishop nodded. "Do you have somewhere we can talk? I wanted to discuss something with you that is for your ears only."

I nodded towards the back. "For sure. Come to my office." After closing the door, I offered him a seat and sat behind my desk. "Have a seat. What's on yo' mind?"

"TBT." He smiled.

I raised an eyebrow. How the fuck did he know about Triple Beam Team?

"I don't follow you."

"I would like to do business with Triple Beam Team. I have some connections that you need. I know powerful people in powerful places. We want to invite you to our table."

I searched his eyes for the meaning behind his words. "I'm listening."

"It's obvious that you are on the rise, and the people I work for see a lot of potential in you to do great things in the city. We would like for you to buy your merch from us and keep the money in the city. In return, you'll get their protection. Their resources. Their favor."

I was surprised by the business offer. "Wow. I would be lying if I said that I wasn't surprised by the offer. I didn't know you was connected like that."

He smiled. "Most people don't. They see me giving speeches and promoting Chicagoans to be their best. And I mean that sincerely. I love my city and the people in it. I want Chicago to do well. But I also know that to get ahead, you have to have connections. That's what I'm offering you. A chance to get ahead and stay ahead."

"As tempting as that sounds, Bishop, I'm going to have to pass. I am loyal to my people. But thank you for considering me. I am humbled."

A determined look shone on his face. "Don't be so quick to make a decision, Carl. This is something that will benefit you and your people. This is a once in a life time opportunity. Give it some more thought."

"I thought about it enough, Bishop. I've made it this far with my people and I'm going to continue to do what I've been doing."

We had a stare off.

"Carl, I have to be honest. The people I work for won't like you not accepting their offer. Chicago is unlike any other city in that we have structure. We stick together. And for those who do not plug in, well, I'm sure you know the rest. I'll be seeing you again real soon."

Chapter 21

I had Lace's nose wide the fuck open!

We were in Chicago, walking around downtown, my arm wrapped around her shoulder, holding her close. This was officially our fifth date and I had pulled out all the stops. We started off at the United Center to watch an NBA game. Lebron was coming to town, so I got courtside seats and watched my Bulls get beat by twenty-five points. After the game, I took her to an upscale piano bar called Bach's. It was a five-star restaurant that had a pianist in the middle of the restaurant playing classical piano music.

"I had so much fun with you today. You showed me a side of you that I didn't know was in there," Lace said, intertwining her fingers in mine as we walked through downtown Chicago.

"So, you thought I was all rough?"

"No. I mean, yes, but not at the same time. The date was very romantic and I was happy to see that side of you. You are a man with layers, and it intrigues me."

"The worst thing a man can do is be plain and predictable," I was saying when my phone rang. I looked at the screen and seen Trav's name. I didn't feel like talkin' to him, so I ignored the call.

"You're not going to answer that?" Lace asked.

"Nah. It's not important enough to take time away from you," I said, putting the phone in my pocket. "Now, what do you say we stop over in the Yves Saint Laurent store and do some shopping? I seen a dress that would look so good on you."

She stopped in the middle of the sidewalk and grabbed hold of my waist. "Or, you can take me back to my hotel and I can allow you to see what's under the dress I already have on."

Fire and desire were lighting her blue eyes like princess cut sapphires. I lifted my hand to her cheek, caressing her beautiful face. "I would love nothing more than to taste every part of your body," I said before tonguing her ass down.

We hopped in my Bentley and headed for her room at the Hilton hotel. When the door closed, our lips locked and clothes started flying. When she was naked, I lay her on the bed and stood looking over her body. I had fucked a lot of bad bitches, and Lace was super bad. Her skin was the color of a peach, her athletic frame flawless. Her titties were perfect handfuls with little pink nipples. She didn't have an ounce of fat on her body. Stomach toned and flat. Waist tiny. And she had a nice ass. Just right for her frame. I knelt on the bed slowly, crawling up her body. She opened her legs for me, exposing her pink and meaty pussy. It was shaved bald and didn't have a hair bump or blemish. Muthafucka was so pretty that I had to stop and commit that bitch to memory.

"C'mon, Carl," she moaned, arching her back and biting her bottom lip.

I lowered my head and kissed her navel before licking my way up to her breasts. I licked and sucked each nipple until they were hard enough to be weapons.

"C'mon, Carl. Give it to me," she whispered, trying to grab my dick and pull it into her pussy.

I remained in control, not allowing her to put me inside as I kissed and licked my way down her body. When I got to that pretty-ass pussy, I started kissing the lips like they were the lips on her face.

"Oh, Carl! Eat me, baby. Please!"

I used my fingers to spread her pussy apart, exposing her clit. I pressed my tongue flat against it and started moving it up and down, creating friction.

"Oh, Carl! Oh, Carl!" she screamed, gripping my shoulders.

I went from licking her clit to sucking it. When she was almost to her orgasm, I slipped two fingers in her pussy and my pinky in her ass, fingering her holes while I sucked that pussy.

"Oh my God! Oh my God! Oooh!" she screamed, her body locking up as she came.

While she caught her breath, I got up and grabbed my tie from the floor. Then I pulled her to the edge of the bed and spread her legs apart. Her pussy lips had gotten fatter from her being turned on and that shit turned me on even more. I aimed my dick and thrust forward into her box. She was hot and wet as fuck!

"Aw shit!" I groaned.

"Carl!" she moaned, grabbing hold of my wrist.

I eased my meat inside, watching it disappear inch by inch. When my shit was all the way in, I paused for a moment, looking in her eyes. They were burning blue with lust. Prettiest shit I ever seen.

"Fuck me, Carl," she purred.

"I'ma be the best you ever had," I said, meaning every word.

I slipped my shit out until only the head was in and pushed forward again and began long-stroking that pussy. Then I gripped her hips and pulled her into me every time I pushed forward.

"Oh, Carl! Oh, baby! I love it! I love it!" she screamed.

I continued drilling her pussy as fast and hard as I could. When I was about to bust, I pulled out and flipped her over onto her knees. Then I used the tie to bind her wrists like hand cuffs behind her back. When she was secure, I slipped my dick in from behind. I put one foot on the bed for leverage, grabbed a fist full of hair with one hand and held her tied hands in my other hand and tore that pussy up.

"Oh, Carl! Oh, my God! Oh my God!" she screamed.

I fucked her until she came again then finally busted my nut. Then we went from the bed to the bathroom and fucked in the shower. An hour later we was chilling in bed, wrapped in each other's arms.

"You are amazing, Carl," she said, looking into my eyes like I was an Egyptian God.

"Not as amazing as you, baby," I said, kissing her lips.

"I can't remember the last time I came so many times. Damn, you know how to put it down."

"What can I say? You inspire me to be great. I told you I wanted to be the best you ever had."

"There's no doubting that that was the best sex of my life. You are amazing," she repeated.

Vibrating of my phone pulled us from the moment. I climbed out of bed to answer it. It was Trav again, so I ignored the call and got back in bed.

"Why didn't you take the call?" Lace asked, suspicion lighting her eyes.

"It wasn't important."

"Who was it? Your girlfriend?"

"Are you asking out of curiosity, or because you don't trust me?"

She thought before answering. "I just want to be sure that I'm not interfering with something."

I searched her face for a moment. "That was a colleague. Well, an employee really. I didn't feel like talking to him."

Curiosity shone in her eyes. "What do you do for a living?"

"I own the tattoo shop, remember?" I said, pointing to the dolphin that Keith had tattooed over her ex-boyfriend's name.

"Not driving Bentleys and spending the kind of money you make. I work in finances and you make more than a tattoo shop owner."

"Will my occupation change how you feel about me?"

"I don't care if you rob banks for a living. I've never felt the things I've felt for you with another man. I don't want this to stop."

I searched her eyes and seen the truth staring back at me. "I'm a drug dealer."

Her eyes grew a little wider. "Really?"

I nodded.

"Wow. You must be really successful at it since you can buy hundred thousand dollar cars."

"I do okay. But I'm having a couple problems."

She looked concerned. "The police? Are you going to jail?"

I laughed. "Nah, relax. It's not that serious. It could be, but it's not yet. And I really don't want to involve you in my shit. I've already said too much."

"What is it? What if I can help? I know people. Lawyers. I have friends."

"It's money problems. But like I said, I really don't want to involve you."

She sat up. "Well, now you have to tell me. I work with money. What do you need?"

It took everything inside of me to stop from smiling and keep my composure. "My businesses can't clean my money fast enough. I need some help."

She looked turned on. "How much are we talking about?"

"Two million dollars."

She smiled. "I think I can help you with that. But first I'll need you to do something for me."

"Name it and it's done."

She threw the covers back. "Give me some more of that best sex I ever had."

***

The next morning I helped Lace pack and we hopped in my Bentley so I could take her to the airport. I had just pulled up to a red light at the intersection when a black Dodge Magnum pulled all the way up on my bumper.

"What the fuck?" I questioned aloud, looking through the rear view mirror. There were two niggas in the car.

"What's going on?" Lace asked, looking in the rear side mirror.

"Muthafuckas all on my bumper and shit," I said, trying to see if I recognized their faces.

"Do you know them?" she asked.

"I don't——"

Before I could finish speaking, lights began flashing on the car and the driver started pointing for me to pull over.

"Is that the police?" Lace asked, alarm lighting her blue eyes.

"We good. We good," I said, trying to remain calm as I pulled over.

The Magnum followed me as I parked and two plainclothes police hopped out with badges hanging around their necks. They walked on either side of the car, their hands on the butt of their guns. The taller one came to my side and tapped on the window.

"What's going on, Officer?" I asked, letting the window down.

He lowered his head to look in the car and I immediately recognized his face. I hadn't seen him in five years, but I would never forget the scar on his cheek or the humiliation him and his boys caused me.

"I do all the questioning, brotha. Turn the car off and get out," he said sternly.

"For what? I didn't do nothing."

He gave me the look a father gives a child that talked back. "I'm not going to tell you again, Carl. Get out the car."

"Wait! What are you doing?" Lace spoke up. "He didn't do nothing."

"Calm down, Goldilocks," the partner said.

I knew how vicious Chicago police were, so I opened the door. "It's okay, Lace. I'ma take care of this," I said, trying to be brave.

"Come to the back of the car with me. You got anything on you I need to know about?" the nigga with the scar asked.

"Nah, I'm clean. I'm just taking my girl to the airport," I said.

"Sit against the car and keep yo' hands where I can see them. That's a nice piece of pork you got in there. Is that how you do when you get money? Kanye was right. Soon as a nigga get some paper, he get a white girl." He laughed.

I didn't find that shit funny, so I just stared at him. "Why you pull me over?"

His demeanor became instantly serious. "Because I wanted to see what the leader of Triple Beam Team looked like. I been hearing a lot about you. I thought it was about time that I introduce myself. I'm Sergeant Snipes. But you probably already knew that because I know we met before. Did I arrest you before?"

"Nah. You don't know me."

He smiled. "I never forget a face, Carl. It'll come to me. But that's not why I stopped you. I stopped you because we need to discuss business. You know Chicago is a treacherous city and you need somebody to watch yo' back. I own these streets, and what I say goes. You see where this is going, right?"

I chuckled. "Yeah. I see where this is going and I'ma have to decline whatever services you offering. I'm good."

Sergeant Snipes smirked. "Nah, I don't think you understand me, Carl. This is an offer that you can't refuse. These is my streets and they say you been eating in 'em for a while," he said, putting his hand on his gun. "You gotta pay dues like everybody else."

We had a long staring contest. He was going to bring problems. I could feel it in my gut.

"How about we talk about this another time? I need to take care of her and talk to some of my people."

The crooked cop smiled. "That's what I like to hear, Carl. I'll be seeing you again real soon. Let's go, Cooper," he called to his partner.

I continued leaning against the trunk and watched them drive away.

"What did they want?" Lace asked when I got back in the car.

I said the only word that fit the situation. "Trouble."

After dropping Lace off at the airport, I went home. Kianna gave me a salty-ass look when I walked through the front door.

"Why didn't you call me back or answer my texts?"

I flopped down on the couch. "Because I was taking care of business. I found somebody to clean the money, but now that that's taken care of, I got two more problems."

"You a God, right? You should be able to figure it out." Kianna smirked.

I wanted to throw something at her to knock that stupid-ass look off her face. "This ain't no game, Kianna. You remember when we got robbed by them police at Cotton's house? Officer Friendly and his boys?"

Her eyes grew wide. "Shit! What happened? They know about Officer Friendly?"

"Nah. I don't think so. But one of them niggas that was there is a sergeant now. He know all about me and TBT and wants me to pay him for protection."

"What the fuck? How does he know all that? We don't even hustle in Chicago."

"I don't know. Then Alderman Bishop Gains came to see me at the club. He wants me to hook up with his people and he ain't taking no for an answer."

"Shit, Carl. What the fuck is going on? Why is all of this happening now? You think it's connected?"

"I don't know. But I gotta figure out something soon because I can't have the police and politicians as my enemies. Shit can get real ugly real quick."

"Damn, Carl," Kianna mumbled before becoming silent.

A knock on the door interrupted the silence. I looked at Kianna. "You expecting somebody?"

She looked surprised. "No. And why didn't the desk call us to let us know someone was coming up?"

"Go grab a pistol!" I said, jumping to my feet. I crept to the door and looked through the peephole. It was Trav. "How you get up here without the front desk calling?" I asked as I opened the door.

"I used to be Special Forces, Carl." He smiled. "Can't no pretend security guard stop me. Can I come in?"

"Who is it?" Kianna asked, appearing with a gun.

I stepped aside and let Trav in.

"Hey, Ki-Ki." He grinned.

"Hey, Trav. Why didn't you call? You had us thinking some crazy shit."

Trav looked at her gun and then back at me. "What's going on, Carl? You good?"

I locked the door and went to sit on the couch. "Not really. More money, more problems. A crooked cop and a crooked politician tryna extort me."

He whistled. "A cop and a politician, huh? Both of them make bad enemies. What you gon' do about it?"

"I don't know yet. But what's up with you? What was so important that you couldn't call and had to sneak past our security?"

"I been calling you for two days. Since you didn't return my calls, I decided to come to Chicago to pay you a visit in person. We need to talk about that raise. I gotta get more for my niggas, Carl."

I let out a long stressed breath. The last thing I wanted to do was talk about a situation I already talked about. "C'mon, Trav. We just went through this a couple weeks ago. If I give you more, other niggas gon' want more. I gotta keep this the way it is. Plus, I might have to add more people to the pay role. I can't keep giving."

Trav sat across from me to look in my eyes. "We not just any ole niggas that work for you, Carl. You got to where you at because of us. We let niggas all over Milwaukee know that TBT was for real. We dropped bodies and had them streets red, my nigga. And a few of our niggas got locked up or killed. These lawyer and commissary bills don't pay they self."

"Listen, Trav. I pay everybody good. And niggas know the risks that come with this shit. They shoulda saved up. We can't take care of everybody. In the game of chess, you need pawns."

Trav looked offended. "So that's what we is to you? Pawns?"

"C'mon, Trav. I didn't say you was a pawn specifically. But some niggas in our organization are more important than others. That's just the facts. And I can't take care of every nigga that screams TBT that go to jail."

Trav looked disgusted. "I didn't wanna have to do this, but if you can't take care of my people the right way, then I'ma have to walk. I love this thang, but you puttin' me in a jam with my niggas and I can't keep getting the short end of the stick."

I searched Trav's eyes for a sign of how serious he was. The soldier didn't blink or waver. And neither did I.

"I got too much going on right now, Trav. I'm taking care of everybody as best I can. I can't give you nothing else."

"I can't give you nothing else either," he said before getting up and leaving.

Chapter 22

"I think we shoulda kept Trav on the team," Chris said.

I took my eyes off the road to glance at him. "I'm not finna be held hostage by nobody, li'l brah. We can't let niggas renegotiate shit they already agreed to. In business, people don't sign contracts and then turn around and be like fuck that, I want more money. That's not how it works."

"But he was too valuable to let get away. He got us all the guns we needed and he had certified killas with him. Low key, they the reason niggas fear Triple Beam Team. They know we hit hard and fuck shit up. And that was Trav, Fantasia's gay ass, and the rest of his niggas. Imagine what could happen if they plug with some other niggas? That's a fight I don't want to have."

"Fuck Trav, li'l brah. He was my nigga, but he walked away. I can't dwell on the past. That shit happened two weeks ago and I don't wanna think about it no more. They gone. TBT still alive and breathing and getting money. That's the only thing that matter right now is eating. We got Lace cleaning the money so now we can have a li'l bit more on the table. Securing the bag is the only thing that matters."

Chris shook his head but didn't say nothing more about Trav. When we got to LAVA, I parked the Bentley and grabbed the bag of money and went inside. Diego was waiting at the bar with a bottle of tequila and three shot glasses.

"Carlito!" The big man grinned.

"What's up, Diego?" I asked, setting the bag on the bar.

"Big news!" He smiled, pulling out his phone. "I bought the yacht! Look at the pictures. I call it the Santa Maria!"

I checked out the pictures of the yacht on his phone. It looked like a spaceship that floated on the water. Everything was shiny and new and state of the art. "So, when do we get to put it on the water? I'm ready to go sailing?"

"It is in Florida. I plan on taking the trip in a few weeks. Get your shit in order because we will be on the ocean for a week."

"I'm ready when you is."

"He means, we ready when you is," Chris spoke up.

"Right. We ready," I chuckled.

"Okay. I'll let you know. So, what do you want? The regular?"

"Yep. That usual ten."

"I'll send Omar to the shop. How are things going? Business good?"

"Yeah, business is good. I found somebody to clean my money. But I ran into some other problems."

His eyebrows scrunched. "Tell me what's going on," he said, pouring drinks.

"I'm having problems with the police and politicians back home. I also had to let go of some of my security because they wanted more money." I explained before downing the shot.

Diego nodded. "You can't put a price on good protection. Can you replace them?"

"We'll see."

"What's this with politics and police? Can you pay them off?"

"The police, yeah. But the alderman wants me to do business with his people. Wants me to spend my money in Chicago."

Diego looked angry. "Do business with his people, hey? Who are they?"

"I don't know. I didn't entertain the offer."

"Find out who they are, Carlito, and let me know. I have connections and I will look into helping you solve the problem. Okay?"

"Sounds good to me. I'll get back to you. And make sure you let me know when you pulling out the yacht. Nothing is going to stop me from sailing on the ocean."

After leaving Diego, I went to see Donovan to make sure he got the work from Omar. When that was done, I drove back to Chicago to drop the money off. Before I could get to the city, I got a call from Lace.

"Hey, baby girl."

"I just got a call from a woman threatening me if I didn't leave you alone. What the hell, Carl? I asked you if there was someone."

I was stunned for a moment. "When did you get his call? Who was it?"

"Her name is Kianna and I just got off the phone with her."

A vision of slapping the shit out of Kianna flashed into my head. "Don't worry about her, baby. I'm going to take care of it."

"Who is she and how did she even get my number?"

"I don't know how she got your number, but she won't be calling you again. I promise you that."

"So, do you have someone or not, Carl? I don't want to get into a messy situation and look like a homewrecker."

Damn. I was busted and needed to put out the fire before it spread. "Listen, Lace. This is not going to get messy. I told you I was going to take care of it."

"So who is she?"

"She is someone from my past that's tryna fuck up my future."

"Why didn't you tell me about her?"

"Because she's not important. Don't worry. I'm going to take care of it. You won't ever hear from her again, okay?"

"Okay. When can I see you again?"

"Real soon, baby. But let me call you back. I need to take care of this shit with Kianna. I'll call you later."

Instead of going to the storage to drop the money off, I drove straight home. Kianna's punk ass needed to be put in her place. I walked in the condo and found her in the kitchen making a drink.

"What the fuck is yo' problem going through my phone and calling Lace?" I snapped, slapping the bottle of Rosé out of her hand.

"What the fuck is wrong with you, nigga?" she flexed up. "Don't be slapping shit out of my hand. And fuck that bitch. Fuck all of your li'l thots."

I grabbed her by the throat and pushed her against the wall. "Bitch, Lace is cleaning my muthafuckin' money! If you fuck up my shit, I'ma beat cho mu'fuckin' ass!"

"Get yo' fuckin' hands off me!" she screamed, pushing me into the cabinet.

I reached my arm back and slapped the shit out of her. "Bitch, I ain't playin' with yo' stankin' ass! Stay the fuck out of my business. I ain't gon' tell yo' ass again."

She held the side of her face and mugged me. "You just put yo' hands on me over a white bitch that you barely know? Fuck that bitch. She didn't help you build this shit. I did. She didn't struggle with you when you was broke. I did. And this is how you do me?"

"This ain't about no struggle. This is about you gettin' in my mu'fuckin' business. You not finna fuck up my money. Don't call Lace no more or I'ma fuck you up. I ain't playin'."

Anger blazed in her honey brown eyes. "Fuck you and that bitch," she spat before walking away.

Feeling like I got my point across, I left the condo, heading for the Bentley. I needed to drop the money off in the Chevelle. I was driving down Michigan when a black Dodge Magnum pulled up to my bumper. A moment later flashing lights bounced in my rearview mirror. Fuck! I looked at the bag of money on the passenger floor. If I reached for it, they would want to know why I was moving around. If I left it in the open, they might get curious. And wasn't no way I was about to let them take three hundred thousand dollars. I thought of a quick plan as I pulled over and parked. Before they could get out of their car, I was already out of the Bentley and walking towards them.

"What's going on, Sergeant Snipes?"

"I remembered how I know you, Carl. Five years ago at Cotton's house. You was there. My old partner, Officer Friendly, took your money. That was you, wasn't it?"

I was surprised that be remembered. "I'm shocked you remembered. I knew you as soon as I seen that scar. Y'all humiliated the shit out of me. I'll never forget that," I said, leaning against the Bentley trunk.

"Different tactics with Officer Friendly. I'm more of a diplomat."

"So, what's goin' on? Is that why you pulled me over?"

"Word around the city is you got the best hand. I'm tryna see if I can use one of those hands to scratch an itch I got on my back."

I nodded. "I think that can be arranged. But you know that one hand washes the other. I just lost some of my security. He was a good nigga with good connections. You looking to fill those shoes?"

The cop smiled. "I wear a size fourteen. Is these Magnum boots big enough for you?"

It was my turn to smile. "Meet me at my club in an hour and we'll work out a payment. TBT could use a few good niggas."

***

I woke up the next day feeling good about the deal I made with Sergeant Snipes. Having the police on my side made me feel a little more powerful and a little safer. And now that I had a valuable asset in the city, I was also considering moving in on the drug trade in Chicago. I didn't like the thought of shitting in my backyard, but with the help of Snipe's squad, I could shit anywhere I wanted. I wanted Triple Beam Team to be everywhere. Global. And with a few more connections, TBT would bigger than any organization America had ever seen.

After a yawn and stretch, I climbed out of bed to hit the bathroom to shit, shower, and shave. When I was clean, I hit the kitchen for a quick snack and ran into Kianna. She was making a drink while talking on the phone. When she seen me, her eyes grew dark and lip twisted into a snarl.

"It's like that?" I asked.

She rolled her eyes and tried to walk by.

I grabbed her arm. "So this how we doing? We ain't talking no more?"

"I don't got nothing to say to you."

I searched her eyes. It looked like they had a lot to say. "Hang up the phone and talk to me for a minute."

She rolled her eyes. "I don't got nothing to say."

"I do. Hang up the phone."

She let out a frustrated breath. "Shawn, I'ma call you when I get to Milwaukee," she said before hanging up the phone. "What do you want?"

"How long you gon' be in Milwaukee?"

"Why? Don't act like you care now. I thought I was old news. Don't you wanna check up on yo other bitches?"

"C'mon, Ki-Ki. You know it's always been me and you."

She laughed and shook her head. "Stop playin' with me, Carl. I'm not stupid. What do you want? I got things to do."

"I want us to be good. I built this thing with you. Why can't you enjoy the fruits of our labor with me?"

"Because you keep disrespecting me. Because you just put yo' hands on me over a white bitch. Because you changed. You not the same person I used to know."

"But that's life, baby. We change. We evolve. And I didn't hit you over Lace. You lettin' your emotions cloud yo' judgment. She is cleaning our money. Millions of dollars. I can't let you fuck up my livelihood."

She stared at me for a long moment. "What is more important to you? Me or the money?"

"You know you mean more to me than money," I lied.

"Prove it," she challenged.

"What you want me to do?"

She started walking towards the living room. "I'm sure you can think of something, god."

I was about to go after her when my phone rang. I didn't recognize the number. "Hello?"

"Carl, this is Alderman Gaines. You got a moment?"

"Not really. How the hell you get my number?"

He laughed. "This is my city, Carl. It ain't much I can't get. And right now I need you to stop what you're doing and meet me at your bar."

"I don't got time right now. I'm busy."

"No, Carl. Trust me, you can't afford to miss this meeting. I'm with Alderman Charles Brown. You should be familiar with him as he is on the board that approved Triple Time's liquor license. There have been several complaints filed against your business and it seems that revoking the liquor license has become a hot topic. Any club that can't serve alcohol isn't really a club at all. You get my drift?"

I was so mad that I was started to see white spots in my eyes. "Man, if you fuck with my——"

"I know you're not about to threaten a public figure, Carl," he cut in. "That's a federal crime, my brotha. I'll be at your club in ten minutes with Alderman Brown. I hope you make the right choice."

He hung up before I could say another word.

"Bitch-ass shit!" I cursed as I ran for the door. I got to my club at the same moment as the aldermen.

Bishop climbed from the passenger seat of a silver Cadillac wearing a smile. "Brotha Carl! I'm glad you could make it."

I walked in his face, allowing him to see the anger in my eyes. "What the fuck you think you doing, nigga?"

He looked offended. "Brotha, watch the language," he scolded before turning to an older man climbing from the driver's seat. "This is Alderman Brown. And those distinguished young men in the black Chevy truck are our insurance policy," he said, pointing to a SUV parked across the street. Three niggas were staring at us intently. "You ready to talk?"

I wanted to kill Bishop's bitch ass right where he stood. But he had the upper hand, so I swallowed my anger. "What you gotta say?"

"First, let introduce you to Alderman Brown. Sir, this is Carlile White, the owner of Triple Time and leader of Triple Beam Team."

The older man extended a hand. "Good to meet you, son. I've been hearing good things about you."

I shook his hand. "Whatever, man. What is it gon' take to get y'all to leave me alone?"

"So eager to get to the feast, huh?"

I stared at him, waiting.

"Okay, Carl. It's simple. You buy from us and you get to go on doing what you've been doing. And you also get our protection. Simple as that. You do business with us and win."

"And if I don't?"

The old man gave me a pitiful look. "You're smarter than that, Carl. Contact us within the next forty-eight hours to arrange the first exchange."

I stood in front of my club feeling helpless as they got in the car and drove away. I needed to find a way out of the headlock they put me in. So I called Sergeant Snipes.

239

"Carl, what's going on, brotha?"

"I got a problem. How soon can you get to my club?"

"Gimme twenty minutes."

When my new head of security walked in the office, I explained to him the situation and the best way I knew to solve the problem.

"You want me to kill Alderman Brown and Gaines?" he asked, his eyes wide with disbelief.

"That's the only way to get these muthafuckas off my ass. I'm not about to be extorted or blackmailed."

"Carl, you might have to consider they offer. If we body some politicians, the Feds gettin' involved. Feds get involved, shit gets ugly. Niggas start talking and all kinds of shit gets fucked up."

"I'm not about to let them muthafuckas make me do shit. And I'm paying you to take care of my security. They threatened me. I need you to take care of that."

Me and the cop had a stare-off.

"Damn, Carl. Let me look into it and see what I can do."

When the cop left, I spent the rest of the day in the club getting some affairs in order and plotting my next move. Around eight o'clock my phone rang. It was Lace.

"Hey, baby girl. I was just thinking about you," I lied.

"Is this Carl?"

I frowned when I didn't hear Lace's voice. "Yeah. Who is this?"

"This is Jeanie, Lace's friend. She's in the hospital. She was hurt really bad. She told me to call you and tell you to come to Milwaukee."

***

The entire drive to Milwaukee, all I could think about was my millions. If something happened to Lace, I was going to be fucked. And whoever brought her harm would pay the ultimate price with their life.

I didn't get to Milwaukee until ten o'clock. I ran in the hospital and spoke with a few nurses before being allowed into Lace's room. When I walked in, I seen a pretty white chick with brown hair sitting at Lace's bedside, holding her hand. Lace was sleeping, her face wrapped up like a mummy.

"What happened?" I asked as I walked over.

"Somebody attacked her with acid," she said, trying to hold back tears.

"Damn. Do they know who did it? How bad is it?"

"I didn't see her, but the doctor said her entire face is gone. She doesn't know who did it. I can't believe someone would do something like this to her. Lace is so nice. She wouldn't hurt a fly."

I stood for a moment, relieved that Lace was okay, but salty that somebody had fucked her face up and put her in the hospital. "If I find out who did this..." I said, stopping myself.

"I can't believe this happened to her," Jeanie said, shaking her head sadly. "I need to run home to take care of some things. She's sedated and might be out for a while. If she wakes up while I'm gone, tell her I'll be back."

"I got you."

When Jeanie left, I took her place at Lace's bedside and held her hand. "Lace, this is Carl. I'm here, baby. If you can hear me, I need you to tell me who did this to you. What happened, baby? Wake up."

Lace stirred. "Carl," she said weakly.

I grabbed her hand tighter and leaned in. "Yeah, baby. I'm here. Who did this to you?"

"It was her," she mumbled.

"Who is her? Tell me who she is,"

"The one that called me. You said you would take care of it, but you lied," she cried. "You lied to me, Carl."

I was going to kill Kianna's funky ass!

"I didn't lie, baby. I'ma take care of it. I promise. I'ma take care of it, baby."

"She took my face, Carl. It hurts so bad. She took my face," Lace sobbed.

I didn't know what to do, so I pressed the nurse call button. "It's okay, baby. I'ma take care of it. I promise. I'm here."

A nurse came in a few moments later. "What's going on? Is she okay?"

"I don't know. She said her face was hurting. I didn't know what to do, so I pressed the call button."

"Let me look her over."

When the nurse started checking Lace, I walked out of the hospital and called Kianna.

"What?" she answered with an attitude.

"Where the fuck you at?"

"Why Carl? Did something happen?" she mocked.

"You think this a game? Where the fuck you at?"

"I don't know what game you talking about, but I'm at my sister's house, where I been all night."

I hung up the phone and called Donovan.

"What's up, Carl?"

"Go to Shawn's house to make sure Kianna don't leave before I get there. And hurry up."

"Okay, I got you. What's going on?"

"I'm finna kill that bitch!" I said before hanging up. When I pulled up to Shawn's house, Donovan was on the front porch arguing with Kianna and her sister. I ran up and snatched Kianna by her hair.

"Bitch, what the fuck I tell yo' stupid ass?" I said before busting her in her shit.

"Ahh!" Kianna screamed.

"Nuh-uh, nigga! Don't be hittin' my sister!" Shawn screamed, looking ready to jump in.

I pulled my pistol and put it in Shawn's face. "Stay the fuck outta my business, bitch!"

She stopped in her tracks. "Stop, Carl. Leave her alone."

I ignored Shawn and began dragging Kianna to my car.

"Let me go, Carl! Let me go!" Kianna screamed, trying to scratch and punch me.

I pistol whipped her ass and threw her in the street. "Bitch, stop! What the fuck I tell yo' stupid ass!?"

"You just hit me with a gun, nigga! Fuck is wrong with you!?"

I opened the door and grabbed her by the hair again. "You what's wrong with me, bitch! Get'cho stupid ass in the car."

We started fighting again and she resisted getting in the car.

"Donovan, help me get this bitch in the car!"

He came over to help and Kianna kicked him in his balls.

"Punk-ass bitch!" he cursed before picking Kianna up and slamming her on the ground.

I felt some type of way about him body slamming her but I let it go because she needed her ass whooped.

"Leave her alone, Carl! I'm callin' the police!" Shawn yelled.

I really wanted to kill both them hoes, but that would be too messy. So I started kicking Kianna. "I told yo' bitch ass I was gon' fuck you up of you fucked up my business, didn't I?" I snapped between kicks. "Don't bring yo' bitch ass back to my house. Fuck you. We done. If I see yo' bitch ass again, I'ma kill you!"

After a few more kicks, I left Kianna on the curb bleeding. I was too mad to see how much losing her would mean to me or how it would come back to bite me later.

TO BE CONTINUED...
Blood on the Money 2
Coming Soon

Submission Guideline

Submit the first three chapters of your completed manuscript to ldpsubmissions@gmail.com, subject line: Your book's title. The manuscript must be in a .doc file and sent as an attachment. Document should be in Times New Roman, double spaced and in size 12 font. Also, provide your synopsis and full contact information. If sending multiple submissions, they must each be in a separate email.

Have a story but no way to send it electronically? You can still submit to LDP/Ca$h Presents. Send in the first three chapters, written or typed, of your completed manuscript to:

LDP: Submissions Dept
Po Box 944
Stockbridge, Ga 30281

DO NOT send original manuscript. Must be a duplicate.

Provide your synopsis and a cover letter containing your full contact information.

Thanks for considering LDP and Ca$h Presents.

Blood on the Money

Coming Soon from Lock Down Publications/Ca$h Presents

BOW DOWN TO MY GANGSTA

By **Ca$h**

TORN BETWEEN TWO

By **Coffee**

THE STREETS STAINED MY SOUL **II**

By **Marcellus Allen**

BLOOD OF A BOSS **VI**

SHADOWS OF THE GAME II

By **Askari**

LOYAL TO THE GAME **IV**

By **T.J. & Jelissa**

A DOPEBOY'S PRAYER **II**

By **Eddie "Wolf" Lee**

IF LOVING YOU IS WRONG… **III**

By **Jelissa**

TRUE SAVAGE **VII**

MIDNIGHT CARTEL III

DOPE BOY MAGIC IV

CITY OF KINGZ II

By **Chris Green**

BLAST FOR ME **III**

A SAVAGE DOPEBOY III

CUTTHROAT MAFIA II

By **Ghost**

A HUSTLER'S DECEIT III

KILL ZONE **II**

BAE BELONGS TO ME III

A DOPE BOY'S QUEEN II

J-Blunt

By **Aryanna**
COKE KINGS V
KING OF THE TRAP II
By **T.J. Edwards**
GORILLAZ IN THE BAY V
De'Kari
THE STREETS ARE CALLING II
Duquie Wilson
KINGPIN KILLAZ IV
STREET KINGS III
PAID IN BLOOD III
CARTEL KILLAZ IV
DOPE GODS III
Hood Rich
SINS OF A HUSTLA II
ASAD
KINGZ OF THE GAME V
Playa Ray
SLAUGHTER GANG IV
RUTHLESS HEART IV
By Willie Slaughter
THE HEART OF A SAVAGE III
By Jibril Williams
FUK SHYT II
By Blakk Diamond
FEAR MY GANGSTA 5
THE REALEST KILLAZ II
By Tranay Adams
TRAP GOD II
By Troublesome

Blood on the Money

YAYO IV

A SHOOTER'S AMBITION III

By S. Allen

GHOST MOB

Stilloan Robinson

KINGPIN DREAMS III

By Paper Boi Rari

CREAM

By Yolanda Moore

SON OF A DOPE FIEND II

By Renta

FOREVER GANGSTA II

GLOCKS ON SATIN SHEETS III

By Adrian Dulan

LOYALTY AIN'T PROMISED II

By Keith Williams

THE PRICE YOU PAY FOR LOVE II

DOPE GIRL MAGIC III

By Destiny Skai

CONFESSIONS OF A GANGSTA II

By Nicholas Lock

I'M NOTHING WITHOUT HIS LOVE II

By Monet Dragun

CAUGHT UP IN THE LIFE III

By Robert Baptiste

LIFE OF A SAVAGE IV

A GANGSTA'S QUR'AN II

By **Romell Tukes**

QUIET MONEY III

THUG LIFE II

J-Blunt

By **Trai'Quan**

THE STREETS MADE ME III

By **Larry D. Wright**

THE ULTIMATE SACRIFICE VI

IF YOU CROSS ME ONCE II

ANGEL III

By **Anthony Fields**

THE LIFE OF A HOOD STAR

By Ca$h & Rashia Wilson

FRIEND OR FOE II

By **Mimi**

SAVAGE STORMS II

By **Meesha**

BLOOD ON THE MONEY II

By J-Blunt

Available Now

RESTRAINING ORDER **I & II**

By **CA$H & Coffee**

LOVE KNOWS NO BOUNDARIES **I II & III**

By **Coffee**

RAISED AS A GOON I, II, III & IV

BRED BY THE SLUMS I, II, III

BLAST FOR ME I & II

ROTTEN TO THE CORE I II III

Blood on the Money

A BRONX TALE I, II, III

DUFFEL BAG CARTEL I II III IV

HEARTLESS GOON I II III IV

A SAVAGE DOPEBOY I II

HEARTLESS GOON I II III

DRUG LORDS I II III

CUTTHROAT MAFIA

By **Ghost**

LAY IT DOWN **I & II**

LAST OF A DYING BREED

BLOOD STAINS OF A SHOTTA I & II III

By **Jamaica**

LOYAL TO THE GAME I II III

LIFE OF SIN I, II III

By **TJ & Jelissa**

BLOODY COMMAS I & II

SKI MASK CARTEL I II & III

KING OF NEW YORK I II,III IV V

RISE TO POWER I II III

COKE KINGS I II III IV

BORN HEARTLESS I II III IV

KING OF THE TRAP

By **T.J. Edwards**

IF LOVING HIM IS WRONG...I & II

LOVE ME EVEN WHEN IT HURTS I II III

By **Jelissa**

WHEN THE STREETS CLAP BACK I & II III

THE HEART OF A SAVAGE I II

By **Jibril Williams**

A DISTINGUISHED THUG STOLE MY HEART I II & III

J-Blunt

LOVE SHOULDN'T HURT I II III IV

RENEGADE BOYS I II III IV

PAID IN KARMA I II III

SAVAGE STORMS

By **Meesha**

A GANGSTER'S CODE I &, II III

A GANGSTER'S SYN I II III

THE SAVAGE LIFE I II III

CHAINED TO THE STREETS I II III

BLOOD ON THE MONEY

By J-Blunt

PUSH IT TO THE LIMIT

By **Bre' Hayes**

BLOOD OF A BOSS **I, II, III, IV, V**

SHADOWS OF THE GAME

By **Askari**

THE STREETS BLEED MURDER **I, II & III**

THE HEART OF A GANGSTA I II& III

By **Jerry Jackson**

CUM FOR ME I II III IV V

An **LDP Erotica Collaboration**

BRIDE OF A HUSTLA **I II & II**

THE FETTI GIRLS **I, II& III**

CORRUPTED BY A GANGSTA I, II III, IV

BLINDED BY HIS LOVE

THE PRICE YOU PAY FOR LOVE

DOPE GIRL MAGIC I II

By **Destiny Skai**

WHEN A GOOD GIRL GOES BAD

By **Adrienne**

THE COST OF LOYALTY I II III

By Kweli

A GANGSTER'S REVENGE **I II III & IV**

THE BOSS MAN'S DAUGHTERS I II III IV V

A SAVAGE LOVE **I & II**

BAE BELONGS TO ME I II

A HUSTLER'S DECEIT I, II, III

WHAT BAD BITCHES DO I, II, III

SOUL OF A MONSTER I II III

KILL ZONE

A DOPE BOY'S QUEEN

By **Aryanna**

A KINGPIN'S AMBITON

A KINGPIN'S AMBITION **II**

I MURDER FOR THE DOUGH

By **Ambitious**

TRUE SAVAGE I II III IV V VI

DOPE BOY MAGIC I, II, III

MIDNIGHT CARTEL I II

CITY OF KINGZ

By **Chris Green**

A DOPEBOY'S PRAYER

By **Eddie "Wolf" Lee**

THE KING CARTEL **I, II & III**

By **Frank Gresham**

THESE NIGGAS AIN'T LOYAL **I, II & III**

By **Nikki Tee**

GANGSTA SHYT **I II &III**

By **CATO**

THE ULTIMATE BETRAYAL

J-Blunt

By **Phoenix**

BOSS'N UP **I , II & III**

By **Royal Nicole**

I LOVE YOU TO DEATH

By Destiny J

I RIDE FOR MY HITTA

I STILL RIDE FOR MY HITTA

By **Misty Holt**

LOVE & CHASIN' PAPER

By **Qay Crockett**

TO DIE IN VAIN

SINS OF A HUSTLA

By **ASAD**

BROOKLYN HUSTLAZ

By **Boogsy Morina**

BROOKLYN ON LOCK I & II

By **Sonovia**

GANGSTA CITY

By **Teddy Duke**

A DRUG KING AND HIS DIAMOND I & II III

A DOPEMAN'S RICHES

HER MAN, MINE'S TOO I, II

CASH MONEY HO'S

By Nicole Goosby

TRAPHOUSE KING **I II & III**

KINGPIN KILLAZ I II III

STREET KINGS I II

PAID IN BLOOD **I II**

CARTEL KILLAZ I II III

DOPE GODS I II

Blood on the Money

By **Hood Rich**
LIPSTICK KILLAH **I, II, III**
CRIME OF PASSION I II & III
FRIEND OR FOE
By **Mimi**
STEADY MOBBN' **I, II, III**
THE STREETS STAINED MY SOUL
By **Marcellus Allen**
WHO SHOT YA **I, II, III**
SON OF A DOPE FIEND
Renta
GORILLAZ IN THE BAY **I II III IV**
TEARS OF A GANGSTA I II
DE'KARI
TRIGGADALE I II III
Elijah R. Freeman
GOD BLESS THE TRAPPERS I, II, III
THESE SCANDALOUS STREETS I, II, III
FEAR MY GANGSTA I, II, III IV
THESE STREETS DON'T LOVE NOBODY I, II
BURY ME A G I, II, III, IV, V
A GANGSTA'S EMPIRE I, II, III, IV
THE DOPEMAN'S BODYGAURD I II
THE REALEST KILLAZ
Tranay Adams
THE STREETS ARE CALLING
Duquie Wilson
MARRIED TO A BOSS… I II III
By Destiny Skai & Chris Green
KINGZ OF THE GAME I II III IV

J-Blunt

Playa Ray
SLAUGHTER GANG I II III
RUTHLESS HEART I II III
By Willie Slaughter
FUK SHYT
By Blakk Diamond
DON'T F#CK WITH MY HEART I II
By Linnea
ADDICTED TO THE DRAMA I II III
By Jamila
YAYO I II III
A SHOOTER'S AMBITION I II
By S. Allen
TRAP GOD
By Troublesome
FOREVER GANGSTA
GLOCKS ON SATIN SHEETS I II
By Adrian Dulan
TOE TAGZ I II III
By Ah'Million
KINGPIN DREAMS I II
By Paper Boi Rari
CONFESSIONS OF A GANGSTA
By Nicholas Lock
I'M NOTHING WITHOUT HIS LOVE
By Monet Dragun
CAUGHT UP IN THE LIFE I II
By Robert Baptiste
NEW TO THE GAME I II III
By **Malik D. Rice**

Blood on the Money

LIFE OF A SAVAGE I II III

A GANGSTA'S QUR'AN

By **Romell Tukes**

LOYALTY AIN'T PROMISED

By Keith Williams

QUIET MONEY I II

THUG LIFE

By **Trai'Quan**

THE STREETS MADE ME I II

By **Larry D. Wright**

THE ULTIMATE SACRIFICE I, II, III, IV, V

KHADIFI

IF YOU CROSS ME ONCE

ANGEL I II

By **Anthony Fields**

THE LIFE OF A HOOD STAR

By Ca$h & Rashia Wilson

BOOKS BY LDP'S CEO, CA$H

TRUST IN NO MAN

TRUST IN NO MAN 2

TRUST IN NO MAN 3

BONDED BY BLOOD

SHORTY GOT A THUG

THUGS CRY

THUGS CRY 2

THUGS CRY 3

TRUST NO BITCH

TRUST NO BITCH 2

TRUST NO BITCH 3

TIL MY CASKET DROPS

RESTRAINING ORDER

RESTRAINING ORDER 2

IN LOVE WITH A CONVICT

LIFE OF A HOOD STAR

Coming Soon

BONDED BY BLOOD 2

BOW DOWN TO MY GANGSTA

Blood on the Money

CPSIA information can be obtained
at www.ICGtesting.com
Printed in the USA
LVHW051730101120
671307LV00011B/1224

9 781952 936371